"THIS IS
BROGNOLA SAID

"I am here to do you a favor," the man said.

"Really?" Brognola was not going to insult the man's intelligence by claiming to be a minor functionary in the Justice Department.

"Your team did exceptionally well in Caracas."

"I see," Brognola said. It was surprising that Nung had so readily admitted to Chinese involvement.

"The world is a very complicated place, Mr. Brognola. It is my job to help guide my country through treacherous political waters. I understand well that you and I share similar vocations which often put us on different sides of the same issue."

"But not in this case?"

"My superiors do not believe that a second attack of the magnitude of 9/11 would be advantageous to our relationship. A shift toward more conservative political thought by your nation could only serve to strain our national interactions."

Brognola felt a cold chill surge through his body. "You have knowledge of a planned attack on the American homeland?"

DON PENDLETON'S

STONY

AMERICA'S ULTRA-COVERT INTELLIGENCE AGENCY

MAN®

HIGH ASSAULT

A GOLD EAGLE BOOK FROM

W✪RLDWIDE®

TORONTO • NEW YORK • LONDON
AMSTERDAM • PARIS • SYDNEY • HAMBURG
STOCKHOLM • ATHENS • TOKYO • MILAN
MADRID • WARSAW • BUDAPEST • AUCKLAND

Recycling programs for this product may not exist in your area.

First edition April 2010

ISBN-13: 978-0-373-61990-0

HIGH ASSAULT

Special thanks and acknowledgment to
Nathan Meyer for his contribution to this work.

HIGH ASSAULT

CHAPTER ONE

October 25, 2007—Beirut, Lebanon

The massive Lockheed L-100 cargo plane circled above the night-shrouded landscape with the relentless patience of a vulture, its four heavy Allison T56-A-15 turboprop engines droning steadily.

From within the civilian version of the C-130E Hercules, Brigadier General Abdul-Ali Najafi watched the operation unfolding below him with the detached scrutiny of the consummate puppet master. Inside the insulated interior cabin, he reclined in an expensive leather wingback chair purchased at Nigel's of London. In front of him rose a stack of HD television monitors fed from glasses-mounted, POV digital cameras that routed their signal through a booster unit in the ground-operations vehicle.

The images flickering on the screen were chaotic and jumbled as the strike team conducted its mission preparations. Najafi glimpsed the barrels of folding-stock Kalashnikovs, the dashboard of the big black

Suburban SUV the hit squad was operating from and the masked faces of the unit. Through the windshield Najafi could just make out the urban residential street along which the target passed each day from work to home.

Najafi leaned forward and hit a key on his laptop. He spoke into the microphone. "Adjust focus," he ordered.

The gunner wearing the headset lifted a hand encased in a black Lycra driver's glove from the pistol grip of his weapon, and the image on the screen shifted as he worked the attachment. The resolution on the display screen sharpened.

"Very good," Najafi said and leaned back into his chair.

From behind him he heard the door to the Lockheed's tactical operation center open. Najafi knew without checking that it was his executive officer, Colonel Ayub. Ayub had come up through the regular Iranian army, but through family connections on the Revolutionary Council he had managed to secure the coveted posting as Najafi's assistant.

"Do you have it?" Najafi demanded.

"Yes," Ayub answered.

Najafi held up his hand, gesturing toward a clear spot on the table in front of him. His nails were manicured, and a gold Rolex Diplomat luxury watch was fitted onto a slender wrist. There was a heavy band of white gold on his ring finger, along with a silver-and-platinum signet ring on his index finger.

"Put it there," he ordered.

Ayub stepped forward away from the TOC's central door and around the dentist's chair secured incongruously in the middle of the control room. He lifted a Schlesinger leather attaché case and set it down. The valise cost a thousand dollars, which Colonel Ayub knew because he had purchased both the case and the item it held on a recent shopping excursion in Tbilisi, Georgia, while doing business with certain Russian bankers in that city.

Beneath his dusky complexion Ayub paled as he looked at the screens. His eyes slid from the monitors to the wingback chair then back to the attaché case before coming to rest on the HD monitors again. His tongue flickered out to moisten his lips under a thin mustache. He released the handle of the case and stepped back.

On the screen there was a sudden flurry of motion. The team leader's arm came up and pointed across his body out the passenger window. The man barked a command into his microphone that was clearly audible through the TOC's sound system. Like dominoes falling in succession, the pictures on the screens of the monitor array flickered to life as one by one the other team members initiated their cameras.

"Now we're moving," Najafi murmured.

The commander drew a slim white cylinder of a fashionable Turkish cigarette from an open pack in his shirt pocket. Ayub responded without thinking, removing the lighter and stepping forward to light the cigarette as Najafi inclined his head.

Gray smoke billowed up in front of the screens. On the monitors, balaclava hoods were pulled into place, turning the hard-eyed killers into anonymous androids. The interior of the vehicle seemed filled with the muzzles of weapons.

Colonel Ayub let his breath out in a slow, controlled hiss and prayed Najafi couldn't hear.

MICHAEL SULEIMAN looked out at the passing street through the bulletproof glass of his limousine's rear windows. He watched, lost in thought, as the tall buildings of Beirut's business district gave way to more residential neighborhoods as they drove up toward the hills east of the city.

In the car beside him, his wife, Suha, read from a children's book to his four-year-old daughter, Taraneh. The little girl had her mother's dark brown eyes and smooth olive complexion, as well as her keen intelligence. Michael Suleiman was always amazed by Suha's insights, even after fifteen years of marriage. In his private moments he doubted seriously if he could have risen to power so smoothly in the Kataeb Party without her support.

His eyes slid past the scars of war left over from the violence of civil unrest dating as far back as the 1980s, despite the reconstruction efforts of more recent years. What his eyes couldn't ignore were the piles of rubble left over from the sectarian violence following the 2006 incursion by the Israeli Defense Forces.

Unconsciously, Suleiman frowned at the thought. Despite international pledges to the contrary, that cross-border assault had only strengthened the hand of Iran in Lebanon, through their proxy puppets—Hezbollah.

In parliament, Suleiman had been using all the leverage he could muster to fight that Iranian influence in his homeland. It was this bitter opposition that had, in no small part, resulted in his newfound need for armed bodyguards.

Four soldiers armed with M-4 carbines drove a scout vehicle ahead of his limo, and even now one of the American-trained protection specialists rode with him, sitting next to his seven-year-old son, Ephraim, listening patiently as the young boy explained the intricacies of whatever new game he was playing on his handheld game system.

The bodyguard smiled indulgently over the boy's head as his eyes met Suleiman's. He looked like a favorite uncle indulging his nephew. Suleiman saw how earnest the boy, a spitting image of himself, was in the explanation and felt an answering grin tugging at his lips. Then the bodyguard's jacket shifted, exposing the handle of the man's machine pistol, and Suleiman's smile faded. He looked away and out through the black-tinted glass of his window and sighed. One day, God willing, his country would be free of the influence of Iran. It was a mission to which he had dedicated himself tirelessly.

He'd be happier once they were safely home.

NAJAFI LEANED FORWARD, drawing deeply on his cigarette, his eyes narrowing as he watched the screen. The white Ford Excursion carrying Suleiman's bodyguards drove past the mouth of his team's ambush street, followed seconds later by the black stretch limo.

The team leader slapped the dashboard, and the SUV gunned forward as the vehicle operator responded to the command. The big automobile shot out of the side street and pulled in behind the cruising limo. The death squad began babbling excitedly, the words coming too hard and fast to differentiate over the microphone pickups. From behind the squad leader came the unmistakable staccato rhythm of a Kalashnikov on fully automatic.

Inside the confined space of the TOC, Ayub could feel his commander's excitement. It rose from the man like heat or static electricity. The head of Iran's elite Special Republican Guard loved the visceral thrill of his work.

On the screen Najafi watched as, ahead of the limousine, Suleiman's scout vehicle swerved into the opposite lane in response to the first burst of gunfire. The interception had been designed to take place on the tight switchbacks leading into the residential hills above Beirut—making it easier to box in the target vehicles. The protective agents were falling neatly into Najafi's trap.

The modified sunroof of the lead SUV slid back and a gunner armed with an American M-4 carbine popped out of the opening. The SUV slowed as the stretch limo sped up, making it easier for them to try to change places.

"Now!" Najafi snarled into his microphone pickup.

Suleiman's bodyguard shouldered up his carbine and triggered a tight burst. On the HD monitor Najafi and Ayub watched the rounds spark off the reinforced glass of the hit squad's vehicle. Ahead on the road a tight switchback suddenly appeared. The bodyguard SUV's brake lights flashed red and the limo driver gunned it even harder.

"Yes," Najafi whispered as if breathing into the ear of a lover.

On the screen, the multi-POV camera angles simultaneously revealed the sudden appearance of the garbage truck on the narrow road. The tail ends of both target vehicles suddenly fishtailed as their drivers slammed on their brakes. The garbage truck slowed considerably and swerved to the right, nose pointed toward the downhill side of the road.

The bodyguard SUV slammed into the back half of

the garbage truck, its front end collapsing with a shriek of metal clearly audible over the repeated bursts of the gunfire pouring from the Hezbollah vehicle. The bodyguard firing from the sunroof was jerked forward like a rag doll, his weapon spinning away like a pinwheel as he was flung into the unforgiving steel of the massive garbage truck. His body seemed to explode with spraying blood as he was smashed to a pulp.

The front end of the limo slid forward at the end of a desperate skid and rammed into the garbage truck's immense bumper. The limo's hood crumpled, and the big V-12 engine block was shoved backward into the front passenger compartment, splitting the reinforced glass of the windshield. The spilled engine fluids caught fire and began to burn.

On the HD screen the garbage truck's passenger door was kicked open. The assassin's folding stock AKMS poured a hailstorm of heavy lead down on the crumpled limo, the muzzle-flash spitting star-pattern bursts of flame as the weapon bucked and kicked in the Hezbollah gunner's hands.

The rounds slammed into the SUV's already compromised windshield at point-blank range, punching divots and gouges and spiderwebbing the safety glass until it began to come apart completely. The black Suburban SUV holding the Hezbollah hit squad drove straight up into the pile, smashing bumpers with Suleiman's limo and pinning it into place inside the killbox.

The Hezbollah hitters bailed out of their vehicles, spraying 7.62 mm rounds at the bodyguard vehicle. From that range, and under the terrific onslaught, glass was pulverized and metal riddled. On the TOC screens

Ayub could clearly see the dark silhouettes of the trapped bodyguards dance and jerk.

On the screen, the team leader peeled off from the main group. A second and then a third Hezbollah foot soldier followed closely as they headed for the trapped and burning limo in a classic fire team configuration. The stretch limo's driver door flew open and a Lebanese army commando in a dark suit and armed with an MP-5K emerged.

He was met with a merciless wall of lead as the team leader and flank gunners unleashed their Kalashnikovs. The HD monitors in the Lockheed's TOC showed the carnage in startling clarity. Najafi ground out one cigarette as he watched the bodyguard come apart, dropping hard to his knees, his jaw going slack as the big bullets knifed through his body armor to scramble his organs. Then his head disappeared in a spray of pink and scarlet, and the brigadier general pulled another cigarette from his pack.

With the reactions of a trained sycophant, Ayub was there to light it. There were dark stains on his silk shirt under his armpits and his forehead was beaded with sweat. Najafi's eyes danced from one monitor screen to the other, not wanting to miss one second of the grotesque action.

On the screen, the Hezbollah team leader gestured with the muzzle of his AKMS, and one of his fire team ran forward to cover the open limo door, his boots splashing through the dead bodyguard's blood like a child stomping in a puddle. The leader spun and his hand appeared in his POV shot, pointing at the rear door, then making a slashing motion.

"Now we're on it," Najafi said, his voice almost a

giggle. "Let this Lebanese Christian learn what it means to displease the servants of the Revolutionary Council."

Ayub muttered something appropriate as he watched, mesmerized, as the Hezbollah team's explosives engineer sprang into action. The man let his AKMS hang from its cross-body sling as he pulled an industrial appliance from a thigh pouch on his web gear. The device looked almost identical to a home construction caulking gun.

The Hezbollah gunner ran forward, the caulking gun up in his gloved fists under the cover of the team leader and secondary gunner. Behind them the remaining hitters had pushed right up onto the wreckage of the bodyguard SUV and were spraying the vehicle's interior with excessive enthusiasm. Two of the gunners peeled off and came over to take up overwatch positions as the explosives trooper prepped the egress point.

The gunman, a powerfully built fireplug of a man, raced up to the rear passenger door of the limo and brought up his applicator. He squeezed the lever against the pistol-grip handle and instantly a Semtex-based foam shot out of the slit-tipped nozzle and stuck to the vehicle in inch-thick strips.

With smooth, practiced motions he outlined the plastique foam around the edges of the door where they met the vehicle frame. Once he had outlined the structure he pulled a thin timing pencil from his black fatigue shirt and hit the plunger on the top to start the five-second countdown.

He inserted the initiator charge in the explosives molding and sprang back, turning his head to the side as the rest of the team fanned out to give the breaching charge room to detonate.

In the C-130, Najafi gripped the edge of the table hard enough to turn his knuckles white. The bright cherry on the end of his cigarette flared like an airstrip beacon as he drew on it, and his eyes fairly bulged from their sockets as he soaked in every aspect of the pregnant seconds before the charge went off.

The crack of the explosive detonating was sharp enough to hurt Ayub's ears through the speaker pickups. The blinding flash of light was followed immediately by a billowing cloud of gray-white smoke. The car door shot straight off the frame and sailed outward ten feet like a cork from a champagne bottle.

The bodyguard inside the rear compartment of the limo came out immediately, his MP-5K up in both hands and blazing. The 9 mm rounds tore the face off the secondary gunner and spread his brains and skull across his team leader. Blood and clumps of flesh struck the POV camera and smeared the lens, obscuring the leader's feed.

The bodyguard landed on the road and went to one knee, swinging the compact subgun around. From half a dozen directions AKMS assault rifles opened up in a brutal symphony. The bodyguard came apart like a grenade exploding and his submachine was shattered as his hands were torn from his wrists.

"Wipe your camera! Wipe your camera!" Najafi screamed at the leader.

Ayub didn't know why Najafi was so excited as the feed from six other cameras showed the scene well enough. On the leader's screen the Hezbollah assassin followed the frantic order of the brigadier general and wiped his screen clear. Smoke was billowing around them as the hit squad collapsed on the breach point into the target vehicle.

Ayub's eyes flickered to the tactical display clock on the wall next to the bank of television screens. Fifty-eight seconds had passed since the initiation of the ambush. The Hezbollah attackers were performing ahead of schedule.

What happened next was ugly.

The big, rough men came out of the car with Michael Suleiman between them. He tried to struggle and they pounded him brutally with fists until he was battered and dazed. The team leader struck him once in the face with the smoking muzzle of his AKMS, tearing the Lebanese politician's nose as the kidnappers dropped him to the ground. One of the men came down with a knee on Suleiman's back, causing the parliamentary leader to scream out in pain.

As a plastic zip tie was tightened around Suleiman's wrists, the man's seven-year-old son came charging out of the ruined vehicle to protect his father. Ephraim Suleiman's young face was twisted in anger, and tears formed tracks down his cheeks as he sprang on the closest Hezbollah killer.

The Iranian-trained terrorist backhanded the boy and the child went tumbling backward. The explosives trooper stepped into the foreground and brought up his AKMS.

CHAPTER TWO

Suleiman screamed in protest, but his cry was cut off by the banging clatter of the Kalashnikov on full auto. The boy's body came apart in chunks of flesh and gouts of blood and most of him ended up spread across the rear bumper and trunk of the limo.

There was a scream so shrill and frantic it cut through the roar of the weapons, and the Hezbollah team leader's camera snapped back toward the breach point on the limo. Suha Suleiman, looking disheveled and battered, clawed her way out of the swirling smoke inside the limo passenger compartment. Behind her the shell-shocked face of her daughter, Taraneh, stared out blankly.

Suha screeched again as she saw the pitiful pile that was all that remained of her son. She opened her mouth and her beautiful face twisted into a mask of hurt and confusion in marked contrast to the tiny mirror image at her side, who simply stared at the trussed-up image of her father on the road.

"Finish it," Najafi said into the microphone, and this time his voice *was* a giggle.

No one on the team hesitated. The terrorists turned their weapons on the wife and daughter of a known Israeli sympathizer. They fired. Michael Suleiman screamed. Green tracer rounds knifed through the roiling smoke. Colonel Ayub felt his heart lurch so painfully in his chest he thought he'd torn it. The woman and girl were punched backward into the vehicle. Suleiman screamed again, but it was only the beginning of the screaming he would do this day.

Brigadier General Najafi moved his finger over and hit the button on the intercom system for the plane, putting him instantly in touch with the pilots of the C-130.

"The package is acquired," he said. "Put the plane down."

"Yes, sir," the pilot answered.

Behind Najafi, Colonel Ayub found his eyes once again drawn to the expensive attaché sitting on the table next to his commander. He thought about what it held. He closed his eyes.

The plane made its descending approach.

THE BIG CARGO PLANE landed on an improved runway controlled by a pro-Iranian Shiite militia. The pilot deftly leveled out and brought the massive bird down on the mile-long runway. As soon as the wheels hit the tarmac the load master in the cavernous bay initiated the cargo-acquisition procedures and the ramp began to lower even as the plane continued to taxi down the runway.

The Hezbollah hit team's Toyota Sequoia raced out from between two hangars and onto the runway. The ramp lowered into position just a few short inches above the pavement and the SUV, with Michael Suleiman trussed up inside, ran up on the platform.

The vehicle driver gunned the Sequoia up onto the platform and drove it straight into the cargo bay of the lumbering C-130, which was large enough to hold five more just like it. Once the SUV was inside, the load master alerted the pilot and began closing the ramp. Instantly the cargo plane's mammoth Allison Turbine engines changed pitch and began racing.

Instead of holding down the speed the pilot applied full throttle, and almost immediately the blunt nose of the airplane began to lift. Inside the cargo hold the snatch team waited for takeoff and watched the load master, now in a jump chair, for the all clear to exit their vehicles.

Inside the TOC both Najafi and Ayub surveyed the hold through a video feed, Najafi calmly smoking while his subordinate stood mute and sweating.

Engines screaming, the C-130 completed its stump-and-jump running landing and left Lebanese soil, heading out to the west toward the sparkling blue waters of the Mediterranean Ocean.

As the plane began a smooth ascent, the load master nodded to the Hezbollah agents in the Sequoia. They sprang into action as Najafi came out and stood on the scaffolding leading up to the TOC's door. Ayub remained in the chamber, studiously avoiding looking at either the attaché case or the dentist chair. It took a considerable amount of willpower.

Outside the door he heard Najafi taunt the prisoner.

"Ah, Michael, so good to see you again," Najafi said. He looked imperiously down from his perch at the top of the scaffolding. In his mind he was Xerxes surveying the beating of an insolent slave at the hands of his Immortals. The Hezbollah thugs jerked the Lebanese parliamentary member from the back of the SUV. His face was purple and black and swollen. Bloody drool hung in ropes from split lips, and he looked up at Najafi with the dull eyes of a wounded animal.

He tried to speak as he was carried up the steps by the masked gunmen but could only manage to gag. His hands and feet had been secured behind him with white plastic zip ties and his business suit had been torn and splattered with blood. He could only manage mewling sounds as he was shoved through the TOC's door and thrown roughly into the dentist's chair.

While the Hezbollah gunners cut the man loose from his restraints and then locked him into the chair, Najafi fitted his impeccable suit jacket on a hanger, then hung that from a hook on the wall. He maintained a calm, playful manner as he donned a blue apron and a pair of black rubber gloves.

"I know we've had our difference, Michael," he purred. "That whole public denouncement of my diplomatic mission as nothing more than a political destabilization operation by Ansar-al-Mahdi was, in particular, quite hurtful—conveyed as it was on your parliamentary floor, in front of television cameras."

Behind the men, Colonel Ayub took an unconscious step backward as Najafi donned a cotton surgical mask and a pair of clear plastic safety glasses. He came up hard against the cold metal wall of the TOC. He could feel the vibration of the plane through the wall as it climbed toward a thirty-thousand-foot ceiling. The Hezbollah agents were inscrutable observers behind their masks, their weapons still reeking of cordite from their recent use.

"Despite that…unpleasantness," Najafi continued,

"I was so sorry to hear about the loss of your family, Michael. These are unfortunate times. The Koran tells us to turn to Allah and the words of the Prophet in times of trouble." Najafi stopped, regarded the battered Lebanese secured to the chair in front of him. "But you don't follow the teachings of the Koran, do you, Michael? You worship this Jesus Christ, like some American lapdog."

"You murdered my family!" Suleiman screamed. "Killer! You disgusting animal!"

The bruised man pushed up against his restraints, disfigured face twisted into rage. His eyes, almost swollen shut, blazed with hate and anger until they were bright points of light. Bloody spittle flew from split lips over broken teeth, and the veins of his neck stood out in sharp relief, like rivers.

Najafi ignored the outburst. He calmly walked over to his attaché case where it sat on the table and undid the gold relief clasps. The springs were tight and the snap of their release was clearly audible despite Michael Suleiman's inarticulate screaming. Suleiman's snarls turned to choking gags behind Najafi and, up against the wall, Colonel Ayub closed his eyes.

Najafi reached into his expensive leather attaché case. The Bosch eighteen-volt high-torque impact wrench was a cordless power drill. Michael Suleiman fell silent as Najafi turned around with the 9.5-inch device in his hands. The power tool was blue with the trigger and brand name printed in a brilliant red. The flat battery pack was secured to the bottom of the drill's pistol grip like a magazine in a handgun. The drill bit was itself five inches long, grooved like a rifle barrel and colored a dull graphite-gray that seemed to absorb light.

Grinning, Najafi depressed the trigger. The 2.4 Ah batteries surged power at 1,900 RPM, generating 350 foot pounds of torque as specially designed cooling rods absorbed the heat generated by use.

"What could you possibly want from me?" Suleiman begged. "What could I possibly know?"

Najafi released the trigger and watched the drill spin down. His sneer was spread across his face as he called over his shoulder to the visibly pale Ayub. "Why do they always think it's about information?"

Chuckling to himself, Najafi turned back toward the helpless Suleiman. "Michael, I already know everything I need to know. There are no secrets in Beirut I do not already possess."

Najafi stepped forward and touched the hard metal of the drill against Suleiman's left leg. The power tool rested on his *vastus medialis,* the teardrop-shaped muscle of the quadriceps located next to the kneecap. His gloved finger rested lightly on the red trigger of the cordless drill.

"Then why?" Suleiman asked, his voice a moan. "Just kill me. You murdered my family. I've suffered enough."

"*I* say when you've suffered enough!" Najafi suddenly screamed. His face was a grossly animated mask of anger.

The drill screamed as the leader of Ansar-al-Mahdi pulled the trigger and pushed downward. The powerful industrial drill bit easily into Michael Suleiman's flesh, burning through skin and tearing into muscle fiber as if they were paper. Scarlet blood splashed as the prisoner screamed, streaking Najafi's pale blue apron and marking his safety glasses with beads of crimson.

Najafi wore a maniacal grin as he pulled the drill free then plunged it down into Suleiman's leg again four more times in rapid succession. Colonel Ayub felt his gorge rising as he tried to look away, but the tortured man's screams drew his eyes despite himself. Blood spilled into the seat of the dentist's chair and puddled on the floor of the TOC.

Suddenly a satellite phone positioned on the table below the POV cam monitors came to life. Najafi straightened, lips pursed as he let the spinning drill power down. Michael Suleiman's head sagged on his neck.

"Always with the interruptions," Najafi snarled. "Always whenever I'm really starting to make progress on a project I am interrupted."

The phone beeped loudly again.

Najafi sighed, almost theatrically. He turned around and walked toward the table. He stopped, looking down at the heavy power tool he still held in his hands. He turned back toward the helpless and bleeding Suleiman.

"Would you hold this for me?" he asked. "Thank you."

The drill screamed into life and Najafi carelessly pushed the impact wrench down into the Lebanese political leader's thigh until it bit into the bone of his femur. The man screamed as it cored into his bone marrow.

The phone rang and without bothering to remove his blood-drenched glove, Najafi snatched it up. "Yes, what is it?" he snapped.

Colonel Ayub, standing only a few short yards away, could hear clearly both sides of the conversation and he recognized the voice on the other end of the connection immediately. It was a voice he feared.

"Is that how you talk to a man in my position, General?" the voice asked.

Najafi's manner and tone instantly changed. "Of course not, Your Eminence," he said. "How may I serve you?"

Behind them Michael Suleiman moaned in agony, the noise very loud in the confined space of the mobile TOC. Najafi scowled fiercely and pointed a finger at the Hezbollah team leader. With a slash of his hand he indicated the bound and helpless Suleiman. Instantly the terrorist stepped forward and threw a right cross down onto the prisoner. The knuckles of the man's hand connected with the sharp prominence of Michael Suleiman's jaw, and the Lebanese political leader's head went limp on his neck.

"There has been a change in certain global geopolitical realities that displease the Revolutionary Council," the voice on the phone said.

"What happened?"

"The Americans in their arrogance have formally labeled our Islamic Revolutionary Guard and the Ministry of Defense and Armed Forces Logistics command as terrorist organizations. The world press is running with the story now."

"The Americans' insolence knows no bounds!" Najafi snarled. "How quickly they forget the humiliation of their embassy hostages on the world stage before that cowboy Reagan came to power."

"The council agrees," the voice replied. "This arrogance will not be ignored. Our own parliament is already constructing a resolution labeling the CIA and U.S. Army as the terrorist organizations they are—but that is only our public face."

"You have something else in mind?"

"We want you to return to Tehran immediately. Your Ansar-al-Mahdi is to be given a new tasking. We'll leave the Lebanese situation to VEVAK officers for now," the voice said, referring to the Iranian Ministry of Intelligence.

"As you command," Najafi said. "I will turn the plane around now."

"Good." The line went dead.

Najafi put the satellite phone down on the table and slowly turned to regard the bound Michael Suleiman. The Lebanese prisoner was only semiconscious, eyes dull and blood pouring from his torture wounds.

"Terrorist organizations," Najafi scoffed, shaking his head with irritation. "You heard that?" he asked Ayub, who nodded. "Those cowboys will soon learn to regret their arrogant presumption."

Najafi walked over to Suleiman and yanked the cordless drill from the man's leg. Suleiman screamed. The drill whined to life, spinning at its fearsome 1,900 RPM. Suleiman's eyes sprang wide in terror and he threw his head back against the chair.

Najafi lifted the drill in an almost offhand manner and plunged it into his captive's left eye. Michael Suleiman jerked like a man in an electric chair, coming up out of his seat against his restraints, then sagging back down limply and falling irrevocably still.

Najafi yanked the drill free. Behind him Colonel Ayub bent double and vomited on his own shoes as the Hezbollah commandos snickered behind their masks. The Ansar-al-Mahdi commander regarded his subordinate with a look of cool distain until he had finished purging.

"Something you ate?"

"Yes, General," Ayub said, wiping his mouth.

"Good." Najafi shoved the gore-drenched power tool

into the colonel's shaking hands. "Clean that so that my briefcase is not stained." He turned toward his Hezbollah surrogates and pointed at the corpse. "Take this piece of shit down to the cargo bay. I'm going to the cockpit. We're on our way back to Tehran. When we're over north Beirut I'll signal the load master and you dump the body out so it can be found."

"Yes, General," the team leader replied.

Najafi turned back toward Colonel Ayub in his vomit-splattered dress shoes. "When you have finished with your valet duties, come up to the cockpit," he told the man. He paused at the door of the TOC after removing his bloody apron. "We are going to figure out how exactly to show these Americans exactly what terror really is."

Colonel Ayub nodded and Najafi went out the door. The politically connected military officer felt the eyes of the Hezbollah gunmen on him. He forced himself to stand straight. He looked at the bloody and mutilated body of Michael Suleiman and he forced his features into a mask of indifference despite the taste of his own vomit on his tongue.

"You heard the commander!" he snapped. "Get the body downstairs and wait for your orders."

But the Hezbollah team was already in motion and they simply ignored the bureaucrat.

CHAPTER THREE

Stony Man Farm, Virginia—Present Day

Barbara Price pushed hard against the pedals of the elliptical machine, her honey-blond hair pulled back in a tight ponytail and her body shiny with sweat. A beautiful woman with a model's looks, she tried to maintain a high level of fitness though her workaholic nature had kept her at the Shenandoah Valley covert operations site almost continuously over the recent months. The War on Terror had left the clandestine Stony Man personnel—both Phoenix Force and Able Team—like paramilitary firefighters, rushing from one global hot spot to the next with little downtime between assignments.

The former NSA mission controller didn't see an end in sight, either.

The cardio trainer machine beeped at her and the readout display informed her that her forty-five-minute workout was almost over. She refocused her attention and began to swing her legs even faster. She was off her normal pace and fought hard to regain the distance before her time ran out.

Her body was fluid in motion. She was trim and muscular, with an assertive but feminine sexuality that caused men's heads to turn when she passed. She took pride in her appearance, but her dedication to fitness was no longer about cosmetic sensibilities. When she was fit, her endurance improved, and when she went days without sleep while exercising a grueling schedule of life-and-death multitaskings, her improved stamina made her a better leader and support system for the men in her command.

Suddenly the cell phone resting on her elliptical machine's console began to ring. Frowning at the interruption, she picked it up and looked to see who was calling the encrypted device before she answered.

"Barb, I need to see you in the War Room of the main house," Hal Brognola announced.

"I thought you were supposed to be in D.C. today," Price replied. "Briefing the Man on our last op in Kenya."

"I was," the big Fed said. "Now I'm in a chopper about thirty seconds from the Farm."

"What have you got?"

There was a pause, and when Brognola spoke again Barbara Price could easily hear the grim note of satisfaction in his voice. "We've finally got a breakthrough on Stage One."

Instantly the Stony Man mission controller stopped running, the machine slowing beneath her. "Really?" she said, her own voice eager. "We have a lead?"

"One for sure and one likely," Brognola answered. "I'll tell you more when I touch down."

"Understood. I'll see you in ten," Price said, and clicked off.

She stepped off the exercise machine and grabbed up a handy towel to mop her forehead and blot the sweat on her arms. She threw it around her neck and then clicked over to the walkie-talkie function on her cell phone. Her thumb pressed the push-to-talk button and she spoke into the phone.

"Bear, you on?"

There was a pause and then Aaron "the Bear" Kurtzman's gruff voice growled out a response. "Go ahead, Barb. What's up?" The brilliant technician served as leader of the Farm's cyber team and was Barbara Price's right-hand man.

"Meet me in the War Room," Price told him. "Hal's coming in now and he has something for us."

"Something big?"

When she spoke Price could hear the same satisfied tone in her own voice as she had just identified in Hal Brognola's. It made the corners of her mouth tug upward in an involuntary grin.

"Hal says we just broke something on our Stage One project."

Kurtzman made no attempt to keep his enthusiasm in check. "Hot damn!" he barked into the phone, making Price wince. "It's about time we caught a break on that one."

"Copy that, Bear," Price agreed. "Is Carmen or Akira near you?" she asked, referring to two members of Kurtzman's team. Carmen Delahunt was an ex-FBI agent recruited into the Stony Man program by Hal Brognola, and Akira Tokaido was a network systems interfacing genius and all around cybercowboy who had conducted digital wizardry for Price many times in the past.

"Carmen's right here," Kurtzman replied.

"Good. Have her alert Able Team and Phoenix Force," Price said. "I want the teams on standby and ready to go the minute we get the rundown from Hal."

"Copy that."

"All right, I'm out. See you in the War Room." The mission controller cut communications and hurried out of the workout center.

The well-oiled machinery of Stony Man had begun ticking with precision timing and practiced competence. Soon men would be out on the sharp end and the blood of killers would begin to spill.

STONY MAN FARM was located in the Blue Ridge Mountains. Despite housing an extensive command-and-control logistics network, an airfield and outdoor training areas, the remote clandestine site maintained a facade as a tree farm, orchard and pulp mill. Security was a fully integrated package of electronic, computer-monitored and human surveillance. The farm workers and general laborers spread around the Farm were actually highly trained soldiers from America's elite military and law enforcement units.

In the past rotational assignments to the Farm had given members of those units access to advanced training tactics and an opportunity to engage in cross-organizational networking. As the wars in southwest Asia and the Middle East had ground on, the short-term assignments to the top secret site had started to provide physically and emotionally exhausted multitour combat veterans with a low-key break from near-constant combat operations.

Such breaks were not available for members of the Farm's premier crews, Able Team and Phoenix Force. While the security corps, designated as blacksuits, maintained protective defensive operations, the Farm's strike teams deployed constantly across the Western Hemisphere and the world on offensive mandates for the U.S. government.

The leaders of those teams now gathered in the basement facility under the Farm's main house in a briefing area called the War Room. Besides Hal Brognola and Barbara Price, Aaron Kurtzman was there with the unit commander of Phoenix Force, David McCarter, and Carl Lyons, Able Team leader.

Kurtzman, confined to a wheelchair after an attack on Stony Man grounds by KGB surrogates had left him paralyzed from the waist down, sat off to one side, running the briefing media presentation components from a keyboard built into his chair.

Built like a power lifter, the barrel-chested Kurtzman still routinely did sets of the bench press with 250 pounds for nearly a dozen reps. In contrast to his heavy build the two big men seated at the massive conference table in front of him seemed built more for endurance, despite impressively muscular builds.

The fox-faced Briton, David McCarter, was a consummate pilot and driver, as well as being a former member of the British Special Air Service. He had seen combat around the world in places as diverse as Oman and Belfast before coming on board as a shooter for the Farm's Phoenix Force. Now, years later, the brown-eyed Englishman commanded that team and had committed violence on behalf of the U.S. government in every region of the globe.

"What have you got for us?" he asked, his English accent mellow after years in United States.

"Tell me it's something good," Carl Lyons answered.

The blond leader of the three-man Able Team was a former LAPD homicide detective. Lyons lived up to his moniker of Ironman. There was no better pistol marksman or fitter athlete than Lyons on the Farm's teams. He had the subtlety of a bull in a China shop, combined with the acumen of a veteran espionage agent. When Carl Lyons ran into a problem he put his head down and battered his way through it.

"We've been waiting for a long time for some actionable intelligence on this," Hal Brognola said. "A long time. Several years, in fact." The Fed's suit was rumpled and he spoke from around the stump of an unlit cigar. He gestured toward Barbara Price, who stood unselfconsciously in her sweat-stained workout gear. "Barb?"

The Stony Man mission controller nodded once curtly, obviously eager to get into the meat of the briefing.

"Gentlemen," she said, "let me tell you about Stage One. Quite a while ago national intelligence estimates began warning the Oval Office about an increased threat focus coming from Iran. These threat focus assessments had little to do with Iraq or with Tehran's burgeoning nuclear program. In fact, the assessments were not Israel centered in nature.".

Intrigued, McCarter lifted an eyebrow and glanced over at Lyons, who shrugged. Behind them, Kurtzman hit a button on his keyboard and an Iranian in an army general's uniform appeared on the monitor at the head of the table.

"The intelligence was disparate, piecemeal and often

obtuse. The Oval Office asked Hal to put Bear and his cyber team on it to try to analyze what we were seeing," Price continued.

Kurtzman powered his wheelchair forward toward the head of the table. "We had precious little to go on," he admitted. "Everything that was Iranian intelligence, Hezbollah, Hamas or Iraqi special groups related had to be screened to see if it fit with any other irregular activities worldwide. We figured out that whatever they were up to, it had something to do with the U.S. directly and not through surrogates or proxies. Mostly we got lost in smoke and mirrors."

"Don't be modest, Bear," Hal Brognola said. "You were two weeks ahead of the golden boys at INR in identification of Stage One." The big Fed referred to the State Department's Bureau of Intelligence and Research.

The bureau had few or no field operatives of its own, but was instead tasked with performing oversight and analysis of information gathered from other branches of the U.S. intelligence community. In both the cases of pre-9/11 threats and the buildup to the invasion of Iraq, the INR had offered up the only dissenting voice in the national intelligence estimates and had subsequently come to be seen as the nation's premier brain trust on intelligence.

Beating them on a point of analytical determination had provided Aaron Kurtzman with a moment of quiet pride.

"If this has been going on for a while, then why are we just now hearing about it?" McCarter asked.

"Because we didn't have any operational intelligence," Price replied.

"You couldn't find anyone for us to shoot or hit over the head?" Lyons asked.

Hal Brognola removed the unlit stogie from his mouth. "Exactly," he said. "Bear and his team were putting together a jigsaw puzzle from half a dozen different boxes while in a dark room."

Barbara Price spoke up. "Stage One is an umbrella term for some sort of operation directed at the United States. It includes several separate but connected operations and projects that are all being run by the Iranian Revolutionary Guard and their black ops unit, the Ansar-al-Mahdi. We were only ever able to tie a couple of low-level couriers and agents to the project. That included this man." She pointed to the Iranian on the monitor screen. "Colonel Muqtada Ayub of a Basij division near Tehran."

"Basij?" McCarter frowned. "I thought they were a local militia, like a National Guard for the Revolutionary Guard."

"Yes and no." Price nodded. "They are an auxiliary paramilitary force. But they also serve in law enforcement, emergency management and social and religious organizing in their respective areas. They also serve as a secret police militia against the general population doing morals policing and suppressing the activities of dissident groups."

"Nut jobs?" Lyons asked. He took pride in a direct approach many often referred to as crass. He also liked to claim it was part of his charm, though he had never met anyone who actually agreed with him about that.

"Highly motivated nut jobs," Brognola specified. "They provided the martyr volunteers for Iran's human-wave attacks against Saddam Hussein's army during the Iran-Iraq war."

"It seems Colonel Ayub is also connected by marriage to a prominent cleric on the Revolutionary Council," Price added. "He's the highest ranking operative we've been able to connect to Stage One so far."

"He's a big, fat intelligence node just waiting to be hacked," Kurtzman added. "With what he can tell us, I'm sure I'll be able to piece together this puzzle in no time."

"Getting him would be a major coup," Price said.

"Where is he now?" McCarter asked. "I assume somewhere we can get to him."

"Yes," Price answered. "Specifically we have him located in a safehouse in Hayaniya, a Shiite-militia-controlled neighborhood in northwestern Basra. Carmen will provide you momentarily with a briefing packet of operational details for you to go over with the rest of Phoenix once we're done here."

"That explains what David's going to be doing," Lyons spoke up. "How about Able?"

Price acknowledged him, then nodded to Kurtzman. The computer specialist used his thumb to strike a key, and the picture changed to a surveillance shot of a Middle Eastern man in civilian clothes. "That individual is Aras Kasim," she said. "A known agent of the Iranian Ministry of Intelligence, VEVAK."

Lyons leaned forward, reading a sign in Spanish in the picture behind the man. "Where's he at? Caracas?"

"Yes. You can thank the very thorough Carmen Delahunt for giving you someone to knock over the head, Carl," Price answered. "Two days ago a CIA interagency memo had Kasim meeting with Ayub in Basra. This morning a brief by DEA agents surveilling Juan Escondito showed him in a meeting with Kasim."

"An Iranian intelligence operative meeting with a

Venezuelan narco-trafficker?" Lyons grunted. "That is big. We can run with this."

"Good. Carmen will have your operational details ready to go in a couple of minutes, as well." Barbara Price looked down at her team leaders from the head of the conference table. "Go out and bring me these men so we can shut the Iranians down."

Both David McCarter and Carl Lyons were grinning as they rose from their seats.

CHAPTER FOUR

Basra, Iraq

Akmed Anjali had been a major in the Iraqi police since the Americans had taken Baghdad. He had been a loyal and partisan son of the Shammar clan all of his life and a follower of the radical cleric Muqtada al-Sadr's Shiite sect since he had been a small boy. His loyalties were not divided; they were prioritized. Allah, family, national duty. He followed them in that order, and if his duties as a Shia patriarch ever conflicted with his responsibilities as police officer, then he had to remember that his land was far older than most Americans could conceive and after the Americans were gone his land and his faith would continue unabated, like the life-mother Tigris River flowing perpetually to the sea.

It was because of this understanding that he went to see the Iranian after he left his liaison meeting with his British counterparts at their Basra international airport headquarters. Diplomatic imperatives had dictated that the British share what they knew with Major Anjali, just as religious obligation dictated that Anjali share what he knew with the Iranian.

Anjali directed his driver away from the airport and toward the northwest Basra neighborhood of Hayaniya. The sergeant, a nephew of Anjali, guided the white Toyota 4-Runner through a maze of backstreets once they reached the neighborhood. The buildings rose around them to heights of five or six stories, and vendors populated storefront properties along the narrow streets, selling everything from chickens to cheap plastic children's toys and a thousand different knockoff versions of name-brand items.

They stopped the police patrol vehicle in front of a baked-brick wall with an iron gate that opened up on an inner courtyard. Anjali nodded to the man guarding the entrance. The sentry, who wore an Uzi submachine gun on a shoulder strap, instantly recognized him and let him in. The sounds of the street life behind Anjali faded as the man closed the heavy iron gate behind him.

"Wait here," the sentry informed the police officer, and Anjali did as he was told.

The man he was here to see kept company with hardened killers. Some were Iraqi insurgents, but more than a few were Quds Force veterans; the Iranian special forces. The network run by the Colonel Ayub was the most efficient Anjali had ever seen in southern Iraq and it ran on impeccable discipline structured around instantaneous and brutal violence.

The sentry reappeared at the inner courtyard door and waved him forward into the building proper. Anjali resisted the urge to unbutton the flap of his sidearm holster. He was walking into a nest of vipers and the only thing that could protect him was the same thing that had always protected him. The good graces of his associates.

He entered a long, low-ceilinged room. Fans ran the length of the chamber, spinning slowly and casting moving slashes of shadows from the harsh white sunlight shooting in from the slats of the window shutters. Anjali paused at the door, blinking his eyes into focus.

There was a blue haze of cigarette smoke heavy in the air. The smell of unwashed male bodies freely sweating in the heat assaulted his nose. The room was filled with armed men in the traditional white robes called *thobe*. Low couches were positioned against the walls, but no one was sitting in them.

A knot of expressionless men stood clustered toward the center of the room. Somewhat hesitantly Anjali started forward. The group of men opened to let him walk through. Cigarettes dangled from their lips, Kalashnikovs dangled from their shoulders and large ceremonial knives dangled from their belts. Flat, inscrutable eyes of black or deepest brown regarded him with either contempt or indifference.

Anjali walked into their midst, and they closed in behind him like the bars of a cell door sliding shut even as more militiamen in front of him stepped back to reveal his Iranian contact.

Colonel Ayub looked up as Anjali stepped forward.

At Ayub's feet an Iraqi in civilian clothes was on his knees. The man's hands were bound tightly behind his back and a bandanna covered his eyes. His face was a checkerboard of bruises beneath the blindfold and he turned toward the sound of Anjali as he stepped forward.

Ayub's arm was extended outward and down toward the captive. In his hand was the largest pistol Anjali had ever seen. It was massive and silver with a long barrel and gigantic muzzle. Ayub's finger rested lightly on the trigger of the big automatic.

"Ah, look," Ayub purred. "The police are here. Just in time."

The crowd of men in the room chuckled lowly as if they shared one voice. It had the disconcerting effect of making Anjali feel even more hemmed in. The police major, who was himself no stranger to either torture or murder, kept his own facial expression as neutral as that of the killers around him.

"I have news," he said.

Ayub nodded. "In a moment. You have arrived just in time to witness the judgment of Allah for crimes of collaboration with the westerners against the free Iraqi people."

At this announcement the man on his knees began to sob and babble, crying out his innocence. Ayub shushed him gently, the way a mother might quiet a frightened toddler. When this didn't work he coldly pressed the muzzle of the .44 Magnum against the man's forehead just above the blindfold and snapped, "Silence!"

The man fell silent.

Ayub's finger took up the slack on the trigger of the massive handgun. Anjali could almost hear the mechanical squeak as the spring was compressed. He silently steeled himself for the sound of the pistol going off. The crowd of men pushed in around them remained very silent.

"So," Ayub said, suddenly changing tracks, "what is your news?"

Anjali felt his eyes glued to the spot where the .44-caliber weapon's muzzle was up against the captive's forehead. The man was sweating profusely, and a fat drop of perspiration slid down cheeks marred by black-heads and a sparse, wiry attempt at a man's beard. The captive was skinny as a rail and his Adam's apple stood out like a knot on his thin neck. He swallowed hard and Anjali saw it bounce like a bobber on a fishing line.

"The British bribed someone," Anjali said. "They know where you are. They told the Americans, who have sent for some commandos."

"Task Force 162?" Ayub asked, referring to the combined unity of Army Special Forces, Navy SEALs and CIA paramilitary operatives that had been formed to track down Saddam Hussein and other high-value targets.

Anjali shook his head. "No. Another group. The briefer didn't specify who they were. Only that they had come from the U.S. for you."

"For me?" Ayub asked. "By name?"

Anjali looked down at the man on his knees. Tears had joined the sweat on his face now. The police major nodded. "Yes. By name."

"Do you see?" Ayub whispered down at the man. "Do you see now? You camel fucker!" he suddenly screamed. "You talk and this does not work! No one must talk!"

"Please!" the man sobbed.

Time slowed for Anjali as a sudden flood of adrenaline coursed through his body. He saw the big silver automatic jump in Ayub's hand just as the report deafened him at that close range. A sheet of flame erupted from the pistol muzzle, scorching the prisoner's skin and setting his oily black hair on fire.

A single smoking shell casing was kicked loose to tumble through the air, and the man's face disappeared in black smoke and red blood as the back of his skull suddenly burst backward, spraying the white, loose flowing robes of the terrorists standing closest to him. The body undulated on its knees then slumped as if the corpse had been deboned.

The crack of the pistol echoed through the room, and out of his peripheral vision Anjali saw a section of the floor tile suddenly burst apart and shatter as the heavy-caliber slug burrowed into it. The man keeled over and dropped to the floor, all slack limbs and gushing blood and spilled brains as Anjali's ears began to ring.

He pulled his eyes from the horrible vision of the murdered captive and felt a surge of surprise so intense it bordered on fear when he saw Ayub already looking at him. The man's mouth was moving as he spoke and the Iraqi police major could see the thin lips forming words over blunt yellow teeth, but the ringing of the shot at such close quarters had deafened him. Then his ears popped and he could suddenly hear the Iranian cell leader again.

"—let the American commandos come. We'll have a surprise waiting for them."

Then Ayub looked down at the cored-out head and blown-apart face of his victim and began to laugh. Immediately the knot of Shiite terrorists around Anjali started laughing, too.

Screw it, he thought and chuckled right along.

Caracas, Venezuela

ARAS KASIM could hardly believe his good fortune. For five years he had labored in Tehran watching dissidents and walking point on guard teams for important Imams, opening limo doors and shoving people clear on the streets. The whole experience had been an exercise in extreme boredom and hardly the reason he had left a Revolutionary Guard marine battalion combat swimmer assignment for a position with VEVAK.

Then he had worked a security detail under a colonel named Ayub and his life had changed almost overnight. Ayub had his pick of intelligence ministry agents, and from within the protective umbrella of Brigadier General Najafi's patronage the colonel got what he wanted when he wanted it. Kasim had earned his stripes in this new operation first by smuggling explosive devices across the southwestern Iranian border into Iraq and then to Baghdad.

Once he had proved himself resourceful and battle tested, Ayub had used him as a insurgent-cell communications facilitator and, finally, as a punitive agent against anyone suspected of disloyalty within the organization. Kasim had executed seven Iraqi insurgents and tortured three times as many under Ayub's direction.

With his competence established Ayub had begun to tap him for more and more serious activities. First travel to the border areas of Pakistan to coordinate with al Qaeda and Taliban operatives there. Then to carry money to cells in Lebanon and the Philippines. There was the torture and murder of a CIA case officer in Ethiopia followed by the meetings with Russian arms dealers in Chechnya.

And finally there was the Juan Escondito network.

The Venezuelan *narco-trafficante* had been a secular blessing to the Iranian intelligence operative. Meetings included fine whiskey, the kindest cuts of cocaine and more young prostitutes than Kasim could ever have prayed existed.

In bed with two of them now, Kasim could only look up toward heaven past the spinning ceiling fan and offer thanks for what the teenage girls were doing to him now. He leaned back against the cool spread of his sheets with their three-hundred-count weave of Egyptian cotton. His body was slick with sweat and the smell of sex was a heavy musk in the room.

On the table was a half-empty bottle of Johnnie Walker Black Label and a mirror piled high with fine-quality cocaine. His head was buzzing and his skin tingled with euphoric sensations. He could feel the press of Marta's breasts against his shin bone on one side and hot damp cling of Juanita's sex on the arch of his other foot as they took turns pleasing him. They would growl and chatter in Spanish to each other and he just knew, though he didn't speak a word, that they were just saying the filthiest of things.

In the morning Program Manticore would begin the operation to bring jihad into the American heartland. Lethal justice would spread through the United States like drugs from the Southern Hemisphere, and the warmongering westerners would relearn what terror really was.

He reached down and put a possessive hand on the top of Marta's bobbing head. Once this was over he would see about parlaying his service into a permanent assignment in South America. The Israelis had a presence here, as well, and the only thing that could please Kasim more than operating against the Americans would be a chance to kill Jewish agents of the Satan state.

He felt Juanita's fingers begin to massage his testicles then slide lower; she knew what he liked best of all. All in all Kasim could not think of a more perfect outcome for his life.

ABLE TEAM'S PLAN was simple.

They would come in on a commercial flight and make it through customs clean. Following that they would pick up a vehicle and make their way to a safe-house used by the CIA and Army special operations. There, Able Team would establish a base before starting surveillance of the target.

Things began to go wrong immediately.

Carl Lyons pulled his carry-on bag down from the overhead compartment just after the unfasten seat belts sign popped up on the TWA commercial flight. They were flying first-class as part of their administrative cover and the team leader had watched, bemused, as Rosario "Politician" Blancanales worked his gregarious charm on a Hispanic flight attendant.

Team funny man Hermann "Gadgets" Schwarz had cracked one stale joke after another as the silver-haired smooth talker flirted shamelessly with the dark-eyed Venezuelan beauty half his age.

There wasn't a person on the plane among the crew or passengers who didn't think the three men were anything but what they claimed; middle-aged divorced tourists on a South American vacation. Blancanales's audacity was role-playing brilliance.

If there was anything bothering Lyons as he exited the plane after the flight attendant had slipped her cell number to Blancanales, it was that circumstances dictated they begin the operation unarmed. Carl Lyons didn't like taking a shower unarmed, let alone entering a potentially volatile nation without a weapon.

"Okay," Schwarz murmured as they emerged into the big, air-conditioned terminal, "we can add a certain

TWA flight attendant named Bonita to our roster of Stony Man local assets."

"Oh, yeah," Lyons replied, "I'm sure she'll be a big help. We can just send Dave and his boys down here sometime and they can all crash at her hacienda. It'll be like the Farm 'South.'"

"You see how it is, Gadgets?" Blancanales said, voice weary. "You try to take one for the team and management doesn't appreciate it. I try to show loyalty through service and all I get is cynical pessimism."

"Can you gentlemen come this way."

The voice interrupted their banter with a tone of undisputed authority. The members of Able Team turned their heads as one to take in the speaker. He was a tall Latino with jet-black hair, mustache and eyes in the crisp uniform of a Venezuelan customs officer. There was a 9 mm automatic pistol in a polished holster on his hip, but the flap was closed and secured.

However a few paces behind him the assault rifles of the military security guards were visible as the soldiers stood with hands on pistol grips and fingers resting near triggers.

Lyons scowled. Schwarz gave the officer his best grin in reply to the summons. Then he turned his head slightly and whispered out of the side of his mouth, "Any chance you want to take one for the team now, Pol?"

Blancanales fixed an insincere grin of his own on his face. "Nope. This time we move right to cynical pessimism," he replied.

VENEZUELAN CUSTOMS separated the three men quickly, hustling them into separate rooms. There they sat isolated for two hours. Carl Lyons found himself sitting in front of a plain metal table on an uncomfortable folding chair while the customs officer pretended to read official-looking papers printed in Spanish with a government seal at the top of the pages.

Fluent in Spanish, Lyons easily read them and saw they were merely quarterly flight-maintenance reports being used as props. Warily, Lyons decided to relax a bit; this seemed a more random occurrence than he had first feared. The Farm had considerable resources, but the operation was miniscule compared to other government agencies, and Stony Man operatives were often forced to rely on logistical support from larger bureaucratic entities. Whenever that happened security became a prime concern, but for now this seemed a more typical customs roust than anything more threatening.

The officer, whose name tag read Hernandez, picked up Lyons's passport and opened it. "Mr. Johnson?" His English was accented but clipped and neat.

Lyons nodded. "That's me."

Hernandez regarded him over the top of the little blue folder. "What brings you to Venezuela?"

"Sunny weather, beautiful women, the beaches. All the usual. Is there a problem with my passport?"

Hernandez carefully put down the blue folder. He ignored the question and carefully tapped the passport with one long, blunt-tipped finger. "There are many countries in South America with beautiful beaches and women."

"But only one Margarita Island—it's world famous," Lyons replied in flawless Spanish, referencing Venezuela's most popular tourist designation.

Hernandez's eyes flicked upward sharply at the linguistic display. His eyes looked past Lyons and toward the large reflective glass. Lyons knew from his own experience as a police officer that was where the customs officer's superiors were watching the interrogation. Hernandez let his gaze settle back on Lyons. He offered a wan smile.

"I'm sure this is just an administrative error," the officer said. "My people will have it sorted out in no time." Hernandez rose to his feet. "Please be patient."

"Okay," Lyons nodded agreeably. "But man, am I getting thirsty."

Hernandez left Lyons and walked into the interrogation room containing Hermann Schwarz. As he moved down the hallway he saw the tall, cadaverous figure in a dark suit standing behind his commanding officer. The man met Hernandez's gaze with cold, dead eyes, and the Venezuelan customs officer felt a chill at the base of his spine. What was he doing here? Hernandez wondered. He stifled the thought quickly—it didn't pay to ask too many questions about Hugo Chavez's internal security organization, even to yourself.

As he walked into the room he saw a burly sergeant had Schwarz pinned up against the wall, one beefy forearm across the American's throat. The officer was scowling in fury as Schwarz, going by the name Miller, smirked.

Schwarz looked over at Hernandez as the man entered the room and grinned. "Hey, Pedro," he called. "You know why this guy's wife never farted as a little girl? 'Cause she didn't have an asshole till she got married!"

The officer rotated and dipped the shoulder of his free hand. His fist came up from the hip and buried itself in Schwarz's stomach. The Stony Man operative absorbed the blow passively and let himself crumple at the man's feet. He looked up from the floor, gasping for breath.

After a pause Schwarz again addressed Hernandez. "You know what this *pendejo*'s most confusing day is? Yep—Father's Day."

His cackling was cut off as the sergeant kicked him in the ribs. Hernandez snapped an order and reluctantly the man backed off. "Leave us!" he repeated, and the officer left the room still scowling.

Hernandez moved forward and dropped Schwarz's passport on the table. He looked down as the American fought his way back up to his feet. Hernandez watched dispassionately as the man climbed into his chair.

"This is a helluva country you got here, pal," Schwarz said. "Tell a few jokes and get the shit kicked out of you. I should get a lawyer and sue your ass."

"You'll find Venezuelan courts unsympathetic to ugly Americans, Mr. Miller."

"Yeah, well, your momma's so fat when she walks her butt claps."

"Why have you come to Venezuela, Mr. Miller?"

"I heard a guy could get a drink. I think it was a lie. Seriously, I'm here with some buddies to check out the sites, maybe see the senoritas on Margarita Island—but instead I get this?"

"Perhaps you shouldn't insult my officers?"

"Perhaps you shouldn't lock an innocent *tourista* up for two hours in a room with a trained monkey like that asshole."

Hernandez sighed heavily, a weary man with an odious task. "I'm sure this is just an administrative error. We'll have it sorted out shortly."

"You're damn well right you will," Schwarz snapped, playing his role to the hilt.

"In the meantime, perhaps you could refrain from antagonizing my officers? Yes?"

"Hey, Pedro—is that your stomach or did you just swallow a beach ball?"

Officer Hernandez turned and walked out of the room, studiously ignoring the thin man standing outside in the hall next to the doorway.

"Hey, who do ya have to screw to get a drink around here?" Schwarz demanded as the door swung closed.

From behind the two-way mirror the thin man watched him with inscrutable curiosity.

AS CUSTOMS OFFICER Hernandez entered the final interrogation room, Blancanales, whose own passport was made out under the name of Rosario, rose from his seat, manner eager and face twisted into a mask of hopeful supplication.

"Listen," he began babbling, "I'm *really* sorry—"

"Shut up and sit down!" Hernandez interrupted. "Yes, I know, I know. You are all here innocently. You are all planning to go to Margarita Island, you are all thirsty and need a drink because you are just typical ugly Americans here to screw our women and drink tequila!"

Face frozen in a look of sheepish innocence, Blancanales settled back down in his chair. He blinked his eyes several times. "Well, er, I guess…yeah."

Face red, Hernandez spun on a heel and tossed the blue passport on the table in disgust. He left the room and slammed the door behind him so hard it rattled in its frame.

Blancanales called after him, "Actually, I am kind of thirsty, *amigo*."

Out in the hallway Hernandez marched up to his superior, who stood waiting next to the thin man in civilian clothes. "Sir, their paperwork checks out. Everything checks out perfectly. They've obviously rehearsed their story—or it's the truth. Should I toss them in a holding cell?"

"That won't be necessary," the thin man said. "Let them go. Apologize for the mistake, wish them well."

Hernandez slid his gaze over to his commanding officer, who glanced at the man next to him, then nodded. "Yes, we have enough. Let them go."

CHAPTER FIVE

Basra, Iraq

The rotors of the Black Hawk helicopter were still turning as the side door to the cargo bay opened to reveal the men Major Anjali had been sent to greet. He surveyed them with a critical eye, noting the athletic physiques, flat affects and nonregulation weaponry hanging off their ballistic armor and black fatigues.

Anjali had seen enough special operations soldiers in his life to recognize the type. The elite always had more in common with each other than even with others of their own country or military. Anjali was a wise enough and realistic enough man to know he himself did not belong among their ranks. It was no matter of ego for him; his interests lay in other directions.

At the moment he remained focused on gaining these mysterious commandos' trust, leading them into hostile terrain beyond the reach of help and then betraying them—making himself a little wealthier in the process.

The first man to reach Anjali was tall and broad with

fox-faced features and brown eyes and hair. Having spent the past five years operating alongside British forces in Basra, the Shiite police officer recognized an Englishman even before he spoke and revealed his accent.

"You Anjali?" David McCarter asked.

Anjali nodded, noting the man did not identify either himself or his unit. Behind the Briton his team paused: a tall black man with cold eyes, a stocky Hispanic with a fireplug build and scarred forearms standing next to a truly massive individual with shoulders like barn doors and an M-60E cut-down machine gun. Behind the tight little group another individual, as tall and muscular as the rest, turned and surveyed the windows and rooftops of the buildings overlooking the secured helipad. There was a sniper-scoped Mk 11 with a paratrooper skeletal folding stock in his hands, the eyepieces on the telescopic sight popped up to reveal an oval peep sight glowing a dim green.

"We were briefed on the flight in," McCarter continued. "You get us past the Iraqi security checkpoints and militia crossings until we're within striking distance, then fall back with the reserve force should we need backup."

"Just so." Anjali nodded. "I'm surprised you agreed to having only Iraqi forces as overwatch. Did you work with us in Basra before?" The question was casually voiced, but still constituted a breach of etiquette in such situations.

"Has there been a change in the situation since our initial briefing?" the black man asked, cutting in.

Anjali turned to face Calvin James, noting the H&K MP-7 submachine gun dangling from a sling off his shoulders down the front of his black fatigue shirt. In his big, scarred hands the man casually cradled a SPAS-15 dual mode combat shotgun, its stock folded down so that he held it by the pistol grip and forestock just beyond the detachable drum-style magazine.

Just as with the rest of them Anjali saw the man's black fatigues bore no unit insignia, name tag or rank designation. His voice was flatly American, however, the accent bearing just a trace of the Midwest, but the major couldn't be sure.

The Iraqi pretended not to notice the pointed disregarding of his own indelicate question. Behind the team the Black Hawk's engines suddenly changed pitch and began to whine as the helicopter lifted off.

Anjali shook his head to indicate no to the black man's questions, then waved his hand toward the armored personnel carrier parked on the edge of the helipad's concrete apron. The Dzik-3 was a multipurpose armored car made by Poland and used by Iraqi army and police units throughout the country.

The 4.5-ton wheeled vehicle boasted bulletproof windows, body armor able to withstand 7.62 mm rounds, puncture-proof tires and smoke launchers. T. J. Hawkins, covering the unit's six o'clock as they made for the APC, thought it looked like a dun-colored Brink's truck and doubted it could withstand the new Iranian special penetration charges being used in current roadside IEDs—Improvised Explosive Devices. He would have felt a lot safer in an American Stryker or the Cougar armored fighting vehicle.

He was used to stark pragmatism, however, and made no comment as he scrambled inside the vehicle, carefully protecting his sniper scope.

It had been easier to coordinate a blacked-out operation through local Iraqi forces than to bring British authorities operating in the Basra theater in on the loop because the deployment had been so frenzied. Hawkins accepted the situation without complaint.

Inside the armored vehicle the team sat crammed together, muzzles up toward the ceiling. Rafael Encizo sat behind the driver's seat holding a Hawk MM-1 multiround 40 mm grenade launcher. As Anjali settled in the front passenger seat beside his driver he looked back at the heavily armed crew with a frown.

"I am in charge of my vehicle during transport and thus am commanding officer for this phase of the operation," he said, voice grave. "I'm afraid I'm going to have to insist that you put your weapon safeties on."

McCarter leaned forward, shifting his M-4/M-203 combo to one side as he did, the barrel passing inches from Anjali's face. He held up his trigger finger in front of the Iraqi major's face and smiled coldly.

"Sorry, mate," he said. "I know you've heard this before but—" he wiggled his trigger finger back in forth in front of Anjali's eyes "—this is my safety." He settled back into his seat. "End of story."

Anjali turned around, face red with fury. He slapped the dash of the vehicle and curtly ordered his driver to pull away from the tarmac of the helipad. As the vehicle rolled out into traffic, he forced himself to calm. It was as the old Arabic proverb, claimed by the English as their own, said: who laughs last laughs best, and Major Anjali planned to be laughing very hard indeed at the end of the next few hours.

PHOENIX FORCE REMAINED alert as the Dzik-3 left the main traffic thoroughfares surrounding the airport and pushed deeper into the city. They rolled through Iraqi national army and police checkpoints without a problem, but as the buildings grew more congested and run-down, and the signs of the recent civil conflicts became more prolific—in the form of bullet-riddled walls, the charred hulks of burned-out vehicles, gaping window frames and missing doors—so did flags and graffiti proclaiming Shia slogans and allegiance.

Now the checkpoints were manned by local force police officers who all wore subtle indicators of tribal allegiance in addition to their official uniforms. Portraits of the firebrand Shiite cleric Muqtada al-Sadr became prominent. They were entering a section of the city where centralized authority had lost its influence and clan leaders and imams were the de facto power structures.

The checkpoint stops became longer and the night grew deeper. In the backseat Gary Manning used the GPS program on his PDA to plot their course as they moved through the city. After a moment he froze the screen and leaned forward to tap McCarter on the shoulder. "We're here," he said.

McCarter nodded and looked out a side window. They had entered an area of urban blight forming a squalid industrial bridge between two more heavily populated sections of the city. The dull brown waters of the Shatt al-Arab, the waterway formed by the confluence of the Tigris and Euphrates rivers, cut through concrete banks lined with empty and burned-out factories, manufacturing plants and abandoned electrical substations. A rusting crane sat in a weed-choked parking lot like a forgotten Jurassic beast of steel and iron.

"Pull over," McCarter told Anjali.

The major looked back in confusion. "What? We

still have two more checkpoints to go before the rendez-
vous point," he protested.

"Pull over. We have our own ops plan," McCarter
stated. "When we give the signal, you and the chase
vehicle can meet us at the RP. We'll insert on foot
from here."

"This isn't what I was told—" Anjali sputtered.

"Pull over."

Anjali scowled. Then he barked an order to his driver,
who immediately guided the big vehicle over to the side
of the road. They rolled to a stop and Phoenix Force wasted
little time scurrying out of the vehicle, weapons up.

Before he slammed the door shut McCarter repeated
his instructions to the Iraqi major. "Get to the RP. Link
up with the chase vehicle and hold position as instructed. When I come across the radio we'll be shaking
ass out of the target zone so expect hot. Understood?"

Anjali nodded. His face was impassive as he replied,
"I understand perfectly, Englishman."

"Good," McCarter answered, and slammed the
Dzik-3's door closed.

As soon as the man was gone Anjali had his cell phone
out. He could feel his laughter forming in his belly and
he bit it down. He'd save it for when he was looking at
the bloody corpses of the western commandos.

Caracas, Venezuela

ABLE TEAM STEPPED OUT into the equatorial sunlight
from the cramped depths of the customs station on the
far side of the international airport. Hermann Schwarz's
eye was swollen slightly and he had a bemused look as
he used a free hand to rub at his sore ribs.

He turned toward Lyons, who was squinting against the hard yellow light of the sun. "Next time *you* play the asshole," he said.

Blancanales chuckled to himself. "It does come more natural to you," he argued.

Lyons shrugged and slid on his shades. He stood in the doorway of the police center and smiled. "Quick, use your cell phone to take a video of me."

Pretending to laugh along with the joke like ugly American tourists, Blancanales quickly opened his cell phone and thumbed on the video function. He started rolling, capturing the scene.

Immediately he saw a cadaverous man in a business suit watching them from beside their interrogator as he pointed the camera over Lyons's bulky shoulder. The man frowned as he saw the Americans taking pictures and then turned and walked away.

"Something to remember Caracas by," Schwarz said loudly.

"Oh, that was great acting," Lyons muttered, walking forward.

"Thank you, thank you very much."

"Did you get it?" Lyons asked.

"You mean, tall, skinny and corpse-looking?" Blancanales asked. "You betcha. I'll see what Aaron's crew can do with it." He hit a button and fired off the short video clip to a secure server service that would eventually feed it into Stony Man.

Stony Man Farm, Virginia

THE E-MAIL TRAVELED with digital speed through security links and into Carmen Delahunt's computer.

Seeing the priority message beeping an alert to her, she quickly lifted her hand, encased in a sensory glove, up to her left and pantomimed clicking on the link with a finger. Inside the screen of her VR uplink helmet the short cell phone video played out.

"Just got something from Pol," she said. "They want an ID on what appears to be a civilian who's buddy-buddy with Venezuelan law enforcement officials."

From behind her in the Stony Man Annex's computer room Aaron Kurtzman's gruff voice instructed her, "Send it over to Hunt's station. His link to the mainframe is more configured to that kind of search than your infiltration and investigation research algorithms. You stay on trying to get into VEVAK systems through their Interpol connection. I'm still convinced that's our best route into Ansar-al-Mahdi computer files."

Tapping the stem of a briarwood pipe against his teeth, Professor Huntington Wethers froze the video image on a single shot then transported it to a separate program designed to identify the anatomical features on the picture then translate them into a succinct binary code. He ran the program four times to include variables for age, angle and articulation, then ran a blending sum algorithm to predict changes for bad photography, low light and resolution obscurity. He grunted softly, then fired off double e-mails of the completed project, one back to Carmen Delahunt and the other to Akira Tokaido.

"There you go," Wethers said. "I would suggest simultaneous phishing with a wide-base server like Interpol and something more aimed, like Venezuelan intelligence."

"Dibs on Venezuelan intel," Tokaido called out.

Speaker buds for an iPod were set in his ears, and the youngest member of the Stony Man cyberteam slouched in his chair using only his fingertips to control the mouse pads on two separate laptops.

"That's just crap," Delahunt replied. "I already have a trapdoor built into Interpol. Dad, Akira's stealing all the fun stuff!"

"Children, behave," Kurtzman growled. "Or I'll make you do something really boring like checking CIA open agency sources like your uncle Hunt is doing."

"Your coffeepot is empty, Bear," Wethers replied, voice droll.

"What?" Kurtzman sat up in his wheelchair and twisted around to look at the coffeemaker set behind his workstation. To his relief he saw the pot was still half full of the jet-black liquid some claimed flowed through his veins instead of blood.

"Every time, Bear, I get you every time," Wethers chided.

"That's because some things aren't funny," Kurtzman said. "I expect such antics from a kid like Akira, but you're an esteemed professor, for God's sake. I expect you to comport yourself with decorum."

"Brother Bear," Wethers said, his fingers flying across his keyboard, "if you ever did run out of coffee you'd just grind the beans in your mouth."

"Bear drinks so much coffee," Delahunt added, her hands still wildly pantomiming through her VR screen, "that Juan Valdez named his donkey after him."

"Bear drinks so much coffee he answers the door before people knock," Tokaido added. He appeared to be hardly moving at his station, which meant he was working at his most precise.

Stony Man mission controller Barbara Price walked into the computer room just in time to catch Tokaido's comment. Without missing a beat the honey-blond former NSA operations officer added a quip of her own.

"Bear drinks so much coffee he hasn't blinked since the last lunar eclipse."

Kurtzman coolly lifted a meaty hand and gave a thumbs-down gesture. Deadpan, he blew the assembled group a collective raspberry. "Get some new material— those jokes are stale, people."

"Bear drinks so much coffee it never has a chance to get stale," Delahunt said calmly. She tapped the air in front of her with a single finger and added, "Hugo Campos—"

"Hermida," Tokaido simultaneously chorused with the red-headed ex-FBI agent.

"Of the General Counterintelligence Agency," Wethers finished for them. All humor was gone from his voice now. "The Venezuelan military intelligence agency."

Sensing the tension immediately, Price turned toward Kurtzman. "Venezuela? What does this mean for Able?"

Kurtzman pursed his lips and sighed. "Trouble."

CHAPTER SIX

Basra, Iraq

Phoenix Force became as ghosts.

They crossed the broken rubble of the abandoned parking lot until they could squat in the lee of a burned-out warehouse. T. J. Hawkins, who had perfected his long-range shooting as a member of the U.S. Army's premier hostage-rescue unit, scanned their back trail through his night scope. The other four members of the team clicked their AN/PVS-14 monocular night-vision devices over their nonshooting eyes.

McCarter waited patiently in the concealed position for his natural night vision to acclimate as much as possible before moving out. A stray dog, ribs prominent under a mangy hide, strayed close at one point but skittered off in fear after catching the scent of gun oil.

The group maintained strict noise discipline as they waited to see if they had been observed or compromised during the short scramble to their staging area. After a tense ten minutes McCarter signaled a generic all clear and rose into a crouch. He touched James on the shoulder and sent the former Navy SEAL across the parking lot toward a break in a battered old chain-link fence next to a pockmarked cinder-block wall.

James crossed the open area in a low, tight crouch, running hard. He slid into place and snapped up the SPAS-15 to provide cover. Once he was satisfied, he turned back to McCarter and gave the former SAS commando a single nod.

McCarter reached out and touched Encizo on the shoulder. The Cuban sprinted for the far side of the lot, his dense, heavily muscled frame handling the weight of the Hawk MM-1 easily. He slid into position behind James and swept the squat, cannon-muzzled grenade launcher into security overwatch.

McCarter leaned over and whispered into Hawkins's ear. "You go after me."

Hawkins nodded and flipped down the hinged lens covers on the NXS 15X scope of his Mk 11 Enhanced Battle Rifle. He took up the EBR in both hands and slid up to the edge of the wall while Gary Manning took his place on rear security, using the cut-down M-60 machine gun to maintain rear security.

McCarter checked once with Encizo, then slid the fire-selector switch on his M-4 to burst mode. There was a fléchette pack antipersonnel round loaded up in the tube of his M-203 grenade launcher, and he had attached an M-9 bayonet just after entering his forward staging area. He got a second clear signal from Encizo and immediately sprang forward.

He covered the distance fast, feet pounding on the busted concrete with staccato rhythm, then quickly slid into position behind Encizo. The muzzle of his weapon came up and tracked left to right, clearing sectors including rooftops with mechanical proficiency.

Satisfied, he turned and caught Calvin James's eye. He made a subtle pointing gesture with his left hand and the ex-SEAL turned the corner and scurried between the break in the fence next to the cinder-block wall. As soon as he was gone McCarter slapped Encizo on the shoulder and former anti-Castro militant followed James through the opening.

McCarter scurried up to take his post next to the breach and then gave Hawkins the all-clear signal. The man raced across the opening with his weapon up and disappeared behind the bullet-riddled wall.

McCarter waited a moment, giving Hawkins a chance to take a good position beyond the wall, then waved Gary Manning over. Trusting McCarter to cover him, the Canadian special operations soldier took up his machine gun and crossed the danger area.

Once Manning was past, McCarter scrambled backward through the opening, remaining orientated toward the open parking lot the team had just crossed, carbine up and ready.

On the other side of the breach he found the unit in a tight defensive circle. A single-story outbuilding lay inside a concrete enclosure. A metal placard in red and white showed the universal sign for electrical danger above black Arabic script. McCarter looked at Hawkins, who immediately moved to lie down and take up a position in the breach.

Gary Manning set his machine gun down and quickly pulled open the Velcro flap of a pouch on his web belt. He pulled an electrician's diagnostic kit from the container while Rafael Encizo pulled a pair of compact bolt cutters from the compact field pack on his back.

"Right, mate," McCarter whispered, "don't electrocute yourself, then."

Manning didn't look up as he quickly assembled his gear. "Do I tell you how to act like a complete jackass?"

"Not once," McCarter admitted, but the corner of his mouth crept upward.

"Then perhaps you can let me do my job wisecrack free?"

"Not a chance, mate," McCarter replied with complete seriousness. "Your ego's already too well developed for my liking."

Manning stopped what he was doing and looked at the Briton. "My ego?"

"Hey, now," McCarter protested, "if you're still mad about that little waitress in Barcelona—"

"Perhaps later would be a better time for this discussion?" James cut in, voice as dry as the Iraqi air.

Manning looked up and nodded toward Encizo. "Ready."

Encizo quickly used the bolt cutters to snap the locking arm of the rusted old padlock connecting the panel access doors. The muscles on his forearms jumped out in stark relief like cables running down to thick wrists. The lock popped free with a sharp crack and dropped to the ground at his feet. Encizo picked up his MM-1 and scooted quickly back.

James helped him put away the bolt cutters as Manning replaced Encizo in front of the access panel. He reached up and pulled the metal hatches apart to reveal a wall of exposed wires, relay switches and conduit housings.

From behind them, T. J. Hawkins suddenly hissed a low warning.

McCarter instantly moved to his side and sidled down low to present a minimal profile as he eased around the corner. Beside him the former Army Ranger lay his finger in the gentle curve of his trigger, taking up the slack. Out on the parking lot a dry wind pushed dead weeds and loose trash around. The area was an island of dark between two illuminated areas of population so the headlights of the approaching vehicles were easily visible.

Hawkins lay the scope on the convoy, quickly working the dampener on his scope's light amplifier to compensate for the illumination of the vehicle's high beams. The images of the Iraqi police squad in three Dzik-3 armored personnel carriers filled the crosshair of his reticule. M-2 .50 caliber machine guns were mounted on the roofs.

"Who the fuck are those guys?" McCarter demanded. "That wanker Anjali's boys? This isn't part of the plan."

Hawkins carefully zeroed in his scope and scanned the crew as they parked their vehicles in a wedge formation facing the abandoned warehouse Phoenix Force had used to shield their initial movements after disembarking from the first wheeled APC minutes earlier.

"They're police for sure," Hawkins answered. His voice was grim. "But to a man they're wearing green insignia shoulder epaulets." He removed his eye from the sniper scope and looked over at the former SAS commando. "David, they're Shia militia. Muqtada al-Sadr's boys."

"Bloody *hell!*" McCarter swore.

Caracas, Venezuela

"GODDAMN IT to hell!" Lyons swore. "We're in country ten fucking minutes and we've got Chavez's head spook nosing up our asses."

His big hand slammed the steering wheel of the rental SUV, a black Ford Excursion. His eyes darted up to the rearview mirror, scanning the flow of traffic behind them for any obvious tails or suspicious patterns. Caracas was a teeming, modern city of three million people and the streets were packed with automobiles, motorcycles, service trucks and pedestrians. Around them, skyscrapers of steel and glass rose in prototypical urban canyons. They would have to be sharp if they were going to spot a surveillance team in that kind of environment.

"At least the Farm was able to get us the information quickly," Schwarz pointed out as he slipped his PDA into a pocket. "It'd be much worse if we weren't aware *el douche* was hot on our ass."

"Having Venezuelan internal security meeting us right there at the airport is a bad, bad sign," Blancanales said. He sat in the back using a PDA of his own to download a software upgrade created by Schwarz into the vehicle's GPS system. "Something got SNAFUed right from the beginning."

"We can't roll on the VEVAK agent till we get to the safehouse," Lyons said. "But we can't lead a team of Chavez's secret police right to a U.S. safehouse, either. Freakin' fine mess."

"I guess we have to identify the shadow unit, then outdrive them." Schwarz shrugged. "I mean, the CIA does everything the CIA can do. The Farm does what the CIA can't."

"Or the FBI," Blancanales agreed. He caught Schwarz's eye in the rearview mirror and winked. "Or the LAPD," he added, voice casual.

Lyons, an ex-LAPD detective, stiffened in response to the inclusion. "Finest police force in the world. You can go to hell. Only reason I left is because SOG has a better dental plan."

"No, no. This is true," Schwarz said. "Absolutely. In fact, if you were to do an unbiased comparison of the three organizations I would say it's obvious the LAPD comes out on top." His voice was completely deadpan as he continued. "This is a no bullshit story, heard it right from the big Fed, Hal, himself. The LAPD, the FBI and the CIA were all trying to prove that they are the best at apprehending criminals. The President decided to give them a test. He released a rabbit into a forest and each of them had to try and catch it.

"The CIA goes in. They place animal informants throughout the forest. They question all plant and mineral witnesses. After three months of extensive investigations they concluded that rabbits do not exist.

"Then the FBI goes in. After two weeks with no leads they burn the forest, killing everything in it, including the rabbit, and they make no apologies. The rabbit had it coming.

"The LAPD goes in. They come out two hours later with a badly beaten bear. The bear is yelling, 'Okay! Okay! I'm a rabbit! I'm a rabbit!'"

"Ten will get you one that bear had done *something,*" Lyons fired back as his two teammates laughed.

Instantly, Hermann Schwarz stopped laughing. "Pol, does that qualify as an actual joke from the Ironman?"

"Close enough, as far as I'm concerned," Blancanales replied in a sober voice, sounding slightly bewildered.

"Screw you both," Lyons replied. He then promptly ran a red light. "Got the bastards! Green current-year Impala, looks like three of them in the rig."

Blancanales turned and quickly looked over his shoulder. "I got 'em. Looks like three in the vehicle," he repeated. There was a sudden blare of horns, squealing brakes and a chorus of angry shouts around them in the intersection. "They just ran the red, too," Blancanales added.

"We're on now," Schwarz said. "Of course if we actively loose these ass clowns then they'll know we're up to something and we'll have to go completely black instead of trying to maintain cover."

"Good," Lyons muttered, and pushed the accelerator to the floor. "I was getting goddamn tired of all the bullshit sneaking around we've been doing."

"Oh, yeah, we've been real below the radar." Schwarz smirked. Then he put his seat belt on.

Basra, Iraq

DAVID MCCARTER scooted quickly backward, leaving T. J. Hawkins in his low-profile overwatch position. Once away from the opening he turned to check on the rest of the team's progress. Gary Manning was coolly using a stylus to work the touch pad on his diagnostic server.

"How we coming, mate?" McCarter asked.

"More time," Manning replied.

"We kind of have company."

"Look, I've got to uplink this substation to the coalition power grid, then trace the connection to our neighborhood before I can shut out the lights. I need more time."

"Right." McCarter turned to the rest of his men. "Encizo, get into position next to Hawkins. If T.J. decides he needs to take a shot I want you to bring the noise."

"Copy." Encizo nodded. The Cuban lifted the MM-1 grenade launcher and slid in next to the prone Texan.

McCarter lifted his left hand and pointed at Calvin James. "We're advancing the plan by ten minutes," he said. "I want you to open the sewer entrance right now and hold the position until we can get Manning through this sabotage gig."

"They're rolling this way." Encizo spoke up for Hawkins. "Moving slow, but it seems obvious they're spooked and looking for something, not just patrolling."

McCarter turned back to the massive Canadian. "Gary?"

"Need time."

"Right, then." He twisted around. "Hold the line," McCarter whispered to Encizo, who leaned over and relayed the information to Hawkins. The Phoenix leader turned toward James and nodded once.

The former SEAL rose into a crouch and glided into the narrow space between the relay station Manning was working on and the cinder-block wall that encircled the work area. McCarter heard the whisper of cloth and leather on the concrete, then James was over the top of the far wall and gone into the night.

James hit the ground on the other side of the wall, his boots making a crunch on the loose gravel as he landed. He was in a small access alley running behind a line of empty buildings. At one end of the lane a worn and deteriorated industrial wharf jutted out into the Shatt al-Arab waterway. In the distance, the lights of a garbage scow moved slowly away, gulls circling it, their night cries sharp against the low rumble of its engine.

James swung around to look the other way. He let the SPAS-15 dangle from his strap and pulled a silenced Beretta 92-SB from a holster on his thigh. Down at the end of the alley opposite the pier ran a larger secondary road, intersecting with the alley where a commercial gas station had once stood. The fuel pumps had been blown clean off their moorings at some point in the war and the building was a soot-covered and burned-out hulk.

Moving carefully, pistol up, James jogged up the alley toward the burned-out service station where a manhole cover was set in the ground. He covered the backs of the building fronting the alley, but all he saw were empty windows, dark doorways and tight, twisted openings leading inward between the structures like tunnels.

Coming up to the manhole cover, James quickly went to one knee and holstered his Beretta to pull a thick-bladed diver's knife from a sheath on his combat boot. A diving knife was, by design, intended to be a pry bar and was built with full tangs and reinforced steel.

Working quickly, James slid the knife into the lip of the manhole cover and pried it up. Instantly a foul miasma wafted up from the opening, causing him to yank his head back in sudden disgust.

As he turned his face to the side, nose wrinkled against the stench, a Mahdi army militia member stared out at him from a weed-choked causeway between two deserted maintenance sheds made out of corrugated tin and aluminum siding. The man had an unlit cigarette dangling from his lips with a blue, cheap plastic lighter held up with his free hand cupped around the flickering flame.

Slung over his shoulder was an AKM.

James popped up out of his crouch like a jack-in-the-box. The Iraqi's eyes grew wide and his mouth sagged open in surprise. James pushed his feet hard into broken ground, springing forward. The militia gunman's cigarette tumbled from his lips and the flame on the lighter winked out as it dropped from his hand.

James crossed the road in a flat sprint, knife up and ready, face twisted into a snarl of rage. The plastic lighter hit the ground at the Iraqi's feet and bounced next to the forgotten cigarette. The man scrambled for the assault rifle slung on his shoulder, fingers fumbling in his fear.

The man tore the strap off his shoulder and swung the Kalashnikov down into his hands, fingers hunting for the trigger as he tried to bring the AKM barrel around. James swung his right hand down and knocked the weapon back into the man's own chest, blocking him like a defensive back on the line of scrimmage.

The man's fetid breath rushed out in a gasp, his spittle spraying James in the face. The dive knife arced up and plunged into the Iraqi's torso just below the sternum, slicing through the membrane of the solar plexus. The man collapsed inward around the thrust and James tore the knife free, blood gushing out to splash into the dust at their feet, making a sticky mud instantly.

James stepped backward to give himself room, then brought the knife back up in a murderous underhand slash. The triangular point of the blade caught the mortally wounded Iraqi militia gunman in his throat just below the bobbing knot of his Adam's apple.

James felt the blade slice through flesh and cartilage. Hot blood gushed out over his fist and the man croaked and his bowels opened up as a spasm rocked his body. James stepped in and shoved hard, pushing the corpse off the end of his knife and letting the man drop like a sack of loose meat.

He whirled and ran back out into street, slipping the blood-smeared knife blade under the web belt of his H-harness suspender. He drew his silenced Beretta and put a finger to his headset mike.

"Let's move this up," he said without preamble. "I just had company at the secondary insertion point. There are bound to be more—he can't have been alone."

"Copy," McCarter confirmed. "Get cover—we have issues here, as well."

"Roger, out," James said.

He dropped to his knee and curled his finger tip under the manhole cover. He jerked upward and threw it clear. Once that was done he rose and quickly unholstered and transferred the Beretta to his left hand while taking up the pistol grip of his SPAS-15 in his right. He backed up quickly to the garbage-filled causeway where he had left the body of the Mahdi army sentry.

In the distance he heard the sudden sharp crack as T. J. Hawkins opened up with his sniper rifle. A second later Rafael Encizo let go with his grenade launcher and Calvin James realized hell had found Phoenix Force one more time.

CHAPTER SEVEN

Caracas, Venezuela

Carl Lyons cut the Excursion hard to the right and shot across two lanes of traffic, threading between cars and trucks. The tires on the big SUV screeched in protest and the vehicle body leaned hard, threatening to roll at the sudden extreme angles.

"This isn't a Formula One car, Carl," Schwarz said, voice cool. "It will roll."

"It won't roll," Lyons answered flatly.

He snapped the wheel back hard in the other direction, cutting off a VW wagon then a red Audi. He crossed over the center divide, bouncing the wheels up and throwing the men around inside the cab.

"We're going to roll!" Blancanales shouted from the back.

"We're not going to roll," Lyons denied.

The Excursion bounced free and Lyons shot down the center of the busy St. Martin Grande roadway. Horns blared and a garish red-and-yellow tourist bus swerved out of the way. Lyons cut between it and a green Honda hybrid running close enough to scratch the paint on the Excursion.

He saw a side street and turned sharply, leaving a trail of rubber behind them on the pavement over a yard long. He got the nose of the big SUV orientated correctly and floored the accelerator. He surged forward as more cars slammed on their brakes around him, but then he felt the back end shake loose and begin to drift.

"We're going to roll," Schwarz repeated.

Lyons didn't bother to answer, but instead turned into the skid and eased off the gas for a moment. He cut the wheel back and just missed running up onto a crowded sidewalk before bringing the heavy vehicle back into line and shooting ahead.

He cut around a late-model four-door sedan and then back in front of it. He quickly looked in his rearview mirror but was forced to keep his eyes on the crowded road in front of him.

"Still there?" he demanded.

"Yep," Blancanales answered from the backseat.

"It's going to be damn hard to outmaneuver them in this behemoth," Schwarz said. "And if we keep this up for too long without losing them, we'll have uniformed officers on our ass and it's right back to playing patty cake with customs officer Hernandez and his jolly crew."

"We're not going to roll," Lyons said preemptively.

The ex-LAPD detective slammed on the emergency brakes, locking up his rear wheels, and spun the big SUV around in a half circle. The blunt nose of the Excursion pointed toward an alley. An ancient flatbed truck blocked half the narrow passage. In the back a lanky teenager handed boxes of ripe tomatoes down to a portly middle-aged man in a shopkeeper's apron.

The SUV rocked on its suspension, leaning so hard toward the driver that the tires left the ground along the passenger side for several inches. The vehicle slammed back down and then the tires squealed as they grabbed traction on the asphalt.

The Excursion's big-block engine screamed as it lurched forward, barreling directly for the delivery truck. The shopkeeper turned and gaped in surprise and the teenager on the flatbed dropped a box of tomatoes and leaped clear. The Excursion shot past them and there was sharp, metallic pop as the driver's side-view mirror was ripped clean off the car door.

Lyons risked a glance back and saw the green pursuit car charge into the alley. He swore violently, then asked, "Can we take them out?"

"Our rules of engagement are pretty liberal," Schwarz said, his voice tinged with dry sarcasm.

"Are we sure we want to?" Blancanales asked. "They're just a surveillance team."

"They're agents of a secret police unit designed to keep an aggressive totalitarian despot like Chavez in power. This country is about thirty-six hours away, at any one time, of going the Night of the Long Knives route. Hell, how many journalists and political dissidents has Chavez's Gestapo already jailed, tortured and killed?" Lyons argued.

"True enough," Blancanales said. "But until we get to the cache point we don't have weapons."

"Don't worry, I have a plan," Lyons said.

"Oh, God, no," Schwarz muttered.

Basra, Iraq

HAWKINS SETTLED his head down and eased into a tight
cheek weld with the buttstock of his weapon. His finger
rested firmly on the trigger, eliminating any slack from
the pull. Poised for the kill, he used the scope to evaluate
the hunter-killer team sweeping toward his position.

Two men stayed behind in each of the Dzik-3
APCs—the driver and a machine gunner using the roof-
mounted M-2 .50-caliber machine gun. A dismount
squad consisting of a three-man fire team from each
vehicle patrolled the area in methodical motions of
cover and movement. The unit commander, an obese
and belligerent-looking soldier in a felt green beret,
walked along beside the center Dzik-3 with a sat phone
in one hand and a U.S. Army Beretta in the other, con-
trolling the search grids of the foot soldiers.

Target number one was the officer, Hawkins decided.
Targets two, three and four would be the exposed machine gunners. Encizo could use the AP rounds in his
Hawk grenade launcher to attack the three fire teams.
With surprise and aggressive use of tactical firepower
their ambush could decimate the platoon. He just wasn't
sure if they could handle any reinforcements.

"Coming closer. Moving careful and being thorough,"
he warned in a tense whisper.

He heard Encizo hurriedly pass the information
along to David McCarter. There was a murmured reply,
and then the Cuban whispered the Briton's instructions
into Hawkins's ear.

"They start crossing the parking lot between the last
warehouse and our position then go ahead and take 'em.
If we can get to insertion point two, we'll be good either

way, but we have to be sure we can hold them off long enough for Manning to finish the electrical job."

"Understood," Hawkins replied.

Encizo gave McCarter a thumbs-up. The Phoenix leader nodded, then turned back toward the big Canadian. Manning nodded without looking up.

"I'm in the schematic pathway," he said. "There's enough juice in these coils to do what we need, but I have to passive link the nodes one at a time to connect with the coalition power grid. It has to be done in order or the transformers will reject the current or overload."

"I understand. Do what you have to. There may be shooting soon, however. Just our normal FUBAR luck."

Manning nodded, apparently unconcerned, his attention entirely focused on his diagnostic and interdiction equipment. He pushed the stylus into the screen then dragged it downward, scrolling the blueprint connection down to the next open port. He tapped the target, then quickly used the miniature keyboard to type in a command.

The node flashed green and he began the process again, this time following representing icons to the left of his screen. Behind him he could hear the big engines on the Iraqi Dzik-3 APCs growing closer. A deep, harsh voice shouted orders in Arabic, and Manning heard others reply.

The undershirt beneath his NATO body armor was soaked with sweat, and beads of perspiration stood out on his forehead. He hummed a little tune to himself to aid in his focus, narrowing his concentration down to a white-hot edge despite the assault of adrenaline on his system.

He heard Calvin James give his sit-rep update over his ear jack and McCarter reply with his instructions. His hand moved and shifted across the pad, sliding and scraping the electronic stylus like a conductor at the philharmonic waving his baton.

Over his shoulder he heard Rafael Encizo suddenly speak up in a conversational voice to David McCarter. "T.J. says he's going to go ahead and kill some people now."

"Grand, just grand," McCarter acknowledged.

There was the heavy supersonic crack of a rifle.

At the end of Calvin James's alley a white Nissan pickup pulled up, blocking the scorched gas station from view. In the bed of the pickup four militia members with green headbands and AKM assault rifles jumped out and hit the ground. The sound of gunfire coming from several buildings over had the irregulars jumpy as junkies, weapons primed. In the passenger seat a sallow-skinned man in a police uniform directed the civilian-clad militia gunmen.

James sank back against the wall of the maintenance shed. Held in a left-handed grip because of the angle, his SPAS-15 was up at port arms as one of the militia called out a name down the alleyway. James looked down at the mutilated corpse sprawled at his feet.

The man would not be answering.

Slowly the Stony Man commando sank into a crouch and then risked a quick look around the edge of the building as the militia squad continued calling out the dead point man's name. The gunmen had fanned out into a loose arrowhead formation and were coming down the alley, Kalashnikovs up and at the ready.

From across the opposite of the alley the sound of explosions punctuated the chatter of automatic weapons.

"I have a flanking element," James subvocalized into his throat mike. "I can hold our position, but I'm outnumbered."

"Copy," McCarter replied. "I'm rolling backup right now."

"Go prone once you clear the wall," James warned. "You're jumping straight into the cooking pot."

"Out."

Letting go of the forestock of the SPAS-15, James reached over to a suspender on his H-harness and pulled free a canister-shaped grenade. He brought it down and hooked the thumb of his trigger hand into the ring then pulled outward with his right. The spoon sprang from the smoke grenade and flew across the causeway to land in a pool of standing blood with a muted splash.

Without looking James reached out around the corner of the building and tossed the canister in an under-handed lob. He heard someone shout in surprise and anger as the grenade landed and began spewing thick white smoke. He went to his left knee, pressing the hard plastic pad secured there into the broken ground, and swung the barrel of his weapon around the corner.

Thirty yards away a wide-eyed Iraqi was moving toward the smoke grenade, AKM up in the crook of his shoulder. James triggered the semiautomatic shotgun, and double-aught buckshot tore into the man, knocking the assault rifle free, tearing off both hands at the wrists in a geyser of blood and smashing into the abdomen and lower chest of the militia irregular.

The man stumbled backward and went down. A Kalashnikov chattered and a hail of 7.62 mm lead rattled the corrugated metal above James's head. He pulled the trigger on the SPAS-15 twice more without bothering to aim as he ducked back around the edge of the building, spreading lethal buckshot across the breadth of the alley in a merciless wall of lead. The recoil hammered backward into his wrist and the smoking shells tumbled outward as he dropped to his belly.

He heard screams and his hand went to his web belt for a fragmentation grenade. Hard steel slugs buzzed and burned around him, slicing through the metal siding of the maintenance sheds as if they were paper. Dirt and bloody mud kicked up just in front of his position and bullets whined as they sliced through the air above him.

Without looking James returned fire, aiming low and filling the narrow alley with more .12-gauge shot. He heard the Nissan pickup engine suddenly surge as the driver gunned it and he knew they were charging his position.

THE IRAQI POLICE commander's head filled the reticule of Hawkins's scope. He put the crosshairs on the bridge of the man's patrician nose. The range was ridiculously close for how powerful the sniper optic was, and he could see the man was sweating freely. Slowly, Hawkins let the air ease out of his lungs. Slowly, he squeezed back on the trigger.

The pull was so smooth the rifle going off almost came as a surprise. The police commander's skull exploded like glass as the rifle recoiled firmly into Hawkins's shoulder. Jagged edges of skull like eggshell mixed with the black syrup of the man's blood as his brains were scattered across the dun-colored armor of the Dzik-3.

Hawkins shifted slightly. The machine gunner in the first wheeled APC filled his scope. The man swiveled in his open turret, swinging the muzzle of the .50-caliber machine gun around in the direction of the shot.

Hawkins put a bullet through his larynx.

A red depression appeared in the man's throat and a fine red mist haloed his head as the back of his neck was blown out by the high-velocity round. Hawkins shifted his sniper rifle.

"Madre puta," Encizo barked over his shoulder. Half a second later there was the distinctive *bloop* sound as the MM-1 fired. Then three more as the Cuban commando unleashed on the dismount fire teams.

"You're in charge of this element," McCarter told Manning just as the 40 mm grenades landed. "Once you're done, over the wall you go."

The sharp crack and dull thump of the explosions drowned out the big Canadian's reply, but he was nodding and McCarter took that as his cue to go. He slid between the substation housing just as Hawkins killed the second machine gunner. As he went over the wall the third weapons operator managed to open up on the Phoenix position and suppress them at least momentarily. The .50-caliber rounds blasted the cinder-block wall into fragments and sent all three Phoenix commandos into a nosedive under the onslaught. Dirt kicking up into his face, Gary Manning continued his tedious task.

MCCARTER LANDED HARD on the other side of the wall and went to his belly. One whole end of the alley was choked with thick white smoke, obscuring his movements from the militia squad. He saw green tracer fire knifing out of the smoke and heard the screaming of a V-6 engine.

Arching his back, McCarter lifted the upper half of his torso from the hard-packed alley dirt and twisted his M-4 carbine sideways. His left hand grabbed the weapon by its shoulder pad and his right went up to the 30-round magazine that served as the pistol grip for the trigger to his M-203 grenade launcher.

The combination weapon recoiled hard in his hand and the 40 mm HE round shot down the alley and into the smoke toward the clarion call of the vehicle engine. The explosion was instantaneous and a ball of fire like a volcano blast billowed out and rolled forward, tossing bodies in pinwheels in front of it.

A flaming figure emerged from the smoke, and Calvin James stepped out of his position and knocked it down with a blast from his SPAS-15. For a second there was only the sound of the burning vehicle in the alley. Then concrete chunks exploded out of the wall beside McCarter and rained down on him in jagged shards.

On the other side of that wall Gary Manning curled into a fetal position around his handheld. He lightly touched the electronic stylus to the last node icon then began typing the final command.

He started singing the song he had been humming during his process. "'That's the night the lights went out in Georgia…'"

A single bar graph metric appeared on the screen. The cinder-block wall above him exploded. The bar turned from green to red and flashed. Heavy-caliber rounds began to hammer the structure in front of him. The red bar suddenly began to drain and a percentage number appeared on the screen just to the left of the plunging line. It dropped from 100 percent to 40 percent to 6 percent to 0 in the blink of an eye.

Then the neighborhoods of southeast Basra went dark.

CHAPTER EIGHT

Caracas, Venezuela

Hector Ramon Casella fought his car back under control. Driving, along with shooting silenced weapons, the implementation of wire taps and the use of a rubber hose during interrogations, was among the premier skills utilized by the General Counterintelligence Agency. The American was good—too good for a mere tourist—but in the clumsy and massive SUV he could never hope to evade a skilled driver in a quicker, more nimble automobile.

Trying to lose them in the parking garage was a mark of desperation, Casella realized. His partner pulled a Glock-17 pistol from a shoulder holster as the GCIA agent sped up a ramp and into the structure after the Americans. Hitting the second story, he turned the car smoothly and aimed for the curved ramp leading up to the next level. His knuckles were white on the steering wheel as he threaded the needle at fifty kilometers per hour.

BLANCANALES LEAPED from the back of the Ford Excursion and slammed the door shut. "Now!" he snarled.

Carl Lyons shoved his foot down on the accelerator. The transmission was in four-wheel drive and all four wheels suddenly started spinning in reverse. The bulky battering ram shot back down the access ramp as the much lighter automobile raced upward toward it.

Ambush set. Ambush sprung.

The hurtling SUV of Detroit steel slammed into the GCIA street car in a heavy metal landslide. The thick rear bumper crumpled the smaller car's grille like an empty beer can and bludgeoned into the engine block at terrific velocity. The oil pan cracked and burst apart and fluid lines tore loose, dumping flammable liquids across the ruined front end of the car.

The dashboard inside the cab buckled under the impact, instantly spiderwebbing the safety glass of the windshield. The passenger, not wearing his seat belt, was thrown forward into the weakened glass and his face punched a hole in it. Instantly his flesh was peeled off his face like the skin of a grape and blood poured down to bubble and sizzle on the heated metal of the exposed engine. The man's lower jaw came away, scattering his teeth like dice, and the jagged glass gouged through his carotid arteries. Blood rolled in a scarlet flood.

A heartbeat later the man in the backseat was catapulted into the windshield and fell limp.

Casella was thrown forward against his seat restraint and felt his ribs along his left side break at the sudden, jerking concussion. His head snapped forward and the steering wheel airbag deployed with a sharp explosion so that his vision was filled with a sudden sheet of white.

His face bounced back from the pneumatic pillow,

wrenching his neck so sharply flashes of light burst in his eyes and a scream was ripped from his lips. Vaguely he was aware of the blaring of his horn then the thump of something landing on the roof of his car.

He tried to rally himself, but this wasn't like kidnapping a teenage college student from the Chavez protest movements. Suddenly he felt strong hands grab him by the point of his chin and the hair at the back of his head. He peeled open his swollen eyes and tried to raise a free hand to swat at the monstrous grip, but suddenly his hair was yanked in one direction and his chin shoved in the other.

He heard a soft muted pop, then saw only blackness.

Rosario Blancanales pulled his hands free and the GCIA agent's head rolled loosely on his broken neck to hang at a bizarre angle. Quickly Blancanales patted the man down and found his Glock-17 pistol.

"Got a handgun here," he yelled over the horn. "Partner's got to have one."

Lyons jumped out of the driver's seat of the Excursion and jogged down the ramp as Schwarz did the same from the other side. Lyons regarded the grisly remains of the dead driver dispassionately. "We have to find a clean car and go completely black."

Schwarz pulled his head from the passenger side door, the mutilated man's Glock-17 in his hands. "Pick your car," he said. He slid the handgun under his belt behind his back. "I got a vehicle appropriation kit through customs by breaking it up into pieces," he said.

"Great," Lyons said. "I'll drive."

"Lovely," Blancanales replied.

Basra, Iraq

RAFAEL ENCIZO LIFTED the reloaded Hawk MM-1 as
.50-caliber slugs tore through the air around him. He depressed the trigger and rode out the recoil as the weapon
spit out a fusillade of 40 mm firepower. The rounds
arched out and slammed into the ground in trip-hammer
shock waves, tossing the corrupt Iraqi police gunmen
in the air and raking them with shrapnel.

The concussive force momentarily stilled the final
.50-caliber gunner, and Hawkins attempted a shot, but
it rang off the roof just to the right of the man. Encizo
fired another two quick shots with the grenade launcher,
but in the heat of the moment the Cuban's aim was wide
with the imprecise weapon and they sailed to either side
of the machine gunner, landing behind him.

The weapon, momentarily silenced, opened up again
and the withering fire of the heavy-caliber machine gun
drove the members of Phoenix down so their noses were
in the dirt.

"Phoenix," Manning said, "we are leaving!"

"It's about time," Encizo replied.

Small arms fired from the surviving police unit
poured into the narrow substation, the 7.62 mm rounds
forming a roof of lead above the cinder-block enclosure
while the M-2 .50-caliber continued punching holes
through the concrete.

"Oh, Christ," Hawkins muttered as he crawled toward the other two men. "This is starting to remind too
much of Mogadishu, guys."

"Sure, that or the Alamo," Manning answered, raising his voice over the din of gunfire.

Encizo rolled over in the dirt on his back and pointed

the blunt muzzle of the MM-1 into the air so that the rounds would just skim the top of the wall. Rounds punched through the rim of the enclosure until it looked like a row of broken teeth. He triggered the Hawk grenade launcher and sent two more rounds over the top of the wall.

The 40 mm grenades landed hard, one right after the other, and the explosions stilled the small-arms fire, but the .50-caliber weapon continued hammering away until there were enough baseball-size holes in the cinder block to let the three Phoenix members see the surviving Iraqi police approaching their position through the Swiss-cheese configuration of the wall.

From behind them where James and McCarter held security on the insertion point, white smoke was billowing up. AKM fire popped up again in ragged bursts, green tracer fire knifing through the air.

"There's no way we're making it over that wall!" Manning yelled.

"Then go through it," Hawkins yelled back.

The ex-Army Ranger threw his Mk 11 rifle to his shoulder and started putting match-grade 7.62 mm NATO rounds downrange through the bullet holes in the wall. Manning snatched up his M-60E and cut loose through the wall with a sudden long burst.

"Do it!" he yelled.

Hawkins pulled an HE grenade from his web gear and primed it. Encizo rolled away from the sound of Manning's machine gun and spoke into his throat mike. "We can't go over the wall, so we're going through— you clear?" he demanded without preamble.

"Do it!" McCarter answered instantly.

"Do it!" Encizo shouted.

Manning let the M-60E cut loose and just ran the 200-round belt out as Hawkins let the spoon on his grenade fly loose. He lunged forward and slapped the high-explosive bomb around the corner of the substation building and into the tight space between it and the wall.

He threw himself back, and all three men turned their body armor toward the explosion. It went off with a deafening boom that popped their eardrums. They scrambled to their hands and knees and snatched up their weapons, crawling for the breach they'd created.

They shoved themselves down the cramped passage as bullets continued firing around them. The high-explosive charge of the hand grenade had created a chasm in the metal housing of the substation conductor and it smoked heavily, sparks showering as an electrical fire flared up.

The cinder block had burst outward under the force of the explosion, leaving a gap hole three times the size of a man in the wall. Manning came off his feet, scooping up the heavy M-60E machine gun, and charged out into the alley. Encizo and Hawkins scrambled through right behind him, weapons up and ready.

They entered a wall of choking, blinding white smoke that swirled around them as they jogged forward. Still moving forward, Encizo turned at the waist and lobbed the last rounds in his grenade launcher back over the wall in the direction they'd come, and a portion of the small-arms fire went silent.

"This way," McCarter called to them from out of the smoke.

Rafael Encizo ran up to where David McCarter crouched beside the open manhole cover. "This wasn't the plan." He grinned.

"You got to use your BFG, didn't you?" McCarter

laughed back. "Down you go. Cal's holding security in the tunnel."

Encizo's bicep swelled up as he lifted the MM-1 by the pistol grip so that the muzzle was pointed acutely vertical. He dropped down to his butt and thrust his legs into the opening until the soles of his combat boots hit the rungs of the service ladder. He ignored the stench of shit that enveloped him and scrambled downward.

Gary Manning turned and held his machine gun in one hand and repeated Encizo's motions, dropping down into the hole. As his head dipped below the lip of the manhole he looked over at McCarter.

"You always take me to the best places," he said, climbing down.

"Everyone in this chicken shit outfit is a bleeding comedian!"

He snapped up his M-4 and began holding security as Hawkins slung his Mk 11 and pulled a second smoke grenade free from his web gear. Behind him from the hole in the derelict substation created by the HE grenade, an Iraqi emerged, AKM up.

McCarter shot him through the face, tossing a loop of black blood up into the air from the man's head as he crumpled like a slaughtered steer in a stockyard. Hawkins let the armed grenade rolled down the alley, intensifying the weakening smoke screen already in place. Gray-white smoke immediately began billowing out, obscuring the breach point from view.

With Hawkins down the hole McCarter triggered an AP round out of his M-203. It shot through the smoke and exploded in a bright flash. Immediately, he let the weapon fall to the end of its sling so that it hung by his waist, and reached out for the manhole cover. He jumped down onto the iron bracket ladder set into the sewer line and scrambled downward, dragging the heavy steel lid toward him.

The swirling smoke above his head twisted and cycloned as rounds sprayed down the alley. Green tracer rounds buzzed like hornets around him as the corrupt Iraqi police unit fired blindly. He heard the sound of the lone Dzik-3 as it approached.

Then the manhole cover settled into place and for a second all of that was gone in the tomblike atmosphere of the reeking hot sewer. He clambered downward several rungs, then stepped back and dropped to the ground. Landing in a tight crouch, he reached up and engaged his IR mono-goggle, turning the impenetrable dark into a green-tinged black-and-white vista.

He saw the rest of his team strung out in a loose Ranger file along the catwalk next to a river of offal and sludge. He saw the body of a dog in the mess, legs stiff with rigor mortis, and twisted his face into disgust. Then he saw the partial body of the baby and he went cold.

He turned his face away and hurried toward where Calvin James crouched at the beginning of the line. He slid past the other members and knelt down next to the ex-SEAL.

"You able to get a signal in here?" he asked.

"Negative," James replied. "I sent a text communication into the repeater service after I couldn't get contact. The server will keep trying to deliver the message so if we get near an open area as we move it should give our sit-rep."

"All right," McCarter raised his voice so all the members of Phoenix could hear him. "We go down fifty yards to a Y-fork. We can hold security there until we see if these assholes figure out how we escaped. Let's go. Manning, you have rear security."

Instantly the commando squad was up and moving. They shuffled along quickly, heads bent low in a toe-heel gait designed to maintain purchase on the slippery strip of stained concrete. They used IR flashlights set next to their mono-goggle to help illuminate the cata-combs. Hawkins ran his gaze across the domed ceiling and saw a mass of crawling cockroaches and squirming worms. Running point, James routinely kicked squeal-ing rats out of his way or stomped the more aggressive ones to a jelly when they refused to give way.

Moving in an awkward, sidestepping shuffle, Manning kept his machine gun up and pointed back toward the in-sertion point as he moved, covering rear security. After a moment of travel the team reached the Y-juncture and took the right-hand fork, disappearing from view.

They went to ground and shut down their IR flash-lights, relying on passive feeds only for illumination. Manning crouched at the lip of the turn, watching the back tunnel with keen interest.

"This thing has been bollixed up," McCarter said flatly. "Someone sold us. Probably that blood ass Anjali. We have to assume our target knows we're coming after him."

"Maybe so, maybe no," James said. "Safe bet says yes, but that doesn't mean he's gone from the area."

"You want to Charlie Mike?" McCarter asked, using military slang based on the phonetic alphabet for "con-tinue mission."

"Gary trashed light and power so the bad guys are living in the dark right now," Encizo said. "We never told the Iraqi liaison what our true insertion plan was so they have no idea that we're coming up from beneath them. We lost strategic surprise, but we still have tactical surprise on our side."

"To do what?" Hawkins asked. "Still pull the snatch? I'd have to say that might be just a bit more ballsy than brilliant."

"Maybe we don't get a snatch," Manning said from the end of the line. "But maybe we could do a soft probe and call in an air strike, or do a hard probe and get a sniper shot off. Plan B may have to be good enough."

"We're risking getting cut off deep in enemy territory," McCarter said. He couldn't keep the smile out of his voice, however. "This snake-out-of-a-hole insertion we came up through seems too good to waste without a try."

"Agreed," James said.

"Agreed," Encizo and Hawkins echoed.

"Gary?" McCarter asked.

"Let's do it," Manning replied. "It doesn't seem like the Iraqis have figured out how in the hell we got away. They could be chasing us all over the neighborhood right now. We should exploit that."

"Then let's roll," McCarter said.

Stony Man Farm, Virginia

BEAR KURTZMAN clicked the icon to accept an instant message. His eyes scanned the screen in rapid movements as he took in the text message. He swore out loud and slammed his coffee cup down on the desk next to his wheelchair. Carmen Delahunt looked up from the computer printout she was reading as both Wethers and Tokaido spun in their chairs at the sudden cursing.

"What happened, Bear?" Wethers asked.

Kurtzman opened his mouth to speak and the door to the Annex computer room swung inward and slammed against the wall. All eyes from the Stony Man cybernetics team swung around as Barbara Price rushed into the room.

"Able is compromised," she said without preamble. "They're going deep black to continue the mission, but we need to get them a new safehouse in a less populated area and arrange resupply."

"When it rains it pours," Kurtzman said.

"What?"

"I got a message from James on the ground in Basra, text based."

"Why text?"

"He couldn't get a signal out so he put a communication in the system for the repeater relay. It's twelve minutes old. They were compromised on initial insertion. They think their Iraqi police counterpart might have set them up."

Tokaido leaned back in his chair and whistled. "Phoenix under fire, Able on the run—this mission is screwed out of the gate."

"Reshuffling logistics for Able shouldn't be too much of a problem," Wethers said. "As long as they stay out of the GCIA's hands they should still be able to move on the target. But I'm not sure what we can do for Phoenix. Grimaldi can be rotors up out of the Basra International Airport as soon as we call him, but it was supposed to be a joint Iraqi mission at British insistence. The Iraqis were supposed to take the credit for nabbing an Iranian."

"Seems shortsighted for them to risk us finding their plant just to wipe out this team," Delahunt pointed out.

"Not if they're so ensconced they think they own the

territory." Price shook her head. "We'll figure out the devious motivations later. For now we need to figure out how to support them."

"They've made it into the Trojan Horse insertion point," Kurtzman said. "For now they're going to continue with at least the recon phase of the op. They're going to see if Plan B is at least an option."

Price nodded. "Akira, call Jack. Have him go ahead and prep the JSOC Predator he's staged with. Once the satellite links are hot and you have control of the drone, put it in high altitude and circle the AO. We'll be ready when they call."

The Stony Man mission controller turned to the other members of the team. "Akira, hack the GCIA system. I want every communiqué in whatever form it might take on what they're trying to do about Able. If a goddamn janitor writes a note on a paper napkin, I want to read it.

"Carmen, you do the same for the Caracas police.

"Hunt, I want you to get a hold of Agency, Joint Special Operations Command, the DEA—hell, try the spooks at whatever code name they're calling the ISA these days, but get me a new safehouse for Able.

"Bear, try and establish contact with Phoenix and then arrange a backup resupply drop for Venezuela. I'll have Cowboy assemble their weapons and explosives. Think of every contingency they could face and then give them two of everything they'll need. Let's spend some taxpayer money, people." She turned and walked out of the room calling out over her shoulder, "Now I've got to go call Hal."

Behind her the computer room exploded into activity. Men's lives hung in the balance and the cyber team had never failed before. They didn't intend to do so now.

CHAPTER NINE

Caracas, Venezuela

Able Team made poor time. Forced to act clandestinely, they avoided the Francisco Fajardo Highway and took secondary streets toward the *casalta* district in the northwest of the city. There the urban center ran up against the Venezuelan coastal mountain range known locally as Cordillera de la Costa.

The lower levels of that mountain range were arid and steep shrub-steppe. The Farm had provided Schwarz with the street address and GPS coordinates of a safehouse used by a U.S. Army Intelligence unit tasked with electronic surveillance and digital interdiction nestled in the rugged terrain.

The house was isolated and set on property at the end of a dirt road. The headlights of the stolen car illuminated the structure, revealing a modest stucco adobe-style hacienda accented by a small courtyard behind a wrought-iron gate and a landscaped garden filled with cactus plants, aloe, silversword bushes and agave.

As Carl Lyons stepped out of the Subaru Outback's driver's side something heavy scuttled across his foot. Cursing, he jumped back and looked down in time to see a softball-size tarantula scurry off under the car.

He spun and saw Hermann Schwarz looking at him, single eyebrow arched.

"Not a word," Lyons warned.

Rosario Blancanales approached the gate to the dwelling's courtyard and worked the security code given him by Barbara Price. The series of miniature lightbulbs set across the top switched from red to a flashing dull amber then blinked a muted green.

He hit a second three-integer numerical sequence, and a small drawer popped out of the bottom of the alarm housing like a feed tray on a CD player to reveal a master key. The Puerto Rican quickly unlocked the gate as Lyons and Schwarz carried their luggage in behind him.

They crossed a modest courtyard of terra-cotta tile to the heavy wooden door, which the master key unlocked, and entered the nondescript hacienda. Just to the left of the inside hall through an open door was a small office set up with four desktop-size CCTV screens showing the outside of the property through live digital feeds. In the upper left-hand monitor they could see their vehicle sitting in the driveway.

Blancanales moved quickly toward the back of the house to where the master bedroom was located. Once there he pulled up first a corner of the carpet, then two specially crafted sections of Pergo flooring to reveal a digitally locked floor safe.

Sitting under the CCTV station, Schwarz fired up a laptop, which he slaved to the U.S. Army portable computer he carried in his kit. Behind him Lyons grabbed a sat phone off a charging port and wandered into the kitchen. He opened the fridge and stood looking at the contents of the commercial-size appliance and grimacing at the supplies.

He shrugged as the sat connection was made and let the door swing shut. Fresh food beat the hell out of MREs. Absently he counted the seven distinct clicks as the signal was routed around the globe in a security shuffle before connecting to Stony Man Farm.

"Ironman?" Barbara Price's cool, well-modulated voice answered. She sounded as aloof and poised as a Wall Street banker, Lyons thought.

"It's me, boss," he answered. "As you can tell, we have arrived."

"No more close calls, I hope?"

"None to speak of."

"You guys are now completely black," Price warned. "Carmen got into the Caracas PD and the GCIA has given them your pictures and you have detectives and uniforms gridding the city. The airports and all public transportation are on alert. And of course all that doesn't count the spooks at GCIA and their pet commando unit they've called in."

"Commando unit?"

"The *negra yaguars*, Chavez's special unit. They shut down dissenting voices in the media, kidnap political agitators and train FARC death squads in Colombia to increase regional instability."

"More people to knock over the head." Lyons shrugged. "Whatever. You got any good news for us?"

"Yes," Price replied. "Your boy Kasim is completely oblivious to the fact that three *el norte gringos* have arrived in town to see him. He's taken no extra security precautions and is blithely unaware of his impending doom."

"I just had that warm, tingly feeling you always give me when you talk like that, Barb."

"I'm very happy for you, Carl. How's the safehouse?"

"Food in the fridge sucks and—wait a second. Here comes Pol with our ordnance."

Blancanales walked into the room with several firearms in his hands. He set them on the table. "Pretty generic. All silenced H&Ks and Berettas. Five total of each gun with ammo and night-vision goggles, as well as some tactical communications equipment. This was obviously a primarily defensive operation prior to us."

Frowning, Lyons looked down at the arsenal on the table. He saw three Heckler & Koch MP-5 SD-3 silenced submachine guns and three Beretta 92-F pistols.

"Barb, damn it," he said into the phone. "All we have are MP-5s and some Berettas."

"So?"

"They're both 9 mm. I've said this before but I'll say it again. The 9 mm was designed for killing Europeans. For serious people you need at least a .45, okay?"

There was silence on the end of the sat connection, followed by a long sigh. "Carl, do your recon. If you need something else, be that condoms or an elephant gun, I have Bear working on a logistic link. Probably a night drop."

"That's all I needed to hear," Lyons said. "I'll call you again after we've been 'eyes on' with the target."

"Farm out," Price said and killed the connection.

Lyons set the phone on the table and picked up a suppressor-equipped submachine gun. He inspected the lethal weapon with a critical eye. "I guess every firearm doesn't have to be my AA-12," he sighed, referring to the Military Police Systems updated version of the Atchisson automatic shotgun. "Let's eat and roll."

Plaza de Sombra, Caracas, Venezuela

HUGO CAMPOS HERMIDA paced the floor. His hands were held behind his back and his head was down as he calmly contemplated his options. Juan Gonzales, commanding officer of the *negra yaguars,* sat in a chair in the corner. At a word from Hermida, the burly man would launch his death squad in an instant, but in the meantime there was nothing to do but wait for an update as the GCIA agent coordinated the sweep of the city on the lookout for the three American spies.

The door to the office swung open and Hermida drew himself up as a short figure in a dark suit entered the room. Hermida instantly recognized the inscrutable features of the only Asian face in the entire building.

"Lieutenant Colonel," Hermida said carefully in acknowledgment.

Lieutenant Colonel Bayo Chin nodded in reply and casually swung the door shut behind him. Chin was the living embodiment of China's attempt to spread its international influence into the Western Hemisphere. An extremely high-ranking member of the People's Party, the Chinese military intelligence officer was fluent in Spanish and an expert in secured communications, digital espionage and passive intelligence-gathering activities.

Chin was here as a political courtesy from China to assist Venezuela in its national security efforts against the United States. He brought resources and techniques far beyond any Venezuela could hope to manufacture domestically, and though Hermida knew the deal was Faustian, he also knew Chin was invaluable.

"I have something for you," Chin said. "Something potentially about your current problem."

Hermida stepped closer, his face glowing with an eager light. In his chair Gonzales leaned forward. "The gringos?" Hermida asked. "You have something on them?"

"I think so," Chin said.

He produced a computer printout from the inside pocket of his military-cut suit jacket. Hermida took it eagerly and opened it, eyes darting back and forth as he scanned the information on the page.

"Members of Chinese special operation mountain reconnaissance troops operating along our border with Afghanistan managed to…acquire…certain pieces of highly encrypted field radios from a U.S. Navy SEAL sniper team," Chin explained. "In Beijing we were able to disassemble and reverse engineer those radios."

"You can listen in on the Americans' communications?" Hermida was stunned. "The spies here, in Caracas? You have eavesdropped?"

Chin shook his head sharply, once. "No," he replied in perfect Spanish. "We have not. Cracking the connection is not possible. However, once you told me about your predicament I instructed my staff to begin searching for signature frequencies."

Hermida lowered his eyes to the paper and eagerly continued reading. "You were able to catch the signal."

Chin nodded. "Just so. We have no idea where the signal ended up—the rerouting technology is too advanced. However, we do have a point of origin possibility. If this spy team makes contact again, we should be able to triangulate their position. Already we know it came from the north of the city."

Hermida turned to Gonzales. "Restage your men at the helipad we have in the Royo Banyos security site. Be ready to move by air or ground as soon as our great friend Lieutenant Colonel Chin gives us the information."

Gonzales nodded. His eyes were the cold, dead orbs of a marine predator, soulless and without mercy. "It will be done," he said.

Basra, Iraq

THE BLAST FROM a vehicle-based suicide bomber had knocked a hole in the street. The explosion had ripped up the asphalt and punched a hole in the ground deep enough to reveal the sewer line. Workers had managed to clear enough rubble out of the crater to keep the sewage stream flowing, but there had not been enough security or money for complete repairs. A line of rubble like a gravel-covered hillside led up out of the sewer to the street.

While the rest of Phoenix crouched in the shadows, T. J. Hawkins eased his way up the uncertain slope to reconnoiter the area. He crawled carefully using his elbows and knees with his weapon cradled in the crook of his arms. As tense as the situation was, there was a large part of him that was grateful to escape the stinking claustrophobia of the tunnel.

He eased his way to the lip of the blast crater and carefully raised his head over the edge. The Hayaniya neighborhood appeared deserted at the late hour. Tenement buildings rose up above street-level shops, the structures nestled against each other. Rusted iron fire escapes adorned the fronts of the old buildings. Brightly colored laundry hung from windows and clotheslines. The roofs were a forest of old-fashioned wire antennas. The street was lined with battered old cars, some of them up on blocks and obviously unusable. Across the street feral dogs rooted through an overflowing garbage bin.

Carefully, Hawkins extended his weapon and scanned the neighborhood street through his scope. He detected no movement, saw no faces in windows and doorways, silhouetted no figures on the fire escapes and rooftops. He looked down to the end of the street and saw nothing stirring, then turned and checked the other direction with the same result.

Satisfied, Hawkins turned and looked down. He gave a short, low whistle and instantly McCarter appeared at the foot of the rubble incline.

"All clear. Come have a look," Hawkins whispered.

McCarter nodded once in reply and then reslung his M-4 carbine before scrambling quickly up the rubble. He slid into place next to Hawkins and carefully scanned the street, as well.

"There," he said. "That building." He indicated a burned-out six-story apartment complex with a thrust of his sharp chin. "That's the building. That'll give us the entry point into the compound."

Eighteen months earlier the building had been as-saulted by an Iraqi national army unit with British SAS advisers after intelligence had revealed it served as an armory and bomb-making factory for the local Shiite militias.

"I haven't noticed any sentries yet," Hawkins said. His gaze remained suctioned to the sniper scope as he scanned the building.

"They're there," McCarter said. "That's the back door to the militia complex."

"Heads up," Hawkins suddenly hissed.

Instantly, McCarter attempted to identify the threat.

Up the street a Toyota pickup turned onto the avenue and began cruising toward their position. The back of the vehicle held a squad of gunmen, and there were three men in the vehicle cab.

McCarter and Hawkins froze, nestling themselves in among the broken masonry of the bomb crater. Slowly the vehicle cruised up the street. Moving carefully, McCarter eased his head down below the lip of the crater and transferred his carbine into a more accessible position.

Beside him Hawkins seemed to evaporate, blending into the background as the pickup inched its way down the street. The former U.S. Army counter terror commando watched the enemy patrol with eyes narrowed, his finger held lightly on the trigger of his weapon.

The vehicle rolled closer and now both Phoenix members could hear the murmur of voices in casual conversation. Hawkins watched as a pockmarked Iraqi in the back took a final drag of his cigarette and then flicked it away.

The still smoking butt arched up and landed next to the prone Hawkins with a small shower of sparks that stung his exposed face. The cigarette bounced and rolled down the incline to come to rest against McCarter's leg.

A gunman in the back of the vehicle said something and the others laughed as the pickup cruised past the two hidden men. Playing a hunch, Hawkins risked moving to scan the burned-out building across the street with his scope. His gamble paid off as a man armed with a SVD Soviet-era Dragunov sniper rifle appeared briefly in a third-story window to acknowledge the patrol rolling past his position.

Hawkins grinned. The pickup reached the end of the

street and disappeared around a corner. "Got you, asshole," Hawkins whispered. "I got a gun bunny on the third floor," the Texan told McCarter.

"Does he interfere with movement?" McCarter scooped loose dirt over the burning cigarette, extinguishing it.

"He's back in the shadow now. I might have a shot with IR," Hawkins replied. "But he's definitely doing overwatch on this street."

"He the only one?"

"Only one I saw," Hawkins said. "But he could have a spotter or radio guy sitting next to him who'll sound the alarm if I put the sniper down."

"What's our other option?"

"I send the team across and hope he doesn't notice until we can be sure of how many we're dealing with."

"The clock is ticking," McCarter pointed out.

"Then I say let me take him."

"Encizo and I will cross the street and try to secure the ground floor before the rest of you come over."

"It's your call, David," Hawkins said simply. He clicked over the amplifier apparatus on his night scope and scanned the windows. A red silhouette appeared in the gloom of the third-story window. "I got him. No other figures present themselves from this angle."

"That'll have to do," McCarter said.

Hawkins held down on his target as McCarter called Encizo up and the two men slowly climbed into position. Encizo had left his Hawk MM-1 behind with Calvin James and held his silenced MP-7 at the ready. McCarter slid his M-4/M-203 around to hang from his back and had pulled his own silencer-equipped weapon, the Browning Hi-Power, from its holster.

"Jack and Jill went up the hill," Hawkins softly sang under his breath. "Jill fell down, skinned her knees and Jack killed some Iraqi snipers…"

CHAPTER TEN

The Mk 11 sniper rifle discharged smoothly, the muzzle lifting slightly with the recoil and pushing back into the hollow of Hawkins's shoulder. The report was muted in the hot desert air and the subsonic round cut across the space and tore through the open window.

In his scope Hawkins saw the figure's head jerk like a boxer taking an inside uppercut. There was an instant of red smear in his sight as blood splashed, then the enemy sniper spun in a half circle and fell over.

"Go," Hawkins said.

Instantly, McCarter was up and sprinting. Behind him Encizo scrambled over the edge of the hole and raced after him. Both men crossed the street at a dead run, weapons up and ready as Hawkins began shifting his weapon back and forth in tight vectors to cover the building front.

McCarter crossed the open street and spun to throw his back into the wall beside the front door of the building. Half a second later Encizo repeated the motion, his MP-7 pointed down the street.

McCarter checked once, then went in through the gaping doorway. He charged into the room, turning left and trying to move along the wall. Encizo came in and peeled right, coming to one knee and scanning the room with his muzzle leading the way. Both men scanned the darkened chamber through their low-light goggles.

The front doors to the building had been blown out during the Iraqi raid and the room saturated with grenades and automatic weapons fire. The two Phoenix members found themselves in a small lobby with a cracked and collapsed desk, a line of busted and dented mailboxes, a pitted and pocked elevator and two fire-scarred doorways. One of the interior doors had been blown off its hinges, revealing a staircase leading upward. The second sagged in place, as perforated as a cheese grater.

McCarter carefully moved forward and checked both doorways before turning and giving Encizo the thumbs-up signal. The Cuban turned and went to the doorway so that Hawkins could see him. He lifted a finger and spoke into his throat mike.

"Come across," he said. "We'll clear upward."

"Acknowledged," Hawkins replied.

Encizo turned back into the room just as he heard footsteps on the staircase. Booted feet pounded the wooden steps as someone jogged downward, making no effort to conceal their movement. Encizo blinked and McCarter disappeared, moving smoothly to rematerialize next to the stairway access, back to the wall and silenced Browning pistol up.

Wearing a headscarf and American Army chocolate-chip-pattern camouflage uniform, a Shiite militia member with an AKM came out of the stairway and strolled casually into the room. On one knee Encizo centered his machine pistol on the irregular.

Oblivious to the shadows in the room, the man started walking across the floor toward the street. As McCarter straightened his arm out, the Browning was a bulky silhouette in his hand, the cylinder of the silencer a blunt oval in the gloom.

There was a whispered *thwat-thwat* and the front of the Iraqi's forehead came away in jigsaw chunks. The man dropped straight to his knees, then tumbled forward onto his face with a wet sound.

Encizo kept the muzzle of his machine pistol trained on the doorway in case the man wasn't alone, but there was no sign of motion from the staircase as McCarter shifted his aim and cleared the second door.

Behind Encizo, James entered the room and peeled off to the left to take cover, followed closely by Manning and then Hawkins. Each member of the unit looked down at the dead Iraqi, his spilling blood clearly visible in their mono-goggle.

"We take the stairs," McCarter said in a low voice. "There's no way to clear a building this size with our manpower so it's hey, diddle-diddle, right up the middle till we reach the roof, then over and in. Stay with silenced weapons for as long as we can."

The ex-SAS trooper swept up his silenced Browning Hi-Power and advanced through the doorway as the rest of Phoenix fell into line behind him in an impromptu entry file. Hawkins took up the final position with his silenced Mk 11, replacing Gary Manning as rear security.

Weapons up, Phoenix continued infiltrating Basra.

Caracas, Venezuela

THE PARQUE CENTRAL COMPLEX occupied the heart of downtown Caracas. Twin fifty-six-story high-rise residential towers rose up out of a huge complex of office buildings, entertainment galleries and civil amenities structures. The complex was the iconic soul of the modern Venezuelan capital, all sleek steel, gleaming glass and streamlined design. In October of 2004 a massive fire broke out in the east towers, its point of origin identified as a suite of government offices that were the subject of a legal inquest at the time. The ten stories between the thirty-fourth and forty-fourth floors were severely damaged and repairs had taken over five years to complete because of the extreme height and massive construction of the tower.

On the fifty-third level of the west tower, Juan Escondito had purchased an entire floor for his personal use. The level was made up of posh business offices close to the elevator bank and a succession of grand suites growing progressively ostentatious down the hallway from the floor lobby.

Aras Kasim had been given use of a VIP luxury suite halfway down the avenue-wide hallway. Hip-hop music blasted from the most advanced stereo that money could buy, the American gangsta rappers talking about the perils of the hood, guns, drugs and the police, along with how hard it was to run hos, earn your money and shoot your friends in the back. Kasim found a lot of wisdom among the profane lyrics.

Three dozen people wandered around the luxurious apartment drinking from champagne flutes and snorting pharmaceutical-grade cocaine from hospitality bowls set around the suite. On a Louis XVI table of oak two European runway models writhed in a tangle of anorexic limbs, sweating and naked, as they enthusiastically wrestled themselves into a cosmopolitan 69 position.

Kasim sat in a plush Gustavian divan, his head spinning from the champagne. Two Venezuelan sisters, ages fifteen and thirteen, their eyes glassy and red, sat on either side of him. His host had promised him that the girls had to be experienced to be believed. He had gone into detail describing the combined sensation of their oral talents, leaving Kasim trembling inside his new Italian leisure suit.

Now he set aside his champagne flute and plucked up the platinum spoon on the chain around his neck. He leaned forward and dipped the utensil into the crumbling, flaky pile of cocaine set on the glass-topped table in front of the twenty-thousand-dollar divan.

He put the spoon to his nostril and snorted hard, leaning back into the divan as his head spun in a swirl of euphoric pleasure. The teenage sisters began rubbing their hands across his chest and thighs in mechanical motions, their young eyes never leaving the pile of drug on the table.

Vision swimming, face numb, with 50 Cent blaring in his ears, the Iranian intelligence agent looked across the table at his host, Venezuelan narco kingpin, Juan Escondito. The man held a Diamond Crypto Smartphone to his ear, the Russian cellular device costing well in excess of one hundred thousand American dollars.

In his other hand he held a blunt the size of a Cuban Presidente cigar, the marijuana pungent and strong as it smoldered. Over his shoulder the runway models switched positions and Kasim reminded himself to take his Viagra pill soon.

Escondito pulled his cell phone from his ear and handed it to the most popular Spanish language soap opera star in the Southern Hemisphere, a former Miss Colombia with an eighteen-inch waist and gigantic breast implants. She held the drug dealer's phone without comment, white powder in a sticky residue on her left nostril. Rhinoplasty had crafted her nose into perfect symmetrical proportions. She had spoken as enthusiastically of the teenage girls' sexual talents as Escondito had.

"My friend," Escondito hollered across the table at the Iranian covert operator. "My associates have just informed me that the shipment was picked up from your Dubai freighter and brought by fast boat to my warehouse in Puerto Cabello." The ugly man grinned, revealing a mouth full of gold teeth. "Once again you have come through." The drug kingpin lifted a hand and snapped his manicured fingers. Kasim saw the bulky frame of the Romain Jerome watch, crafted out of steel salvaged from the hull of the Titanic.

Instantly a steroid-enhanced gorilla with a military-issue Glock-18 machine pistol in a shoulder holster stepped from his post by the wet bar and crossed to Escondito. The drug prince pointed at Kasim and nodded before settling back in his seat and taking a gigantic pull off his blunt. The Colombian soap opera star whispered something in his ear and he grinned like a demented jack-o'-lantern, eyes glued to the deep valley of her improbable cleavage.

As the bodyguard handed the Iranian a padded

manila envelope, Escondito looked over at Kasim. "Hey, friend," he said. "Did you know Marta has her tits insured with Lloyds of London for five million British pounds?"

Kasim leaned forward and took the envelope from the bodyguard, his eyes following Escondito's blunt-tipped fingers as they waved at the beautiful woman's breasts. She giggled as the Iranian stared and then thrust her chest forward and shook it at the intelligence agent. Lacking a bra inside her Halston dress, the globes bounced and jiggled.

"If the weapons are half as good as my man in Puerto Cabello tells me," Escondito continued, "I might let you do a line or two off them."

"It's better than a mirror any day." The television star laughed in a smoky alto. "Isn't that right, girls?" she asked the sisters bookending the Iranian.

Dutifully, with responses of zombies, the teenagers smiled and nodded. Kasim put his glass down and opened the bubble-wrap-padded envelope. Inside he saw a clear plastic shock case around a miniature 80 mm CD.

"That gives you what you need," Escondito said. "That's my lifeblood right there. The information on that disk will give you everything you need to run along my network up through El Salvador into Mexico and as far north as Chicago. Most of the space on that disk is taken up by security ICE," he explained, using the slang acronym for Intrusion Countermeasure Electronics. The man turned deadly serious. He sat forward and used a sharp elbow to knock the former Miss Colombia back away from him. "I want my submarine. I gave you what you said you needed. I gave you the underground railroad into America and all the support that goes with it."

He kissed his fingertips like a French chef. "Those weapons that just came off your freighter? That's a good start—but I want the connection with the Russian navy. I want my fucking submarine."

Kasim slid the envelope away. Colonel Ayub would be pleased. He intended to inform his superior just as soon as he finished with the girls. Miss Colombia had confided in him that they worked harder if you spit on and slapped them. He was fairly tingling with his eagerness to tear into the teenagers.

"We will get you the contact," Kasim assured him.

The Iranian agent's assignment to South America had already proved to be everything he'd heard. It beat the hell out of trying to run a Shia cell in Baghdad or an assassination operation in Lebanon. He'd heard that working with the Russians was like this—all parties and whores, but Kasim hated vodka and the cold. He would give Juan Escondito anything he wanted to stay in his position.

Around him the apartment erupted into frantic cheers as the runway models unveiled their sex toys. Kasim snorted more cocaine and thought about the streets of America's cities running red with blood.

HERMANN SCHWARZ GRASPED the TTY iPhone in his left hand and the handle above the passenger window with his right. He spoke into the ISA-provided device and his words were transferred to text, encoded and transmitted through satellite relay to the Farm.

"I appreciate the fact that Akira is flying one of the Farm's Predators for Phoenix, but the Agency confidential informant was wrong. I need the schematics for the west tower of the complex. Preferably before Carl fucking kills me with his driving."

Barbara Price's voice answered with cool proficiency over the ear-jack pickup. "Carmen's running it down right now. I think we can simply give you security and engineering overrides to the whole building. There's no way anything less than the hardware we're running is going to crack those firewalls anyway."

"Fine," Schwarz acknowledged. "What do I need to do to shut down the alarms and commandeer the elevators, then?"

"Bear is telling me that if you can manage to crack into the building through a local access port, he can slave the commands to your PDA."

"Fine. That's not a problem," Schwarz replied. "Walk in the park. All I need is a computer inside the building and its AV in/out port."

"We're good to roll, then," Price said. "Standby for transmission of west tower blueprints and electrical schematics."

"Copy. Able out," Schwarz said.

FOURTEEN BLOCKS AWAY Chinese technical officer Chin entered GCIA agent Hermida's office. The Venezuelan counterintelligence operative came to his feet instantly. The Chinese liaison handed a second computer printout over to Chavez's secret policeman.

"You have them?" Hermida asked.

"Yes. Still no voice verification—that remains impossible. We do have a firm lock on the signal, however, allowing for triangulation," Chin replied. "They're in downtown Caracas right now and on the move. With the codes I just provided, you should be able to follow and track that signal at will."

Hermida turned toward the stone-faced Gonzales. The commando leader rose smoothly from his seat. "Alert your team," Hermida ordered. "Once you're in the air, I'll have tech services provide you with coordinates."

"Yes, sir," the grim-faced killer replied.

Basra, Iraq

RAFAEL ENCIZO opened his hand.

Greasy hair slid through his loosened fingers as he plucked the blade of his Cold Steel Tanto from the Iraqi militia member's neck. Blood gushed down the front of the man's chest in a hot, slick rush and the gunman gurgled wetly in his throat.

Standing beside Encizo, Calvin James snatched up the man's rifle as it started to fall. The eyepieces of the two commandos' night optics shone a dull, nonreflective green as they watched the man fall to his knees. Encizo lifted his foot and used the thick tread of his combat boot to push the dying Iraqi over.

The final Shiite soldier on the building roof struck the tar paper and gravel as the last beats of his pounding heart pushed a gallon of blood out across the ground. As James set the scoped SVD sniper rifle down, Encizo knelt and cleaned his blade off on the man's jeans before sliding it home in its belt sheath.

Seeing the sentry down, McCarter led the rest of the team out of the stairwell and onto the roof. They crouched next to a 60 mm mortar position beside the parapet and overlooked the cluster of buildings in the Basra slum. Below them, in the shadow of the militia sentry building, a large flat-roofed home stretched out behind an adobe-style wall. Armed guards walked openly or stood sentinel at doorways. In the courtyard near the front gate, a Dzik-3 with Iraqi police markings stood, engine idling.

Hawkins went to one knee and began using the night scope of his Mk 11 to scan surrounding buildings for additional security forces. As David McCarter took up his field comm Manning knelt behind him and began to loosen the nineteen-pound grappling gun from the Briton's rucksack.

"Phoenix One to Stony Bird," McCarter said.

"Stony Bird copy," Akira Tokaido acknowledged.

"You have eyes on us?"

"Copy that," Tokaido confirmed.

At the moment the Predator drone launched by Jack Grimaldi from the coalition-controlled Iraqi airport floated high enough that it was invisible to the Iraqi special groups HQ below. Despite that, the powerful optics in the nose of the UAV readily revealed the heat signature silhouettes of the Phoenix team to Tokaido where they crouched on the Basra rooftop.

It was a little known fact that most of the larger drone aircraft seeing action in Afghanistan, and to a lesser extent Iraq, were piloted by operators at McCarren Air Force Base in Las Vegas, Nevada.

As soon as Kurtzman and Price had seen the remote-pilot setup used by both the Air Force and the CIA they had gone to Brognola with a request for the Farm to field the same capabilities using the Stony Man cyberteam as operators.

Both Kurtzman and Carmen Delahunt had proved skilled and agile remote pilots, but Hunt Wethers had been the most adept at maneuvering the UAV drones and he had consistently outflown the other two in training.

But Akira Tokaido, child prodigy of the video game age, had taken the professor to school. The Japanese-American joystick jockey had exhibited a genius touch for the operations and Kurtzman had put the youngest member of the team as primary drone pilot for the Farm.

Now Tokaido sat in the remote cockpit unit, or RCU, and controlled an MQ-1C Warrior from twenty-five thousand feet about Basra. He had four AGM-114 Hellfire missiles and a sensory-optics package in the nose transplanted from the U.S. Air Force RQ-4 Global Hawk, known as the Hughes Integrated Surveillance and Reconnaissance—HISAR—sensor system.

From a maximum ceiling of twenty-nine thousand feet Tokaido could read the license plate of a speeding car. And then put a Hellfire missile in the tailpipe.

Having seen the effects of the coordinated air strikes during training with the FBI's hostage-rescue team at a gunnery range next to the Groom Lake facility known as the Ranch, David McCarter was more than happy to have the air support.

The ex-SAS leader of Phoenix touched his ear jack and spoke into his throat mike. "You see the wheeled APC at the front gate?" he asked.

"Copy."

"That goes. I want a nice big fireball to draw eyes away from us while we come in the back door."

"That should obstruct the main entrance to the property," Tokaido allowed, voice calm. "That changes the original exit strategy Barb briefed me on."

"Acknowledged," McCarter responded. "But the truth on the ground has changed. Adapt, improvise, overcome."

"Your call, Phoenix," Tokaido allowed. "I'll put the knock-knock anywhere you want."

"Good, copy that. Put one in the armored car and shut down the gate. You get a good cluster of bad guys outside in the street, use Hellfires two and three at your discretion. Just save number four for my word."

"Understood." Tokaido paused. "You realize that if you're inside that structure when I let numbers two and three go you'll be extremely danger close, correct?"

"Stony Bird," McCarter said, "you just bring the heat. We'll stay in the kitchen."

"Understood. I'll drop altitude and start the show."

"Phoenix out." McCarter turned toward the rest of the team. "You blokes caught all that, right?" Each man nodded in turn. "Good. Hawkins, you remain in position. Clean up the courtyard and stay on lookout for snipers outside the compound."

Hawkins reached out and folded down the bipod on his Mk 11. "I'll reach out and touch a few people on behalf of the citizens of the United States of America." The Texan shrugged and grinned. "It's just a customer service I provide. Satisfaction guaranteed."

"Just try and stay awake up here, hotshot," McCarter said. "I'll put the zip line on target. The rest of you get your Flying Fox attachments ready."

"I'm going first," Manning said. "You hit the mark with the grappling gun but we'll use me to test the weight."

"Negative. I'm point," James said. "The plan calls for me to slide first."

Manning shook his head. "That was before we got burned. Those assholes down there know we're coming. We'll only get the one line. I should go first." He stopped and grinned. "Besides, Doc, if you fall, who'll patch you up?"

McCarter lifted a hand. "The moose is right, Cal. We'll send Gary down first."

James took up his SPAS-15. "Doesn't seem right, a Canadian going before a SEAL, but I'll make an exception this time." He reached out a fist and he and the grinning Manning touched knuckles.

"Get set," McCarter warned.

He lifted the tactical line-throwing system launcher to his shoulder. The device sported 120 feet of 7 mm Kevlar line and launched the spear grapnel with enough force to penetrate concrete. Despite himself McCarter paused for a moment to savor the situation.

He felt adrenaline slide into his system like a bullet train on greased wheels. He knew that he was not only among the most competent warriors on the face of the earth, but he was their leader. He could sense them around him now, reacting not with fear, but with the eagerness of dedicated professionals.

They were exhausted from their hard slog through a stinking sewer and the sudden violence of their betrayal and ambush. They smelled like shit and sweat and blood and gunpowder. They had the brutal acumen of men about to face impossible odds and achieve success. McCarter smiled to himself in cold satisfaction as he recalled the motto of the SAS—Who Dares Wins.

As his men, other than Hawkins, slid on their protective masks, McCarter's finger took up the slack in the grappling gun.

There was a harsh *tunk* sound as the weapon discharged, followed by the metallic whizzing of the line playing out. The sound of the impact six stories below was drowned out by the sound of Tokaido's Hellfire taking out the Dzik-3 APC. A ball of fire and oily black smoke rose up like a volcano erupting. The blazing hulk leaped into the air and dropped back down with a heavy metal crunch that cracked the cobblestone court.

"Now we're on," Encizo said, and Phoenix Force sprang into action.

THE MEN SLOWLY CHEWED their food as they watched the body hanging from chains set into the wall. The imman had dared to speak out against the random violence that claimed the lives of Basra's women and children, preaching before the prayer mats in the mosque that the Koran did not direct the slaughter of Muslim innocents in the name of Allah.

On his way to the market an Iraqi police car had stopped the imman and two officers had thrown a sack over his head and pushed him into the vehicle. When his hood had been ripped off the cleric found himself chained to the wall and in the hands of the very extremists he had railed against.

He saw two men, one in the uniform of the Basra police, calmly eating. The two men continued eating as other men caught his tongue in a pair of pliers and cut it off with a bayonet. They had continued eating as the torturers had taken a ball-peen hammer to first his fingers and then his toes. Then, when his naked body was slick with his own blood they had driven the slender shaft of an ice pick into his guts, perforating the large intestine and allowing his own fecal matter to flood into his system, causing sepsis.

Then a vengeful god had rained fire from the sky.

Colonel Ayub jumped out of his chair at the sound of the explosion. Around him his men scrambled to respond and he looked across the table to Anjali, the Iraqi police officer.

"It's *them!*" He roared, stunned.

"Ridiculous. They never could have gotten close. It must be an air strike. I told you to leave the city," Anjali fired back.

Ayub thought about Brigadier General Abdul-Ali Najafi sitting in Tehran like a spider at the center of his web. He thought of telling the Ansar-al-Mahdi commanding officer how he had failed, how the Americans had driven him from the Shia city of Basra.

"No," the Iranian said simply. "I'm safer here."

"I'm not!"

Then they heard the gunfire burning out around them and they knew it was more than an air strike. They knew then that against all odds the unknown commandos had made it into the Shiite slum, had come for them. They both realized that whoever these clandestine operators were they would never give up.

Instantly they rose and ran to rally their men.

"Fall in around me!" Anjali snarled.

"To the roof and perimeter!" Ayub said in turn.

Men were scrambling into positions and snatching up weapons.

THE LINE DIPPED under Manning's weight as he rode the Flying Fox cable car down the Kevlar zip line. He sailed down the six stories and applied the hand brake at the last possible moment. He swung his feet up and struck the roof of the building with the soles of his combat boots.

Because of the size of his primary weapon, the cut-down M-60E, he couldn't roll with the impact and instead bled off his momentum by sliding across the roof like a batter stealing second. With the last of his forward energy the big Canadian sat up and took a knee, swinging his machine gun into position and clicking off the safety.

Behind him he heard the sound as Calvin James hit the roof and rolled across one shoulder to come up with SPAS-15 ready. Above them they heard the muffled snaps as Hawkins cut loose with the silenced Mk 11 from his overwatch position. Below them in the courtyard around the sprawling house they heard men scream as the 7.62 mm rounds struck them.

Covering the exposed roof, Manning turned in a wide arc as Rafael Encizo slid down to the roof, putting his feet down and his shoulder against the line to arrest his forward motion. The Cuban came off his Flying Fox and tore his Hawk MM-1 from where it rested against the front of his torso.

McCarter landed right behind Encizo and rushed across the roof, M-4/M-203 up and in his hand. Gunfire burst out of a window in a mosque across the road. Manning shifted and triggered a burst of harassment fire from the hip. His rounds arced out across the space and slammed into the building, cracking the wall and shattering the lattice of a window. Red tracer fire skipped off the roof and bounced deeper into the city.

Above the heads of Phoenix Force in their black rubber protective masks, Hawkins shifted the muzzle of his weapon on its bipod and engaged the sniper. He touched a dial on his scope and the shooter suddenly appeared in the crosshairs of the reticule on his optics.

The man had popped up again after Manning's burst had tapered off and was attempting to bring an M-16 A-2 to bear on the exposed Americans.

Hawkins found the trigger slack and took it up. He let his breath escape through his nose as he centered the crosshairs on the sniper's eyes. For a brief, strange second it was as if the two men stared into each other's eyes. The Iraqi pressed his face into the eyepiece on the assault rifle. The man shifted the barrel as he tried for a shot.

The silenced Mk 11 rocked back against Hawkins's shoulder. The smoking 7.62 mm shell tumbled out of the ejection port and bounced across the tar-paper-and-gravel roof. In the image of his scope the Iraqi sniper's left eye became a bloody cavity. The man's head jerked and a bloody mist appeared behind him as he sagged and fell.

Autos fire began hammering the side of the building below Hawkins's position. He rolled over on his back, snatching up his sniper rifle. He scrambled up, staying low, and crawled through the doorway of the roof-access stair. He intended to shift positions and engage from one of the windows overlooking the compound in the building's top floor.

Below his position McCarter found what he was looking for. He pulled up short and shoved a stiffened forefinger downward, pointing at a enclosed glass sky-light that served to open up and illuminate the break-fast area. The opening had appeared as a black rectangle on the images downloaded from the Farm's Keyhole satellite, and from the first McCarter had seized on the architectural luxury as his entry point.

"We have control," Manning barked, and from half a world away Barbara Price and the Farm's cyberteam watched from the UAV's cameras. "We have control," McCarter repeated.

To create a distraction on the hard entry, Gary Manning had prepared an explosives charge. Since they were unable to precisely locate their target before the strike, nonlethal measures had been implemented. Working with Stony Man armorer John "Cowboy" Kissinger, the Canadian demolitions expert had prepped a series of flash-bang charges using stun grenades designed to incapacitate enemy combatants in airplane hangars, factories or warehouses. In addition to the flash-bang charges, Manning and Kissinger had layered in several additional payloads of CS gas.

McCarter slipped into his own protective mask, then gave Calvin James a thumbs-up signal. "Five, four, three, two, one."

The ex-SEAL jogged forward and pointed the SPAS-15 at the skylight. The semiautomatic shotgun boomed and the spray of buckshot shattered the reinforced commercial-grade Lexcan window.

"Execute, execute, execute!" McCarter ordered.

Instantly, Manning stepped up and threw his satchel charge through the hole. As it plunged through the opening the entry team turned their backs from the breach, shielding their eyes and ears. Instantly the booming explosion came. Smoke poured out of the opening like the chimney of a volcano.

James spun and stepped up to the ledge before dropping through the hole. He struck the ground and rolled to his left out along the side of his body, absorbing the impact from the ten-foot fall. He came up, the SPAS-15 tracking for a target in the smoke and confusion.

A running body slammed into him, sending them both spinning. Ignoring the combat shotgun on its sling, James reached out with his left hand and tore the AKM out of the figure's grip, tossing it aside as he rolled to his feet. His Beretta appeared in his fist. He pulled the guy closer but didn't recognize the stunned terrorist and put two 9 mm bullets through his slack-jawed face.

David McCarter dropped down through the breach into chaos.

He saw James drop a body and spin, his pistol up. Around him the whitish clouds of CS gas hung in patches, but the interior space was large enough that the dispersal allowed line-of-sight identification. McCarter saw a coughing, blinded gunman in an Iraqi police uniform stumble by and he shot him at point-blank range with the M-4.

The man was thrown down like a trip-hammered steer in a Chicago stockyard. McCarter went back down to a knee and twisted in a tight circle, muzzle tracking for targets. Behind him a third body dropped like a stone through the skylight breach.

Rafael Encizo landed flat-footed then dropped to a single knee, his fireplug frame absorbing the stress of the ten-foot fall. His MM-1 was secured, muzzle up, tightly against the body armor on his chest, and his MP-7 machine pistol was gripped in two hands.

Through the lens of his protective mask Encizo saw two AKM-wielding men in headdress and robes stumble past. The Cuban lifted his weapon and pulled the trigger, firing on full auto. He hosed the men ruthlessly, sending them spinning into each other like comedic actors in a British farce. He turned, saw a Iraqi policeman leveling a folding-stock AKM at him and somersaulted forward, firing as he came up. His rounds cracked the man's sternum, struck him under the chin and cored out his skull. The corrupt Iraqi dropped to the ground, limbs loose and weapon tumbling.

Gary Manning dropped through the breach, caught himself on the lip of the skylight with his gloved hands and hung for a heartbeat before dropping down. He landed hard with his heavier body weight and went to both knees. He grunted at the impact on his kneepads and orientated himself to the other three Phoenix members, completing their defensive circle as he brought up the cut-down M-60E.

Without orders the team fell into their established enclosed-space clearing pattern. Manning came up and charged toward the nearest wall, clearing left along the perimeter of the room while James followed closely behind him, then turned right. Encizo tucked in behind Manning as he turned left, and McCarter, also charged with coordination, followed James.

Manning kicked a chair out of the way and raced down the left wall of the room. Weapons began firing in the space and he saw blinking muzzle-flashes flare in the swirling CS gas. He passed a dead man hanging by chains from the wall. A close-range gunshot had cracked the bearded man's skull and splashed his brains on the wall behind his head.

Manning suddenly saw Anjali standing with a pistol, three men with Kalashnikovs in a semicircle in front of him. The Canadian special forces veteran triggered the M-60E in a tight burst and the 7.62 mm rounds tore the first police bodyguard away as he rushed forward. From behind him Encizo used the MP-7 to cut down the left flank bodyguard before the Iraqi police officer could bring his weapon around.

Manning took two steps forward and shoved the muzzle of his machine gun into the throat of the final bodyguard as Encizo swarmed around him. The Iraqi stumbled backward at the blunt-tipped spearing movement, his hands dropping his weapon and flying to his throat. As he staggered back, Manning lifted up a powerful leg and completed a front snap kick into the man's chest, driving him farther backward and into Anjali.

Both men fell as Encizo reached the fumbling Iraqi police major. The Cuban thrust the muzzle of his smoking hot machine gun into the coughing and half-blinded Anjali's face, pinning it to the floor. With his other hand Encizo broke the man's wrist, sending his pistol sliding away.

Hot shell casings rained down on Encizo as Manning cracked open the bodyguard's chest with a short burst from the M-60. Blood splashed Anjali's face as he grimaced in pain and the stunned and terrified traitor squeezed his eyes tight shut.

Manning halted his advance and swung the machine gun up to cover them as Encizo flipped the Iraqi over onto his stomach and used a white plastic zip tie to bind his hands. Anjali screamed in pain as the shattered bones of his wrists were ground against their broken ends by the Phoenix commando's rough treatment.

A block of light appeared in the gas-choked gloom. A knot of well-armed reinforcements surged through the open door from the outside. Manning shifted on a knee, swinging around the M-60. He saw one of the reinforcements fall, the side of his head vaporizing, then a second fell and realized Hawkins had found his range even at such an acute angle.

Manning pulled back on the trigger of his machine gun and the weapon went rock and roll in his grip. He scythed down the confused Iraqi terrorists, cutting into their ranks with his big 7.62 mm slugs. The men screamed and triggered their weapons into the ground as they were knocked backward. He let the recoil against his hand on the pistol grip climb the muzzle up and his rounds cut into the terrorist bodies like buzz saws.

"Phoenix, we have company," Tokaido warned over the team's ear jacks. "Hellfire number two is away. Danger close."

CHAPTER ELEVEN

Caracas, Venezuela

Across the street from the west tower of the plaza complex Able Team watched the building. Inside the vehicle behind the steering wheel, Carl Lyons carefully slid the brochure on urban transportation in Caracas away into an inside pocket. Behind him in the back of the vehicle Schwarz was busy finishing up his daisy chain linking of what explosives had been available at the safehouse, including the C-4 stripped from four Claymore mines and a small amount of Semtex.

"I think that'll do it," the electronics wizard said.

"Good," Lyons said. He turned to Blancanales. "You ready, Pol?"

The Puerto Rican looked up from his own PDA, where he had been memorizing the building architectural plans. He tucked the device away and reached for the door handle on their stolen automobile.

"I'm ready. Create the distraction, then get in hard on our six as I move through the building."

"You get a good copy on all that back on the Farm?" Lyons asked into his throat mike.

"We're picking you up solid," Carmen Delahunt replied. "It'll be myself and Hunt on the line tonight. Akira and Bear are handling a Phoenix operation. I have zero official police chatter about you guys so far. Hunt is handling other government agencies."

"Let's roll," Lyons said. He reached down beside the steering column and hit the release on the sedan's gas tank.

The doors on the vehicle flew open and the Stony Man commandos slid their silenced H&K MP-5 subguns beneath their jackets. The hour was late, past midnight, and there were only a few pedestrians, most in their early twenties, on the street.

Blancanales and Schwarz immediately left the automobile and began walking up the sidewalk. Lyons casually strolled to the back of the vehicle and unscrewed the cap to the gas tank. Behind him Blancanales and Schwarz crossed the street a full city block up from the entrance of the west tower.

Lyons let the gas cap dangle and reached into his jacket. Like a fisherman playing out line he quickly unwound a yard of det cord attached to the firing system of one of the Claymore mines Schwarz had stripped at the safehouse.

Blancanales, followed by Schwarz, stepped off the street and up onto the sidewalk fronting the side of the plaza west tower. They reached an ornate concrete divider holding heavy planters and leaped the barrier.

Lyons slid the silver metal blasting cap detonation trigger at the end of the det cord down into the fuel tank of their stolen vehicle. Casually, he backed away from the vehicle, playing out the det cord as he strolled down the sidewalk.

Up the street Blancanales and Schwarz disappeared behind a wall of vibrant, blooming azaleas and arboreta shrubs. Lyons heard drunken, laughing voices and looked up to see a young couple approaching his IED.

"Oh, Jesus Christ!" he snarled, and pulled out his MP-5. Then in perfect Spanish he called, "Excuse me, people—violence going on here." He triggered a burst from the silenced submachine that sent geysers of dirt from the sidewalk lawn into the air. The couple screamed and froze. Growling, Lyons waved the muzzle of the H&K to shoo them away and they both turned and ran.

"Carmen, I just had to play the big bad with some love birds. The Caracas PD should be getting calls very soon."

"Copy, Ironman," Delahunt replied. "I'll monitor and delay as appropriate. This should help cement the action as an Escondito rival's hit team."

"Absolutely," Lyons replied as he worked. "Getting ready to make some noise."

He quickly rolled out the last of the det cord until he was left holding the preprepped plastic Claymore trigger, often called a clacker. The Able Team leader went to one knee behind the front of a conveniently placed Audi sports car and took a last look around before squeezing the lever action on the device.

There was a *whump* as the explosion sucked up the surrounding oxygen, then a brilliant ball of flame rolled into the sky, carrying the four-door sedan upward on it. The vehicle rolled up end over end, then crashed down in the middle of the street directly in front of the building's entrance.

Casually, Lyons rose, throwing the Claymore trigger down after wiping it clean of fingerprints on his shirt. He stepped out from behind the bumper of the Audi and

casually strolled across the street as the burning automobile rolled over on its side and flaming engine fluids
spilled out in a river from the blazing pyre.

Down at the doors of the west tower the ex-LAPD
police officer saw a uniformed security guard appear,
then three more. He hopped the concrete barrier and
pushed his way through the bushes to come up against
the side of the building.

Blancanales and Schwarz, MP-5s out and up, stood
beside the first-story floor-to-ceiling window that com-
prised the construction on this aspect of the west tower.
Blancanales lifted his submachine gun and triggered a blast,
raking 9 mm bullets down the length of the glass wall, un-
zipping it like a dress. The sound of the blazing vehicle
muted the sound of shattering glass and the leaping flames
cast wild shadows in the window reflections, making the
three Americans look like demons in the uncertain light.

Weapon up, Blancanales entered the building, stepping over the threshold of broken glass. Behind them
Lyons pulled the pins on two smoke grenades and tossed
them on either side down the building. The smoke can-
isters spit out their concealing fog and added to the
overall confusion on the scene.

As Schwarz entered the building after Blancanales,
Lyons stepped forward and followed him in. So far he
could detect neither an audible building alarm nor the
sounds of approaching response sirens.

Inside the building the team entered a network labyrinth
of office cubicles, computer workstations, copy centers
and partitioned walls of the IT suites. Each member of
Able Team reached up and pulled his night-vision goggles
into place, transforming the office space into a surrealistic nighttime theater of muted greens and grays.

"Up ahead, on the left," Blancanales said. He jogged forward, turned a corner, ran down three steps on a memorized route, then turned a right-hand corner. He lifted his MP-5 and fired on the move as he ran forward.

The single 9 mm round struck the glass of the interior door and shattered it. He ran up to the breach and used the silencer on his submachine gun to knock loose glass down to the carpet. Following behind him, Schwarz ran through the opening and entered the blade farm.

"I'll secure the access door," Lyons said, and peeled off.

He ran down a transparent wall separating the building's CPU and blade server farm from the IT workstations. Inside the vault were several hard drives locked in transparent plastic cases and carefully stacked atop plasti-alloy filing cabinets. On the other side was a small rectangular box of polished Brazilian walnut. The containment unit was surrounded by a cluster of sophisticated electronics: climate-control sensors, humidity readouts, seismograph, gas analyzer, barometer and temperature gauge. On the other side of the glass Hermann Schwarz used a sliver of his thermite to burn out a security door lock as Lyons raced for one of the doors in the office complex that opened up onto the nonpublic access parts of the massive skyscraper.

"That was it, boys," Carmen said. "We have the call. I'm moving to insert cross-channel traffic to slow down the communications, but the clock is ticking."

"Understood," Blancanales said.

While Blancanales pulled security in the other direction, Lyons cracked the door and looked out on the service hallway and toward the private elevator bank situated there. He looked back to see Blancanales covering the primary entrance to the IT offices.

Schwarz, speaking in a calm voice, broke squelch over the comm link ear jacks. "I'm linked up to the system, Stony Man."

"Copy that, Gadgets," Delahunt replied, using the team's nickname for the man. "I'm initiating our Trojan program now."

A burst of angry Spanish came from the front of the office, and Lyons had to stifle his instinct to turn and spray the potential danger. They may have been trying to create the illusion that they were a drug cartel hit team, but they had no intention of murdering innocent civilians to perpetrate the charade.

Three security officers in brown uniforms rushed through the doorway. Each man had a radio on his belt with a handset attached to the epaulet on his shoulder. In their hands they carried side-handled batons and cans of pepper spray.

Blancanales stepped out of the shadows, lowered his MP-5 and fired off three short bursts. The 9 mm slugs tore the red exit fire sign above the door into twisted pieces of metal and a shower of sparks. The second bursts punched holes in the Sheetrock on either side of the security officers as they crowded through the door.

"Jump back!" Blancanales yelled in flawless Spanish, and the frightened men stumbled over themselves to make their escape.

"Able, listen, I have a sit-rep from the professor," Delahunt broke in, using Wethers's nickname. "He's lifted an internal e-mail from the GCIA saying they're scrambling a squad of *negra yaguars*. It doesn't say why or to where, but it's suspicious."

"Chavez's thug unit?" Blancanales asked. "The timing's not good for us, but it could be something else."

"No such thing as a coincidence," Lyons cut in.

"Trust an ex-cop not to believe in serendipity," Schwarz said.

"Seren-what? Is that even a real world?"

"Done!" Schwarz interrupted. "I have taken control of the building. Do not attempt to modify your vertical or horizontal. Let's get to the elevators."

A second later the building went black.

Stony Man Farm, Virginia

BARBARA PRICE HURRIED into the computer room, where she saw Huntington Wethers hunched over his workstation keyboard, fingers flying, while Carmen Delahunt was pulling her VR helmet back on.

"How's it going with Able?" Price demanded.

Wethers looked up and smiled. "The plaza firewalls were very good, but no match for our computers. I negotiated primary control to Gadgets's PDA interface just a minute ago. We'll still run all the software packages, but our computers will take their cue from his gear."

"The GCIA launched an elite unit by helicopter," Delahunt broke in. "It seems coincidental since Caracas police are scrambling to the site, but we don't know what they're dealing with yet."

"I don't like coincidences," Price said flatly.

"Nobody does," Delahunt agreed. "But so far we have no indication that the commando unit is trick to Able—just that they launched. Chavez has a lot of dirty deals going down in-country and even though his spooks are aware that Able is up to no good, that doesn't mean they know exactly what that 'no good' is."

"Fine," Price allowed. "Keep me informed, and I want to know the second they have the target."

"Understood," Wethers said.

Price left the room and pulled out her cell phone. She strode down the hallway toward the tram car on the underground track connecting the Farm's Annex with the older structure of the main house. She nodded to the burly blacksuit standing sentry at the miniature subway station.

Her encrypted cell phone rang as she climbed into the car and started the short ride. The walls of the tunnel flicked by as she picked up speed. At the other end of the signal Hal Brognola picked up on the third ring.

"Talk to me, Barb," he growled.

"Able has engaged, and Phoenix is knee-deep in the hoopla as we speak. Akira's just dropped two Hellfires into Basra."

"Christ," Brognola sighed, "when it rains, it pours. We got lucky that it's the time of year it is, so that we have hours of darkness overlapping between Iraq and Venezuela. To be honest I'm worried about Able's plan."

"It makes me nervous, too," Price said. The open tram car began to slow. "But that's Carl for you."

"True enough, but another firefight in Iraq is nothing. They blow up the biggest landmark in Caracas? *That* could be an international incident."

"There's something else," Price said. The car came to a stop and she stepped out and proceeded into the basement of the main house.

"Something else? What?" Brognola demanded.

"We're not sure if it's significant, but one of Chavez's elite death squads got scrambled about the time Lyons blew his distraction and the team made entry into the building."

"What's the chatter from the Venezuelans? They made our boys? How?"

"We don't know. We just don't like the timing."

"You think they could have cracked our commo?"

"There's no way they busted our ice," Price said. "No one can bust our ice. Okay, maybe the British or the Chinese—but not that quickly and not even really that likely," the former NSA mission controller said. She stepped into the elevator and hit the button. "Though maybe…"

"Maybe what, Barb?"

"Maybe if their gear was updated or augmented they could catch the signal itself. Not break the encryption or trace us through the cutouts, but maybe they could catch the initial beacon transmission."

"How much of a maybe is this?"

"Bear doesn't think it likely of Chavez's operatives. I tend to agree," Price said.

"But?"

"But I guess it's possible."

"So Able could be compromised?"

"Only as to a triangulation of their location, not to their actual mission objectives. Also the Venezuela spooks wouldn't know for sure that the people using the comm unit were the same as the ones who shook them at the international airport. It'd be them throwing manpower at everything hoping to get lucky."

"I'll hold off telling the Man, then," Brognola said. "I want to know as soon as Phoenix and Able are both in extraction phase from their ops."

Price stepped out on the main floor of the farmhouse and began walking toward the front door. "Understood," she said.

"Goodbye." The line went dead.

CHAPTER TWELVE

Basra, Iraq

Calvin James spun, bringing up the SPAS-15.

The combat shotgun boomed like a cannon in his hands, and steel shot scythed through the CS-tinged air to strike two AKM-wielding figures. The Iraqi terrorists were thrown backward and spun apart, arms flying in the air, weapons tossed aside by the force of the blasts.

One of them tripped over a wastepaper basket and went down hard. The second bounced off a wall and tumbled into a chair. James moved between them, double checking as he went. The one on the floor was leaking red by the gallon from a chewed-up throat and torn-open chest. The second was missing enough of his face that his brains were exposed.

There was a burst of rifle fire and the SPAS-15 was knocked from James's hands. Heavy slugs slammed into the ceramic chest plates of his Kevlar body armor. He staggered backward and grunted. His shoulder hit the wall and he went to one knee. Reflexively, his hands flew to his Beretta. As he drew the handgun David McCarter lunged past, the M-4 carbine up and locked into his shoulder, the muzzle erupting in a star-pattern blast.

He saw the figure wearing an expensive black silk *thobe* at the last moment and pulled his shot. The 5.56 mm rounds struck the man in his legs and swept him to the floor of the building. Bright patches of blood splashed in scarlet blossom on the figure's thighs.

Behind them the front of the building exploded as Tokaido's Hellfire struck.

McCarter was thrown to his knees. He grunted with the impact as something heavy and wet struck him between the shoulder blades. He looked down and saw a severed arm lying on the floor. He felt the heat of the raging blaze burning behind him.

He struggled to his feet.

"Talk to me, people!" Tokaido shouted over the line. "Talk to me!"

McCarter didn't answer but lunged forward. Ayub was screaming from his shattered thighs, but the Iranian colonel was pulling a Jordanian JAWS pistol from out of his robes. McCarter slashed out with his M-4. His bayonet caught the man across the forearm, slicing a long, ugly gash. The Iranian screamed again as he dropped the pistol.

Still on all fours, McCarter scrambled forward, the M-4 up in one fist. The blade of the wicked bayonet jabbed into the soft flesh of Ayub's throat and pushed the man backward.

"Freeze!" McCarter snarled in Persian. "Move one fucking inch and I'll put your brains on the wall!" He lashed out with the bayonet again, lancing the tip into the meat of the Iranian's shoulder and opening a small wound.

"Speak to me, Phoenix!" Tokaido hollered again.

"Manning up. That was very fucking 'danger close,' my man," the Canadian special forces veteran said.

"Pescado is good," Encizo said. "I'm knee-deep in tango guts, but that blast blew the front off the building."

"Copy that," Tokaido said. "They had two platoon-size elements as reinforcements at the door. Forty, fifty guys all bunched up at the entrance."

"McCarter up," McCarter said. "But Cal took a round and I have our boy." He paused. "If we're clear, I need help."

Instantly there was a reaction from behind him and the massive frame of Gary Manning appeared by his side as Encizo scrambled over to pull security near the prone Calvin James.

Encizo leaned in close, his eyes hunting for enemy motion from behind the lenses of his protective mask. "Speak to me, Cal," he demanded. "You okay, bro?"

James turned his head and opened his eyes. He opened his mouth to speak but no sound came out. Encizo, ears still ringing from the Hellfire blast, shook his head to clear his hearing.

"Speak to me!" the Cuban demanded.

James lifted his head and the muscles along his neck stood out. His lips formed the words under his protective mask and his eyes bulged with his effort under the lens but no sound came out. Finally there was a rush of air through the blunt nose filter.

"That hurt!" he wheezed. "Jesus, that hurt. I think I cracked my ribs."

"Is he good?" McCarter demanded over one shoulder. His weapon's muzzle never wavered from Ayub's face. "Is he good?"

Beside the Briton, Manning fired his M-60E in a short four-round burst. A crawling Iraqi terrorist shuddered under the impact of the 7.62 mm slugs and lay still. Encizo turned toward the Phoenix Force leader and shouted back.

"Yeah, he just had the wind knocked out of him. Maybe bruised ribs, maybe cracked—we don't know, but he's ambulatory!"

"He's also right goddamn here," James snapped, sitting up. "He doesn't need you talking about him as if he were incapable of speech."

"Good," McCarter replied, his voice echoing weirdly under the mask. "'Cause I got our boy, but the bitch needs patching up before we yank him back to Wonderland." McCarter switched to his throat mike. "Akira, how we look out there?"

"You got vehicles coming up the street. You'll have more bad guys on site very shortly. I'm still sitting on Hellfire number three."

"Fine. Hit 'em at the gate and cause a further chokepoint, but save number four for my direction."

"Understood."

McCarter pulled back as James moved forward, medic kit in hand. Ayub looked at the black man with real hatred as the ex-SEAL began to treat the Iranian's wounds.

"Give him morphine," McCarter said as he rose. "We're going to have to carry him anyway with those leg wounds. It'll keep him docile."

Encizo spoke up. "What about the son of a bitch Anjali?"

McCarter looked over at the Cuban commando. "You guys tag and bag him?"

"Yep," Manning interrupted as he rose. "We got him against the wall." The big Canadian began to move down the length of the room toward the blazing hole in the building, checking each of the downed bodies as he did so.

"We aren't prepped to carry two deadweights out of here," McCarter pointed out.

"What's the penalty for treason?" Manning asked.

"Firing squad," Encizo said, an ugly smile splitting his face.

James looked up from bandaging the glowering Ayub. "Where will we find volunteers?"

McCarter turned, lifted his M-4 to his shoulder and pulled the trigger. Across the stretch of floor broken by the rapidly thinning clouds of CS gas the corrupt Iraqi police officer Anjali caught the 3-round burst in the side of the head.

Blood gushed like water from a broken hydrant and the blue-gray scrambled eggs of his brains splashed across the floor with bone-white chips of skull in the soupy mess. McCarter lowered his smoking M-4.

The ex-SAS commando leaned down close to the wounded Iranian. "Ayub, you see I'm a serious bastard now?"

The Ansar-al-Mahdi colonel paled under the scrutiny of the cold-blooded Stony Man commando. His eyes shifted away from the death mask McCarter's face had become. Then he jerked and winced as James unceremoniously gave him an intramuscular shot of morphine.

James smiled with ghastly intensity at the captured Iranian terror master. "Don't worry," he said. "If we shoot you, it'll only be in the gut."

Manning and Encizo reached down and jerked the sedated Ayub to his feet. McCarter spoke into his throat mike. "Akira, how we look?"

"Clock's ticking. You got stubborn bad guys trying to dig their way through the burning barricade I made out of the first-wave vehicles. I'm still sitting on my last Hellfire."

"Good copy," McCarter said. "We'll be rolling out the back door in about ten seconds. Why don't you go ahead and blow me a hole out the back fence now?"

"One escape hatch coming up," Tokaido replied.

"Phoenix," McCarter said to his teammates. "We are leaving."

Caracas, Iraq

ABLE TEAM rode in the elevator up the west tower.

With the building completely under Schwarz's control, he had shut everything down except for the service elevator they had commandeered.

"Shall I hit the sprinklers and fire alarms now?" Schwarz asked. "Get everyone in the building running out just as the police and fire emergency show up?"

"Wait till we hit the floor," Lyons said.

"Sure," Schwarz replied.

The team stood there in silence as the elevator smoothly rose up toward the top of the building. Time seemed to drag out to improbable lengths as the floor numbers grew steadily larger.

The elevator slowed beneath their feet and slid to a stop at their floor. The doors parted with a pneumatic hiss, revealing a small, bone-white service area. Able Team stepped out, Schwarz using commands from his PDA to keep the elevator firmly in place.

Inside the service area there was a bucket with a mop in it and a silver metal room-service cart with an empty champagne bottle on it. The American commandos freed their submachine guns from beneath their jackets.

"Will that elevator hold even against a firefighter override key?" Lyons asked.

"We're in so deep to this building's control system that that elevator will hold until I say even if they cut the goddamn cables." Schwarz laughed.

"They have room service?" Blancanales asked. He pointed at the fancy wheeled cart with the empty champagne bottle. The room smelled vaguely of disinfectant and the fluorescent lights were stark and industrial, casting everything in a bright, harsh light that Blancanales associated with hospitals.

"The building has a concierge service," Schwarz told him. "It's only available to the top five floors."

"Fine," Lyons said. "Go ahead and hit the fire alarms. When the authorities get here I want thousands of people streaming out. I want us to disappear in a real mob scene."

Blancanales reached out and pulled open the door to the service lobby as Lyons stepped forward, lifting his H&K MP-5 SD-3. Behind them Schwarz, grinning like a mischievous child, quickly typed a command into his PDA. The encrypted signal bounced along its traverse to the Stony Man Farm computers, which interpreted the command and fed it back into the building's network.

As they stepped out into the hallway all hell broke loose.

An electronic siren began to screech. The lights on the top half of the tower went out just as the ones lower to the ground floor had. Red glowing emergency lights clicked on low to the ground. Overhead the sprinkler systems opened up and began to flood the area. An audio system of extensive power that had been blaring hip-hop music from behind one of the many hall doors suddenly cut out.

Able Team moved down the center of the hallway ignoring the chaos they had caused. They were in a luxurious hall of marble tile, titanium-gold fixtures and black walnut woodwork. Four burly Hispanic men in expensive suits came away from a teak desk and comfortable office chairs set in the middle of the hallway near the residential elevator doors decorated in gold filigree and Italian cut crystal.

Blancanales, the muzzle of his H&K submachine gun pointed down, walked forward, lifting his left hand up, palm out. "Good evening, my friends," he said in rapid-fire Spanish. "We have a fire in the kitchen of the restaurant on the top floor. Everyone must evacuate using the stairs because of the gas leak."

Ingram M-11 9 mm submachine guns appeared from beneath the desk.

"Why are you armed!" one of the Hispanic bodyguards demanded. "Who are you? Who is the gringo!" Water from the spewing sprinklers began to pool on the desktop and run over the edges.

Doors began opening up along the hallway, drunken partygoers stumbling out in confusion, men cursing and more than a few females screaming in fear. The blinking red emergency lights illuminated the scene with a surrealistic quality.

Lyons stepped from behind Blancanales even as Schwarz floated out farther to the left. The Americans revealed their silenced weapons and the narco-soldiers understood the situation instantly. There was a triple echo of harsh, sound-suppressed coughs as the German weapons fired, the three American commandos moving forward in a synchronized line.

Able Team's bullets tore down the wide hall in a pyramidal pattern designed to avoid the clusters of intoxicated partygoers stumbling out of the rooms. Bullets stitched into the bewildered bodyguards and the pooled water from the sprinklers turned a diluted crimson.

The dead men flopped to the ground as confused and intoxicated guests flooded the hallways. The fresh, leaking corpses were trampled on by a dozen different men and women in expensive party clothes and cocaine-induced tunnel vision.

Lyons lowered his submachine gun to make it less obvious and stepped in front of Blancanales and Schwarz. He turned a big shoulder to the press of hysterical humanity and began to rudely push his way through, searching faces as he made for the door to the main suite.

Behind him Blancanales and Schwarz threw punches to knock the cartel hangers-on away from them. The soldiers who reached for pistols were executed, their bodies dropping down to the cold, water-slick tile like sacks of loose meat.

A topless woman tripped over one such corpse and sat up screaming, her face and hands painted red. Reflexively, Schwarz stopped and grabbed her under one arm to help her. She shrieked and raked his exposed face with her nails, clawing for his eyes.

The ex-Special Forces soldier jerked his face back and shoved the screeching woman away, barking out his pain and surprise as three red stripes were gouged into his face. The hissing woman stumbled backward, eyes rolling wildly. The heel of her pump broke as she forced herself to her feet—then the crowd surged around her in the dark hallway and she was gone.

"What the hell," Schwarz swore, amazed.

"Hey, I wanted a building's worth of people clogging the halls and spilling out into the street when the police showed up," Lyons said. "But these guys are *muy loco, hombre.*"

"Cocaine and Johnnie Walker Black Label will do that to you," Blancanales replied.

The team shouldered their way to the door, the thick crowd thinning out steadily as they approached the far end of the hallway. The door to the master suite foyer hung open and Able Team approached the entrance with caution, weapons held low but ready.

From inside, even over the scream of the fire alarm and the rushing howl of the sprinkler system, they could hear a man shouting angrily in Spanish. Lyons moved through the door and stepped left, coming up against a table. Behind him Schwarz followed through and peeled off to the right. Blancanales anchored the door just to the right of the opening.

Inside the room a man they recognized from their briefings as Juan Escondito was snarling into an expensive cell phone. Standing close by, a group of bodyguards watched him, hair plastered against their heads by the sprinkler system. As if controlled by a single hive mentality, the squad of gunmen turned to face the intruders, hands darting beneath jackets to dig for the grips of pistols.

Lyons stepped forward and lifted his H&K MP-5 as one of the bodyguards pulled a Skorpion machine pistol from inside a sky-blue suit jacket. The German-made submachine gun shook in the big American's hands and the 9 mm Parabellum unzipped the narco-soldier from belly to sternum.

Blood splashed the front of the man's shirt as his stomach was opened up and he stumbled backward. Schwarz knocked the Venezuelan gunman standing next to Lyon's kill down with a 3-round burst to the head. From the doorway Blancanales hammered a third kill down with his own weapon as the other two swiveled to deal with the remaining bodyguards.

The room flashed with light and cracked with the detonation of heavy calibers as unsuppressed weapons returned fire.

CHAPTER THIRTEEN

Basra, Iraq

Phoenix unfolded into action with the choreographed smoothness of a dance troupe on display or a surgical team in an emergency room. Taking out the last three 40 mm rounds for his Hawk MM-1, Encizo laid his grenade launcher on the ground. He pulled a fragmentation hand grenade from his web gear, armed it, then trapped the spoon under the weapon's weight to create a high-explosive booby trap.

Manning jerked their prisoner to his feet and threw a hood over the frightened man's head as Hawkins snatched the man up under his arm. Still gathering himself after his close call, James readied two smoke grenades. McCarter, waiting by the door to the terrorist redoubt, looked back at his team, then nodded once when he saw they were ready.

"Hit it," he ordered.

"Copy, danger close," Tokaido responded immediately. There was a long moment of silence. During the elastic minute the team's ringing ears recovered slightly and they could hear the shouts of men coming from the street outside the compound gate, the racing of engines and the stutter barks of automatic weapons. There was the crackling of vehicle fires clearly audible through the walls of the building. Inside the hazy room it stank of sweat and blood and fear. Their eyes watered and their noses ran as they stripped off their protective masks to facilitate their coming sprint.

Hawkins grabbed the sweat-soaked Iranian under one arm while the gigantic Manning held him tightly on the other side.

"Here it comes!" McCarter shouted.

The ex-SAS trooper swung away from the open door and went to a knee. Outside there was a final heartbeat, then the Hellfire slammed into the back wall of Ayub's compound. The missile shrieked in screaming as it darted toward the cinder-block wall. It struck with the force of an automobile and detonated with a deep, resonant boom. The concussive waves rolled through the building and shook the team, threatening to knock them down.

Ayub swayed and the Phoenix operatives jerked him back upright. Outside, through the open door past McCarter, a cloud of smoke and dust rolled by. The Phoenix leader came up off his knee and turned toward the door.

"Go! Go! Go!" he yelled.

James ran forward and threw his two primed smoke grenades into the swirling mess toward the blocked compound gate where the burning armored car smoldered. Thick smoke began to pour into the already obscured area, reducing vision to inches.

McCarter slapped Encizo on the shoulder as James threw his grenades. The Cuban rushed out and ran toward the breach in the wall created by Akira Tokaido's Hellfire. Broken chunks of masonry and rubble were scattered across the courtyard, threatening to turn his foot under his boots. He moved forward, weapon up, pushing through the smoke until he found a breach big enough to drive a truck through.

He rushed forward through the smoke until he broke out on the other side. He stood in a dirt-lane alley running along one side of Ayub's compound. To his right he could see the building and street the team had used to infiltrate the enemy combatant stronghold. Seeing no movement, he spun in the other direction and went to one knee.

"Clear!" he hollered.

"Coming!" Manning shouted through the swirling cloud of smoke and dust. A second later the big Canadian burst through the smoke, the stumbling Iranian between him and Hawkins. The men orientated on Encizo and approached him, walking fast, weapons up in their free hands.

A second later James emerged from the smoke, his submachine gun ready, and half a heartbeat after him came David McCarter. There was the sound of Kalashnikov fire from above them and gouts of dirt geysered up from the alley floor in a sloppy staccato pattern.

McCarter and Encizo spun as the bullets hammered toward the group. The Briton's carbine swung up and he cut loose with a series of 3-round bursts as Encizo cut loose with his backup weapon. An Iraqi in a third-floor window was driven back from the opening as the team's bullets hammered around him. In the brief lull

McCarter triggered his M-203 and launched a 40 mm HE round through the opening. The black projectile lobbed upwards, then sailed into the window.

The crack of detonation was followed by a surge of dark brown smoke, and body parts flew out the window.

"I'm overhead," Jack Grimaldi's voice filled their ear jacks. "Three blocks due west is our LZ," the Stony Man pilot reminded them. "But the streets around you are crawling with bad guys," he warned.

Hawkins felt a chill surge through him as he was forcibly reminded of his time in Mogadishu. He snarled in response and lifted his weapon as more Iraqi gunfire began to be directed toward the fleeing team.

"Phoenix," McCarter shouted, "let's move!"

In the buildings around them Iraqis awoken by the explosions and gunfire appeared in their windows, looking down on the chaos below while others tried to shepherd their family toward cover. The occasional militia member or armed neighborhood youth took the opportunity to snipe at the American unit below even as Ayub's own militia floundered in confusion.

Overhead Jack Grimaldi's Black Hawk helicopter appeared. The Farm's premier pilot spun the aircraft around, the rotor wash beating down on the struggling men. He got the chopper's nose pointed to the team's six o'clock and sent two 7-inch rockets down the alley behind them. The missile rounds flew like arrows through the tight passage for a hundred yards before slamming into the corner of Ayub's compound, pouring fire and smoke in a wild, wide pattern and driving the civilian gunmen for cover.

Running hard with one hand under the Iranian's arm, Hawkins saw movement and reacted without conscious thought. He pivoted at the waist and brought up his submachine gun. An Iraqi teenager armed with a folding-stock AKM staggered backward in a doorway, red blossoms opening up his chest.

There was a blaze of gunfire from a second-story window on Manning's side, and the big Canadian staggered as a round struck his vest. Two 7.62 mm rounds struck their prisoner in the hip and right leg. The terrorist screamed out loud and staggered, trying to fall.

Hawkins swung around and put a shoulder into the Iranian terror master's gut, scooping up the wounded man in a fireman's carry. Manning let go of the prisoner and twisted toward the fire, swinging up the cut-down M-60E. He cursed savagely and cut loose with the heavy machine gun.

Red tracer fire lanced upward as he poured twenty rounds through the open window. There was a shrill, high-pitched scream as the heavy-caliber slugs ripped into the building and a shattered Kalashnikov forestock still attached to a nylon shoulder sling tumbled outward.

"I've got the bastard!" Hawkins yelled. "Just cover us!"

"Got it!" Manning yelled back.

Around them James and Encizo and McCarter were firing, as well. Above them a cascade of smoking, gleaming brass shells fell around them as the hovering Grimaldi worked the trigger on his chain gun.

"Phoenix," the pilot's voice broke squelch, "it looks like an anthill from up here. You've got men and vehicles pouring into this area from all sides. I have RPGs on the roof and snipers in almost every window."

"Another day at the office, Jack," McCarter replied. "Block and a half. We can do anything for another block and a half."

"Negative," Grimaldi replied. "Your primary route is filled with enemy gunslingers. You need to move to Route Bravo."

Hearing that, James shouted, "Plan B, people. We are switching to Plan B."

"I thought this *was* plan B," Encizo shouted, his machine pistol chattering in his hand.

Bullets knifed through the air around them. Manning cut loose again with the M-60, trying desperately to suppress the growing enemy fire. Above the team Grimaldi banked the helicopter hard and swung away to leapfrog one street over from their position. McCarter fired his last 40 mm grenade from his M-203, aiming at a rocket team on a building above them.

The HE round arced up like a basketball sailing smoothly from the hands of a talented player in a fade-away jump shot. Just as the two RPG gunners knelt and shouldered their weapons the 40 mm grenade slammed into the roof. The round tore the ambushers apart, spraying chunks of their body out in a spinning whirlwind and punching a hole through the structure's ceiling. Both of the RPG-7 warheads were detonated, and the resulting explosion ripped the roof off the building, scattering bricks in the air like raindrops.

"This way!" James shouted.

Manning sprayed the street behind them as the other Phoenix pros quickly ducked down an open alley and cut across to the next street. With each step the burdened Hawkins took, the Iranian prisoner screamed in anguish and the ex-Ranger was soaked in the man's blood.

Phoenix Force emerged on the next street over, McCarter leading the way. A bullet parted the hair on his head and tugged at the sleeves of his black fatigue shirt. A step behind him, James and Encizo both saw the gunner at the same instant and fired simultaneously. Their bullet streams crossed as they poured tight bursts into the man's body and he was punched to the ground.

Up ahead of them by thirty yards Grimaldi swiveled the helicopter in a tight pivot. His voice came over their ear jacks, eerily calm in the din of the massive street fight. "It's the same as the sat photos showed," the Stony Man pilot reported. "We've got a chain-link fence bisecting the alley."

"Copy," McCarter replied. "Blow it."

A rocket sprang to life and leaped from the pod on the Black Hawk. A second later a ball of fire rolled up into the air, funneled like a chimney between two buildings. At the rear of the team Manning sensed motion and heard a high-pitched, almost rhythmic wailing from behind him. He spun, swinging the M-60E into position, its barrel still hot.

He paused, finger on the trigger. He felt his throat choke in shock and horror, his eyes bulging wide in surprise. From behind a heavy black cloth burka he saw an Iraqi woman racing toward him, wailing her prayer. From behind her body two middle-aged Iraqi men fired from the safety of a basement doorway. The woman's hands appeared empty at first glance and were held above her head as she raced. Each step she took caused her ankle-length dress to flare outward.

Manning squinted in confusion as the men's AKM fire snapped and popped around him. Thrown hastily over the woman's concealing outfit was an OD-green vest with multiple pockets. Red-and-green wires ran out of the pockets and up past her veils to a square, black plastic detonation device in the woman's hand.

"Jesus Christ!" Manning swore in horror as he realized the woman had to be wearing over twenty pounds of plastic explosives in her suicide vest.

His finger tightened on the trigger.

CHAPTER FOURTEEN

Caracas, Venezuela

Muzzle-flashes erupted like yellow blossoms from the barrels of the narco-soldiers. The three bodyguards cut loose with sustained blasts as they closed ranks to protect their boss. Carl Lyons knelt, his H&K MP-5 already up and firing as he dropped. Above him 9 mm rounds slammed into the ornate paneling of the luxury suite, gouging wood and drilling holes through the walls. He heard the buzz of a round cutting through the air next to his right ear and he felt his hair blow back from the bullet's passage.

The MP-5 danced in his hands as he triggered a hasty burst. Across the doorway from him the spinning Schwarz's weapon responded with its own *thwat-thwat-thwat* of suppressed fire. They both heard Rosario Blancanales grunt in pain as he was struck.

Lyons saw one of the bodyguards go down under his fire. The man fell backward, weapon spraying wildly as blood splashed out in inky scarlet jets. The falling thug struck his boss, Escondito, in the shoulder and staggered the intoxicated man as he tried to bring a Beretta 92 to bear. On the other side of the cocaine kingpin the last bodyguard did a drunken two-step as one of Schwarz's 3-round bursts nearly decapitated him. Lyons surged to his feet and thrust his submachine gun to the full stretch of his arms and snapped his finger against his trigger three times.

The German submachine gun shook in Lyons's hand, sending vibrations up his arms as shells spit out of his ejection port. All nine 9 mm rounds hit the drug lord center mass, shredding his sky-blue silk shirt. The man folded inward under the impact of the pistol rounds, his shoulders slumping, his knees buckling. His face, frozen in a visage of disbelief, snapped forward as his head fell forward on a loose neck.

The man dropped straight down, pistol flying to the floor, then flopped over onto his back. In an incongruous moment it registered with the American that the man's pants were unbuckled and open at the waist, revealing a flash of silk boxer shorts the same sky-blue as the man's shirt.

Operating on instinct and adrenaline, Schwarz directed a blast that carved the Venezuelan's jaw off and shattered the man's spine just below his skull. The Able Team commando spun toward his partner, finger easing off the trigger to lie along the guard.

"Pol!"

Blancanales was on one knee, his face twisted into a grimace and his left hand clutching his chest. With an exercise of sheer willpower he rose, bringing his weapon into play.

"I'm fine," he gasped. "Let's go!"

Lyons was already moving forward. He caught a flash of movement and spun, dropping the smoking barrel of his MP-5, his finger finding the smooth metal curve of the trigger. In the manner of all trained hostage-rescue experts the former LAPD detective's eyes went to the rushing figure's hands. The rule was a simply dichotomy: weapon equals shoot. No weapon equals no shoot.

His finger slacked off the trigger of his weapon just before he almost fired a tight burst. He saw empty, slim brown hands tipped by long, bloodred nails. He blinked out of his operational tunnel vision and saw the complete picture. The woman was nude, a sheer G-string revealing a bikini wax and silicon bags blowing her bare breasts up to the size of beach balls, the nipples and areola very dark against the *café aula* of her flawless skin.

In an adrenaline-stretched moment Lyons saw a glittering diamond necklace above the swaying, bouncing breasts and a beautiful face twisted in terror, brown eyes tinged red as she screamed past perfect, pearl-white teeth. He saw her eyes find the bloody, mutilated corpses of Escondito and his bodyguards and he saw something snap in her mind.

She screamed again and darted for the door.

Lyons stepped forward and thrust the heel of his left palm into her sternum. The blow knocked her backward, tossing her anorexic frame onto a divan. She gasped at the impact and flew back before bouncing into the cushions. He lowered the smoking MP-5 and trained it on her face.

She looked up, eyes white in terror, her lipstick smeared across her face. He leaned in close, menacing and huge, eyes angry slits. He spoke in perfect Spanish, his voice an angry bark.

"Where's the Iranian?" he snarled.

"In there," she sobbed. A skinny arm thrust out and a scarlet-nail-tipped finger pointed toward a double set of ebony wood doors across the room. "I swear to God, he's in there with the girls."

"Go," Lyons ordered. He jerked his weapon muzzle toward the door, indicating the path. "Get out of here."

The woman sobbed in relief and sprang up off the couch. She sidestepped in a skittish dance past the bloody corpses of her former lover and his men, then raced out of the room. Blancanales, still recovering from the impacts to his body armor, covered her until she left the room, then took a knee again to provide rear security.

"Get ready," Lyons told Schwarz, voice low.

Schwarz nodded and took a flash-bang from under his coat. Lyons moved forward toward the door. "Come out, Aras Kasim!"

From inside the room a pistol boomed five times. Able Team ducked as bullets slammed through the door, spraying splintered wood. The bullets cut through the room in wild, desperate patterns, none striking close to the Americans.

"Hard way. Always the goddamn hard way," Schwarz swore.

Lyons carefully lifted and aimed his MP-5. He triggered a 3-round blast. The 9 mm Parabellum rounds struck the handle of the interior doors, shattering the lock housing. Instantly two feminine voices screamed in terror from inside the room.

Schwarz and Lyons ran forward, each taking up a position by the door. Behind them they heard Blancanales's weapon cycle as he fired the suppressed submachine gun at targets outside the room.

Schwarz let the spoon fly off his flash-bang as he primed the grenade. Lyons leaned forward, reaching across the door and snagging the twisted metal handle connected to the shattered lock housing. He yanked his arm back and jerked open the door. A pistol fired three times from inside the room. Schwarz tossed the stun grenade through the opening and both men turned away.

The metal canister landed on thick carpet and rolled to a stop. The voices of the teenage girls screamed again and a man cursed in fear. There was a brilliant flash and a sharp, deafening bang as the grenade detonated.

The occupants of the room cried out in pain and fear as dozens of hard rubber balls exploded like shrapnel, cutting through the room and raising welts on naked flesh. There was the distinct sound of shattered glass, and Schwarz turned and charged through the bedroom door, his MP-5 up and ready. He darted inside and cut left as Lyons popped up out of his crouch and swung around the open door to enter the room and cut right.

Schwarz danced left in a sidestep like an NBA guard trying to cut off the center's drive to the basket. His own submachine gun up, Lyons sprinted right, the muzzle snapping through vectors as he cleared his assigned spaces. The room was dark, but floor-to-ceiling balcony doors revealed a million-dollar view of the Caracas skyline and provided light from the buildings around them.

Cold air rushed in through the shattered windows and sheer, gauze drapes fluttered like flags. Schwarz saw a California King waterbed in the shape of a heart, the covers and blankets tangled into piles, a dozen pillows scattered around. To the left of the big bed, on his side of the room, he saw two skinny but eerily beautiful teenage girls, one dressed in jet-black lingerie and stockings, the other in gleaming white. He felt a queasy sense of disgust as his adrenaline-sharpened eyes recognized the girls as looking so alike they could only be sisters.

The two young girls huddled in the corner of the bed. "Stay down," he ordered in Spanish, and put a burst into the bed, slicing the sheets and kicking up stuffing. "Clear!" he snapped in English.

Lyons charged forward on his side of the room, clearing his vectors. He saw a tall, thin man in a pair of fire-engine-red briefs. The swarthy-skinned and black-haired man was laid out on his stomach. A 9 mm pistol lay on the floor several yards away.

Kasim moaned, still blinded and deafened by the stun grenade, and attempted to push himself up on shaking arms. Lyons ran forward and kicked him in the gut. The man gagged, almost puking at the impact, and sagged back down. The Able Team leader spun around and stomped the fingers of the Iranian's right hand, breaking three of them, then hopped forward and kicked the pistol across the room toward the shattered glass window.

Schwarz stepped closer, keeping his muzzle pointed in the general direction of the teenage girls, but watching the downed Iranian intelligence agent with a reflexive suspicion. Lyons moved closer to the man as he gasped for breath and let his submachine gun hang from its strap. He dropped down, driving his knee into the man's unprotected kidney.

Kasim shouted at the pain and spasmed up like a fish yanked into the bottom of a boat. Lyons snatched the man's arms while he was too hurt to resist and slapped on a pair of handcuffs. Once the bracelets were secure he popped back up and pulled the Iranian to his feet. He reached down and squeezed the intelligence agent's fingers together, grinding the broken fingers in a viselike grip.

Kasim screamed. Lyons leaned in close, maintaining pressure, and whispered in Spanish, "You are fucking coming with us. If you give me a moment of problem, I'll break your arm at the elbow. If you try and run, I'll machine gun your kneecaps. Do you believe me?"

Kasim didn't answer, panting from the pain. Lyons snarled and crushed his hands harder. "Do you believe me?" he repeated.

"Yes, yes—I believe you." Kasim nodded.

"Good. Let's go."

Lyons shoved the injured Iranian forward, driving him out of the room despite the man being dressed in nothing but underwear. Kept up on his toes by the painful hold the ex-cop kept him in, the bewildered and overwrought Iranian meekly complied.

Schwarz danced backward toward the door, searching the room for possible intelligence or dangers. He saw the Iranian's clothes in a pile at the foot of the bed and he stooped down to rifle the pockets quickly. He took the man's wallet, cell phone and a manila envelope containing a miniature disk. As he secured the finds he looked over at the girls. They had stopped crying and watched him with huge, dark eyes.

"Stay in school," he told them as he backed out of the room. "And just say no, okay?"

The girls hugged each other until they were sure the killers were gone. Then they went out into the gore-painted suite to steal money and drugs from the dead men.

BLANCANALES LED THE WAY down the dark hallway. He moved quickly, stepping past the occasional corpse of an Escondito bodyguard and ignoring the spraying sprinklers. The water was two inches deep on the floor and Able Team splashed as they hurried toward the elevator.

Lyons initiated his throat mike. "Stony, we have the package. We're making our exit now."

"Copy," Price replied immediately. "Everyone okay?"

"Pol took a few rounds to the vest, but he's mobile," Lyons acknowledged. "What's the status of forces at the moment? I can hear a whole shitload of sirens outside, even this far up."

"You have a massive police presence, according to Carmen," Price relayed. "However, the Caracas fire service was not able to break Gadgets's lock on the elevators with their master override keys. The elevators are still shut down and under your control so those police teams are going to have to climb fifty stories to try to find you."

"Good to hear," Lyons said.

"Americans!" Kasim sputtered, outraged. "You dare—!"

Casually, Lyons squeezed down tighter on the man's broken fingers. The Iranian spy went up on the balls of his feet in agony as shocks of anguish burst through his body. Nonchalantly, Lyons swung a big hand out and slapped the prisoner across the face, cutting of his words and outcry.

"You shut up," Lyons snapped. "There'll be plenty of time for you to talk later."

The Iranian gasped at the pain, but stopped talking. Schwarz pulled his sat-linked PDA clear as the team approached the service elevator room. Furiously he began typing on the miniaturized keyboard.

Lyons shoved the Iranian into a corner of the room. Blancanales kept the service room's door open an inch, watching the hallway outside with his weapon at the ready.

"What about that helicopter response crew Hunt picked up?" Lyons asked.

"Radio silence on that," Price told him. "Nothing going across the GCIA network. If they're coming for you they have gone operational quiet. The regular police and fire emergency services are screaming up a storm, but that's it for the moment."

"If they're screaming now, just wait," Schwarz said, grinning. He hit Enter on his pad. "Let's go!"

"Able over," Lyons said into his throat mike, and shoved Kasim into the elevator car.

"Stony copy," Price said, and went silent.

"Christ, heads up!" Blancanales said from the door.

"What do you have?" Schwarz demanded, finger on the button of the elevator.

"I got a SWAT team with flashlight-mounted shotguns and assault rifles. They just came out of the stairwell at the other end of the hallway," Blancanales replied into the dark room.

Lyons narrowed his eyes and squinted past Blancanales to look out through the crack in the door. The flashlight beams cut through the sprinkler drizzle and cut swathes through the dark hallway. "Impossible," he said, voice low. "No way a team in full helmet and body armor makes it up fifty-five floors that fast. I don't give a crap how good they are."

"Helicopter from the roof?" Schwarz offered.

"Only way," Blancanales agreed. He eased the service door shut and began backing away.

"Help! He—" Kasim shouted in Spanish, voice shrill from inside the elevator.

Lyons pivoted and punched the man in the stomach as Schwarz automatically threw a sharp elbow into the man's jaw. Kasim folded then sagged, his voice cut off as Blancanales jumped into the elevator.

Schwarz closed the doors and emergency lights flickered on, casting weird shadows as the elevator lurched and began descending. "Going down?" he asked.

"You've been waiting to say that all night," Lyons said.

"I take it where I can get it." Schwarz shrugged.

"This asshole alerted that team," Blancanales said. "They'll come for the room, see us descending and radio down."

Lyons shrugged. "Nothing for it now. They aren't going to be able to guess what we're up to, anyway. We just have to ride it out." He looked over at Schwarz. "You still got that hundred-mile-per-hour tape?" he asked.

Schwarz produced a small roll of the OD-green military electrical tape from his fanny pack. "Always."

"Good. Tape this asshole's mouth shut."

Kasim started to protest and tried to rise up off his knees, but Lyons silenced him by pressing the still hot muzzle of his submachine gun between his eyes. "Shh," the ex-cop said. "You're already pushing my buttons, Mr. Aras Kasim of the VEVAK. Now hold still while my good friend here tapes your pie hole shut or I'll shoot you in the shoulder."

Kasim went very still and with impersonal, utilitarian efficiency Schwarz wrapped several loops of the heavy, industrial-strength tape around the man's head, pinching his lips shut. "Tsk, tsk," Schwarz whispered. "A man your age in bed with two little girls like that? What would the Revolutionary Council back home say? I thought it was only the suicide martyrs who get dispensation to party like an infidel."

"We got other problems," Blancanales pointed out. "How the fuck that team know to come down from the roof? You think regular Caracas police got SWAT teams just flying around in a chopper in case someone tries to steal an Iranian spy from a local drug runner?"

"No, I do not," Lyons agreed. "Occam's razor makes me think that they were the GCIA crew Hunt tripped onto. Has to be."

"Still doesn't explain how they knew about us," Schwarz said. "GCIA might fly around, but mostly to kill reporters and torture students—they don't roll backup on regular police operations."

"We have to assume they've been on to us from the airport," Lyons said.

"Then we can't go back to the safehouse," Blancanales said.

"No, we've got to adapt, improvise and overcome," Schwarz said. "Once we blow this building we've got to disappear 'cause they're going to pull out all the stops to get us—bring the military in, shut this city down."

"This mission hasn't gone the best," Blancanales pointed out, voice rueful. "But we don't say die."

"No, we just make other fuckers die," Lyons snarled, and poked Kasim in the head. He looked up at Schwarz. "Get the Semtex ready. Once these doors open I want to be ready to roll the hell right out of here."

"No worries, we'll be ready." Schwarz grinned.

THE TWO POINT MEN of the heavily armed *negra yaguar* unit came through the door hard and fast, weapons up and fingers poised on the triggers. Right behind them a third man rushed into the room and then a fourth. Four gun muzzles swept tight vectors in the crammed space, and four fingers tightened on the smooth metal curves of triggers. Adrenaline-charged hearts hammered in heavily muscled torsos as safety-visored eyes clicked around the room. Flashlight beams played through the suffocating dark, searching.

"Clear!" each man barked in succession.

Immediately, Hernandez entered the room, pistol out and ready. Behind him his cohort of highly trained killers crowded in around him like hunting dogs at the foot of a cliff where a big cat has gone to ground.

The officer strode forward, face twisted with frustration, and stood next to the elevator. Above the doors a red digital light clicked off numerals in descending order as the car plummeted downward.

"How in the hell do they have control of the elevator!" he demanded. "How can we be locked out of the building like this?"

The men shifted uneasily, unable to answer and not liking the feeling of futility that ensnared them. They were action players, used to effecting changes on their environment. Now their initiative had been stolen, their energy subverted and their motivation rendered futile. It was an unaccustomed feeling and it sapped their morale.

"Open the doors!" Hernandez snapped.

The members of the elite Venezuelan unit leaped to obey. One man, tasked by designation as breaching specialist, produced a claw-ended pry bar in the shape of a

comma from his kit. Two men, burly with regular inges-
tion of anabolic steroids, hovered close, ready to leap
forward and assist.

The breach trooper crammed the end of his pry bar
into the seam between the elevator doors and worked it
in. Once the tip was in tight the big man threw his body
weight against the resistance. The doors opened with a
slight screech of metal on metal and a hydraulic hiss.

Weapons snapped to shoulders, and the red cyclo-
pean eyes of laser sights danced in the black opening.
In front of the commando squad, the elevator cables
sped by as the lift car smoothly fell away below them.
Hernandez moved forward and peered down the shaft.

Seemingly satisfied, the man stepped back. His face
was an ugly, brutal mask of impassivity. His eyes were
the cold, dead eyes of a remorseless predator.

"Stop them," he snapped.

Instantly two men stepped forward and around their
commander. Grenades were snatched off Kevlar vests
and the pins yanked free. Lever safety catches sprang
free and fell away. The two men looked at each other
and nodded before stepping forward and tossing their
grenades into the open shaft underhanded.

The black eggs fell away down the long pit and disappeared into the dark beneath the open doors. The men
stepped back, waiting for the twin explosions to follow.

Standing with his hands folded behind his back, feet
spread shoulder width apart, Hernandez allowed himself
a small, ugly smile.

CHAPTER FIFTEEN

Basra, Iraq

The woman shrieked, her voice as penetrating as an air raid siren. Manning, an explosives expert, automatically calculated the blast radius from the detonation of plastique in the vest as he hesitated to fire.

The sum of his calculation was obvious. If the woman wasn't stopped, then every member of Phoenix Force would die right there, strewed in chunks across the dusty Iraqi street like bloody piles of garbage.

His finger spasmed on the trigger.

The shot wasn't smooth and his burst was ragged, but instinct and training ensured his accuracy even if he couldn't consciously bring himself to do what needed to be done. The woman took the rounds and fell to the ground, the detonator flying from her grip.

Manning shifted his still rattling machine gun and poured fire past the spot where the woman's body had been and into the doorway where the cowardly Iraqi fighters crouched. The rounds from the heavy machine gun chewed through mortar and wood, reducing the structure to shards and splinters. The rounds chewed into the men like buzz saws and ripped them apart mercilessly.

"Come on! Come on!" McCarter screamed.

James raced past Manning and up to the dead woman. He reached down and snatched the det cord from the suicide vest and threw it away, rendering the device inert. "Let's go!" he shouted.

Bullets whipped and whined around them, tearing up the road and filling the air with angry lead hornets capable of dashing a man's brains out in an instant. Hawkins dug in hard, running for the alleyway in a stumbling sprint. McCarter led the way, his carbine up and barking. Iraqi gunmen fell with each discharge of his weapon, Kalashnikovs spinning away and white muslin headdresses tumbling into the dirt.

Encizo shuffled along directly behind the burdened Hawkins, covering him with his machine pistol as the man charged forward toward the dubious safety of the alley. The Cuban saw a flash of motion above him on the one-story roof of an earthen brick business. Encizo lifted his MP-7 and fired on reflex as the sniper leveled his weapon. The man screamed as six rounds tore into his gut, and he crumpled at the waist and pitched forward. The sniper fell, struck a cloth sun awning and flipped over to land in the middle of the street in a broken heap.

McCarter ran up to the edge of the alley and turned the corner. Immediately an Iraqi neighborhood gunman reared up in front of him, the man screaming in angry surprise. The Iraqi tried to lift his AKM and bring it to bear in the short distance separating the two men.

Directly behind the first Iraqi a second man with an

RPG-7 lowered his weapon and clawed for an automatic pistol in his belt, eyes wide as he watched his friend struggle with the big Englishman.

McCarter snarled and lashed out with his M-4 carbine, using his bayonet to catch the Kalashnikov just behind its fixed iron sights and knock it aside. The Iraqi's hand came off the forestock as the M-9 bayonet slashed the old Soviet weapon aside. The man triggered a frantic, useless burst and the sound of the weapon firing echoed in the confined space of the alley.

McCarter stepped in close and swept his bayonet up before thrusting it forward and catching the man in the throat just under his Adam's apple. The blade punched through skin and cartilage, spilling bright blood in a gush. The Iraqi's eyes bulged in pain and terror, then filmed instantly in death as the tip of the bayonet shattered his spine at the back of his throat.

The Iraqi militiaman tumbled backward and McCarter's M-4 twisted in his grip as the stuck blade tried to drag his weapon down. Behind the falling Iraqi the RPG soldier had his hand on his pistol and was yanking it clear. Desperate to clear his weapon, McCarter triggered a 3-round burst.

The 5.56 mm rounds tore through the dying man's throat at point-blank range, the muzzle-flash setting his shirt on fire as the high-velocity rounds shredded all organic material in front of them, freeing the tip of the blade from where it had become anchored in the man's spine.

The RPG gunner lifted his pistol as McCarter pivoted and jerked his assault rifle upward. The Iraqi's finger tightened on the trigger as the ex-SAS trooper fired a second 3-round burst, then a third and fourth. At the extremely close range all nine rounds smashed into the man with supersonic force.

The pistol went off with a single, sharp bark then tumbled from slack fingers as the Iraqi was cut open from belly to sternum by the blast. Blood exploded outward like water from a child's balloon. The bearded man went down and looked up toward the sky with fixed and sightless eyes.

McCarter looked beyond the RPG team and down the alley. He cursed violently as he saw the jumbled mess blocking movement for his team. From behind him the street was on fire and deafening with the sound of automatic weapons. Bullets slapped the mud brick wall above his head and burrowed into the ground with lethal force.

He spun and fired at a building across the street as first James then Manning entered the alley. Both immediately turned and began spraying the street behind them with withering streams of fire as Hawkins sprinted into the opening closely followed by Encizo.

"Manning!" McCarter bellowed.

The big Canadian turned and looked toward his team leader, his machine gun still bucking and kicking in his hands, the belt-fed links spilling from the green plastic drum attached to the weapon. Empty shell casings poured in a shining stream from his ejection port as he let the weapon run and the barrel had begun to glow red-hot from the continuous barrage.

Making eye-contact acknowledgment with his demolitions expert, McCarter jerked a thumb over his shoulder at the alley. Manning followed the gesture with his eyes and saw the old BMW sitting there, stripped of tires and doors. Crammed into the narrow lane beside the dented old vehicle were garbage cans, filthy mattresses, coils of barbed wire, rusted oil drums and piles of stinking garbage and refuse including the bloated corpse of a mongrel dog.

Manning stopped firing and rose up off his knee, dancing backward as bullets sliced through the air around him. He sized up the task in a moment's study and frowned as he looked at his team leader.

"That's not a precision job—it's a fucking mess," he said. "No need to try to place my charges strategically. I'll just pile what I have at the bottom and hope they do the job."

"We can't go back out into the street to avoid the blast," McCarter shouted.

Next to them Hawkins had dumped his wounded prisoner on the ground beside the dead RPG team, splashing the already blood-soaked man in their gore. The former Delta Force trooper lifted his primary weapon and started laying suppressive fire of his own down.

"I can slide it to the other side under the car," Manning offered.

"Good enough!"

McCarter let his M-4 drop to the end of its sling and took Manning's piping-hot M-60 from him as the Canadian unhooked two OD-green cloth satchels from where they hung around his neck.

"Down! Down! Down!" McCarter hollered as he rushed forward to the lip of the alley. The members of Phoenix threw themselves belly down as Manning worked to arm his Semtex satchel charges.

A knot of Iraqi militia began advancing up the street from behind the cover of a .50-caliber machine gun mounted in the back of a white Nissan pickup. On the rooftops armed figures scrambled into position or took hasty shots at the cornered commandos.

There was such a milling mass of humanity in the street that the Phoenix Force operatives hardly bothered to aim, instead simply pouring their fire into the congested mass of humanity charging toward them, weapons blazing.

The .50-caliber opened up and tore baseball-size chunks of masonry from out of the wall above their heads. The stench of cordite hung in the air and stung their nostrils with every breath they took. Their empty shell casings rained down on each other and tinkled into piles on the ground like mounds of loose change.

Encizo looked over as Manning suddenly appeared and threw himself down. Instinctively the Cuban ducked his head and thrust his face into the dirt. James saw Ayub blink his eyes in sudden lucidity and try to get up. The ex-SEAL dropped his weapon and threw himself bodily across their prisoner.

Suddenly the air was sucked from his lungs and his eyes were stung by a searing flash of light then a deafening explosion boomed out, the blast force channeled up and over the team's crouched forms, followed by a rolling cloud of dark smoke and thick dust. Manning and Encizo and McCarter bounced instantly to their feet just as a burst of machine gun fire sprayed the alley from the rooftop of the building across the street.

Manning grunted in a sharp exhalation as two 7.62 mm rounds smashed into his flak vest and NATO body armor. He staggered backward and fell from the concussion, his face twisted in a grimace as he hit the dirt for a second time.

Encizo cursed in sudden, shocked surprise as a

heavy-caliber round struck his right shoulder and a second round gouged out a furrow of flesh on his bicep. He spun like a child's top and staggered against the alley wall, his arm going numb and turning red in a splash of blood.

McCarter popped up, lifting his carbine to direct the team as the burst found him. Three machine gun rounds hit his flak vest at the gut and were only slowed when they buried themselves in the Kevlar weave of his body armor. He folded up like a book closing, his breath driven from his body in ruthless fashion.

He went facedown on the ground hard enough to draw blood from his nose. His teeth went through his lip in a bright sensation of pain, and blood filled his mouth and funneled down his throat as he fought to breathe.

He gagged at the slippery rush of copper-tasting fluid and threw up into the ground as smoke and dust billowed around them. Green tracer fire lanced through the cloud of debris, burning paths around the huddled team.

James came up off Ayub and jerked the Iranian terror master to his feet. "Go! Go!"

He snarled in adrenaline-charged anger and shoved the prisoner forward. Hawkins rose up off his belly and ran forward. He grabbed McCarter up under one arm and hauled the man to his feet. Beside him Manning rose up, still gasping, face a mask of dirt while Encizo struggled to his feet.

Hawkins spun as he saw his teammates trying to gather themselves. His weapon erupted from his hip and he swung the muzzle in a loose figure eight, filling the street with loops of hard-jacket slugs. James came up behind the stumbling Ayub and roughly shoved him over the dented hood of the BMW wreck. As the Iranian flipped over to the other side, the ex-Navy SEAL jumped the obstacle and hauled the man up.

Encizo ran forward, the first to recover, and hurtled the obstacle. He was followed by the lumbering Manning. Hawkins felt a presence at his shoulder, and suddenly McCarter was beside him, hammering out covering fire with Manning's M-60. The barrel of the machine gun was so hot the superheated rounds came out sideways, rendering the weapon completely inaccurate but still putting out a wall of lead to cover the team's retreat.

"Go!" Hawkins yelled above the din.

"Get out of here! That's an order," McCarter yelled back.

Hawkins made to argue, then shut his mouth, knowing it was futile. He fired a last, long burst into the dust-choked street before following the rest of the team over the wrecked car and into the alley. McCarter kept the trigger of the machine gun wide-open as he shrugged his shoulders and ducked his head underneath the strap, freeing himself.

The last 7.62 mm round cycled through the weapon out of the green plastic drum and the weapon bolt froze in the open position. The Briton heaved the weapon from him and turned, snatching up his own M-4 carbine. A black metal sphere arched out of the smoke and landed at his feet. McCarter lashed out with his foot in a soccer-style kick and punted the grenade back out of the alley. The little bomb rose up off the ground and cleared the edge of the building.

McCarter spun as a bullet caught him high on the back and punched him back to the floor of the alley. His

M-4 skidded away, lost in the swirling dust as the grenade exploded behind him. Instantly he went deaf from the concussive force. Shrapnel peppered his legs, drawing blood in several places.

Bursts from assault rifles poured into the alley as smoke from the hand grenade added to the obscuring cloud of dust. McCarter came up to his hands and knees only to realize his left arm was numb and useless. He tried to crawl and tumbled back down to that side. With a soft pop his hearing returned and his head was filled with a ringing sound. He heard angry screams as if from under water and turned to see two Iraqi gunmen charge into the alley.

Flat on his back, McCarter drew his Browning Hi-Power as the confused fighters searched for a target. He lifted the pistol and shot the lead man first in the crotch then in the throat. The second man turned as the other fell, and McCarter squeezed the trigger on the Browning again. The handgun jumped in his hand and the Iraqi's throat disappeared in a flash of red and pink punctuated by white shards of spinal bone. The man dropped down as McCarter got his legs under him and heaved himself up, his left arm still useless.

McCarter turned and ran toward the blackened BMW, his Browning up in a port-arms position while his left hand dangled limply from his useless arm. Running forward, the ex-SAS trooper leaped for the hood of the ruined vehicle and rolled across the top.

Hawkins appeared out of the dust on the other side of the vehicle, his weapon up. A star-pattern flash blinked from the American commando's muzzle and bullets struck targets behind the rolling McCarter.

The Phoenix team leader hit the ground on the other

side of the car, grunting at the impact. Firing one-handed, Hawkins reached down and hauled him to his feet. McCarter saw movement at the hostile end of the alley and lifted his pistol, putting three rounds into the figure.

Hawkins turned and ran, pushing the Briton in front of him. Blood stained the legs of McCarter's trousers. A channel had been blown between the debris and trash choking the alley by Manning's satchel charges and the two forced their way through.

Coming out into the street on the other side, McCarter instantly saw Grimaldi. The Stony Man pilot lowered his helicopter into a vacant lot half a block down from their position. A building had been caved in and set on fire by the helicopter's rockets. Rotor wash sent billows of grit and sand and masonry dust rolling out in clouds.

McCarter squinted against the blinding sheets. He saw James and Manning running with the captured Ayub between them, trussed up like a Christmas turkey, while Encizo ran just off to their side, firing his machine pistol in an almost futile attempt to cover their movements.

"Come on!" McCarter shouted to Hawkins, but the American was already running forward.

The rifle in Hawkins's hand cracked and a bloody crater appeared in the face of an Iraqi in a random doorway. McCarter turned and shot two men through the heart at thirty feet before he was even fully conscious of the threat.

The two men sprinted forward as James and Manning threw their prisoner into the helicopter cargo bay. The Iranian screamed as he landed and the two big commandos threw themselves in after him, battering him with their bodies. The pitch of the helicopters engines changed as Grimaldi prepared for liftoff.

A screaming Iraqi in a soiled headdress popped out from behind a pile of brick and rebar, an AK-74 chattering in his hand. Encizo took the top off the man's head with a wild burst from his machine pistol. The Kalashnikov rounds hammered into the Cuban, smashing the MP-7 apart and punching into his flak vest and body armor.

Encizo staggered backward and Hawkins saw his eyes roll up, showing whites as he was knocked unconscious from the impacts. The Cuban toppled backward, falling flat out, his hands bleeding profusely from where broken parts of his weapon had sliced into them.

Suddenly, Gary Manning was there. Two strong hands reached out and snatched the falling Encizo up by his combat harness. A third hand, starkly black and belonging to James, appeared between Manning's and Encizo was yanked up into the helicopter.

Bullets burned past Hawkins and McCarter, slamming into the body of Grimaldi's helicopter. Divots appeared in staccato patterns and rounds ricocheted wildly as the last two members of Phoenix ran forward. The landing skids broke free of the ground and lifted off. Hawkins dived forward and threw himself through the open cargo door. An RPG rocket burned past, missing the tail rotor by inches before sailing out into the lot and exploding.

McCarter put one foot up on the helicopter skid as it rose two feet up off the ground. He lunged forward toward Calvin James, who leaned out, hands spread wide to catch him.

Then the bullet struck him in the side of the head and the world went black.

CHAPTER SIXTEEN

Caracas, Venezuela

Carl Lyons jerked his head upward in surprise.

Two metal thunks sounded, clearly audible overhead on the roof of the elevator car. The red digital readout on the floor indicator flashed past 1 as they dropped toward the basement.

The twin detonations came hard, denting the roof with intense bangs. The lights on the ceiling bulged outward and exploded from the concussive force. The elevator went dark and shards of plastic sprayed outward. Above them the explosion of the hand grenades snapped the cables instantly and the elevator car plunged downward.

Carl Lyons was thrown hard against the side of the elevator. He rebounded wildly and his feet got tangled up in each other and he went down, landing hard on their prisoner, Kasim. The man grunted in pain as the big American struck him.

Hermann Schwarz felt his center of gravity suddenly

shift and his feet flew out from under him so that he landed hard on his ass, snapping his teeth together with the force of a trap. His outflung arm struck Rosario Blancanales, who was falling himself. Both men went down in a tangle of arms, weapons spinning out of their hands in the sudden, violent plunge.

Blancanales threw an arm up and grabbed for the side railing on the elevator wall but a loose weapon struck him in the face and broke his nose in an instant, blood gushing across his face. He cursed out loud, then heard Lyons doing the same.

The elevator car crashed down fifteen feet and slammed into the bottom of the shaft. Lyons was picked up and thrown forward by the force of the impact. He struck the front of the elevator with his back and his breath was bludgeoned from him. He gasped and flipped down on his face.

In the darkness a sharp, unwilling cry was forced out of Blancanales as his left leg, folded unnaturally beneath his body, was broken at the ankle. Kasim screamed at the impact then gagged. Schwarz moaned and rolled over, pinning the Iranian agent's head down beneath his body weight.

"Jesus," Schwarz said. "We good?"

"As good as can be expected," Lyons replied. "Pol, you okay?"

"I broke my ankle." His voice sounded nasal and thick from his broken nose. "We tape it up, I can move no problem, but we've got to get out of here before they drop any more grenades."

Lyons was already up, a wide-bladed fighting knife in his hands. He reached out in the dark and felt for the seam of the elevator doors. Blancanales had been correct; they were sitting ducks at the moment. His searching fingers found what they were looking for as the rest of Able Team prepped themselves behind him in the dark, cramped space.

He dug in with his fingertips and slipped the point of the knife blade into the seam. He got a purchase then violently pried the doors open. They slid back with a sluggish, unwilling motion to reveal a concrete wall and the lip of the basement floor about a yard high. Red emergency lights cast shadows across the room. Lyons threw himself upward, caught the lip with his belly and scrambled over.

"Give me the asshole," he muttered.

Schwarz forced the moaning and disorientated Kasim to his feet, imagining more grenades falling down the shaft with paranoid clarity even as they worked. "They drop any more bombs," he warned in Spanish into the man's ear, "and you're a goner just like the rest of us."

"Yeah," Blancanales added as he helped shove the man up. "I'm guessing these guys aren't exactly 'hostage rescue' so much as 'search and destroy,' savvy?"

Kasim didn't answer, but went willingly into the viselike grip of Lyons. The ex-LAPD detective hauled the man up out of the elevator car, then turned and pushed him to the ground. He held out his grip for Schwarz, who took it and stepped upward onto the basement floor. Then both men turned and pulled the injured Blancanales upward.

"Let's clear the area and get to the extraction site," Lyons said.

Schwarz put a hand under the Iranian's sweat-drenched armpit and helped the big blond team leader haul the prisoner to his feet. Behind them Blancanales used the wall as a crutch to hobble after them.

Twenty feet down they paused to activate their night-vision goggles and after that they made better time.

HERNANDEZ WATCHED HIS MEN unfold into action with a cool disposition. His face remained impassive as the descent team secured their 250-foot nylon ropes and shrugged into their rappel harnesses. He'd already sent fire teams down each stairwell to try to pinion any survivors, but the rappellers would cover the vertical distance in two big leaps at ten times the speed. He would follow them down. Two SWAT troopers in black uniforms stood for a moment in the open elevator shaft, weapons secured on slings across their ballistic vests.

Faceless behind protective masks and night-vision monoculars, the men turned and nodded once to each other. In unison the two stepped off the edge and plunged into the darkness of the elevator shaft, leaving only the whisper of metal carbiners on nylon fibers to mark their passing.

Instantly, a second pair moved forward and snapped into a second set of lines. Working quickly, they were over the edge and down their ropes in a matter of well-orchestrated seconds. After the second pair of rappel troops had dropped, Hernandez stepped into position and hooked up to his line.

He counted off the seconds with patience. Then the team leader of the rappellers informed him in clipped tones that the relay point had been reached and the second set of ropes put into position. He acknowledged them and began his own drop into the black.

HERMANN SCHWARZ PULLED the two rolls of engineering tape from his belt pouch and stuck a single finger through the center of them. Using his finger like a dowel, he began quickly wrapping the tape around Blancanales's injured ankle over the outside of his boot while Lyons pulled security.

The Puerto Rican soldier set his mouth in a firm, thin line against the sharp pain of his broken ankle as he kept an eye on their prisoner. Behind them, across the vast expanse of the tower's basement, IR illumination beams, visible only through night-vision goggles, suddenly played across the pitch-black room.

"Company," Lyons warned. His finger rested on the curve of his H&K's trigger.

Schwarz played out the last of the tape in the makeshift cast and looked up at his teammate. "You good?"

Blancanales shifted his submachine gun and nodded. "You bet. Let's finish this."

Moving quickly, Schwarz tossed aside the denuded cardboard tape rolls and produced a blocky object the size of a catcher's mitt from his pouch. Kasim's eyes grew wide as he took in the digital display on the thermal detonator placed atop the PPC, or Precision Penetration Charge.

Seeing the Iranian's fear, the Able Team electronics and demolitions expert grinned wickedly. "¿Que pasa, hefe?"

"Everybody belly down," Lyons ordered. "I've got to keep them off us."

Immediately, his silenced submachine gun cycled in a series of 3-round bursts. From across the basement there was the sound of confusion and erratic movements followed by angry shouts. Then the return fire began to pour in.

Crawling on his belly, Schwarz moved up to the cinder-block wall of the basement. He held up a laser stud finder used by building construction crews and scanned the wall. Stray bullets took chips out of the concrete wall above his head. Behind him Blancanales added his own firepower to Lyons's while maintaining close surveillance of their prisoner.

Schwarz began peeling strips of industrial-strength two-sided tape off one aspect of the trapezoidal-shaped PPC. He worked calmly to place the high explosive even as enemy fire peppered the room around him.

When Schwarz hit Enter, the digital display changed from a subdued green to a dull red.

"We're ready!" Schwarz barked. "Everybody move to my right."

Kasim began moving without help even with his hands bound behind his back, scooting frantically along on his stomach. Lyons held up his MP-5 and burned off the better part of a clip to provide cover fire as the team moved farther down the wall away from the shaped charge.

Blancanales fired three ragged bursts, then pushed himself forward and somersaulted over one shoulder to spare his injured ankle. Behind them Schwarz snatched up the prisoner by the back of his shirt and hauled him forward while crawling quickly. Despite the specific explosive trajectory of the shaped charge, where most of the force would be channeled through the wall in a blade to create the breach while the back blast was directed off in a funnel pattern, Schwarz did not want to press his luck by remaining in unnecessary proximity to the detonation.

"Move!" Schwarz barked.

IR flashlight beams scythed through the dark and off toward the other end of the room where unsuppressed muzzle-flashes flared in star patterns. Bullets whined around the frantically scrambling team. The lead slugs smacked into the wall, causing craters and spinning shards of masonry out in deadly fragments.

Blancanales grunted as his injured ankle turned as he pushed off it, the pain causing white points of light to appear in front of his eyes. He threw himself down next to the cursing Kasim and threw his hands over his head. Beside him, Schwarz shoved the captured Iranian into the floor and rolled over on top of him.

Lyons dropped flat on his belly, but stubbornly continued to fire, punishing the approaching SWAT unit for any bold motions. Then like the crack of a falling redwood the PPC breaching device detonated.

HERNANDEZ LET THE ROPE slip quickly through his gloved hands. His feet struck the devastated roof of the elevator car and he quickly unsnapped his carbiner. He dropped down through the elevator hatch and looked out. Ahead of him he could see his men fanned out across the basement in defensive positions, trading fire with the foreign gunmen.

He scrambled clear, brought his own weapon up and shuffled forward, throwing lead downrange in the general direction of his targets to add to the assault momentum. Red tracer fire zipped past and lit up his IR goggles like laser bolts and he saw one of his men go down, the side of his head dented inward like a soda can.

He snarled and barked out orders like an angry dog, driving his men up out of their defensive positions and toward the enemy. His unit had the numbers and firepower on their side to drive what the Chinese suspected was an American commando team into a box trap and finish them. To utilize that advantage he would need to be ruthless in his expenditure of resources.

Hernandez got them up and moving forward, submachine guns, assault rifles and combat shotguns blasting out a wall of covering fire. Through his night-vision goggles he saw bizarre shadows twist in the winking bursts of muzzle-flashes.

His head twisted and turned even as his primary weapon jerked on automatic in his hands as he madly searched for targets. Two of his men executed a pincer movement and he held his finger off the trigger as they passed in front of him.

Off in the darkness behind a support beam he heard a man scream in agony and another start cursing horribly in Spanish. He twisted on the ball of his foot as the soldiers deployed to his left began to fire their weapons with renewed intensity.

He took three steps forward in a fast, bent-over shuffle, weapon up at his shoulder. He stepped around the splayed legs of one of his fallen officers and ground his teeth in impotent fury. The Americans would pay.

Ahead through the monochromatic lens of his NVD Hernandez suddenly saw the blurred-at-the-edges heat signatures of his prey. He saw a broad-shouldered silhouette raise an arm and a submachine gun with glowing red muzzle spit a white-hot star-pattern burst. A black-clad soldier on the Venezuelan commander's left was thrown backward.

Hernandez twisted and leveled his submachine gun. His finger took up the slack on the trigger and the laser sight engaged. The red beam cut out like a searchlight cutting through the black and cordite-stench-filled basement. The big man in Hernandez's IR vision suddenly dropped his weapon and put his head down.

Hernandez opened his mouth to bark an order when he had the sudden strange sensation of all the air in his lungs being sucked clean of his body. Some instinct made him squeeze his eyes shut in the heartbeat that followed.

The concussive force slammed into him like a freight train, driving him backward and jerking him off his feet like a puppet on a string. A burst of brilliant light flashed past his eyes, searing them white.

He grunted as the sledgehammer force slammed into him and his breath was pummeled from his body. He hit the floor of the basement hard enough to rattle his teeth and his jaw slapped upward like a trap. Blood poured as his teeth tore of a chunk of his cheek and a small piece of his tongue was bitten off. His skull smacked the concrete hard enough to put stars in his already dazzled eyes.

He felt nausea sweep over him in a tidal wave as his lungs fought to drag in a breath, then the darkness took him.

CHAPTER SEVENTEEN

Stony Man Farm, Virginia

"Goddamn it!" Barbara Price snarled.

The Stony Man mission controller ripped off her headset and threw it on the desk. Around her Kurtzman and his cybernetics team looked grim as they waited for their instructions in the face of this new wave of successive crises.

"Bear," Price said, her voice coldly devoid of emotion. "Get on our backdoor link and see if the Basra British commander is willing to give us a reactionary force. Tell them we need medical, our chopper is down and our Iraqi counterparts may be compromised by militia loyalists. We need armor or mechanized infantry and we don't have much time."

"I'm on it," Kurtzman replied, taking up a sat comm unit and rolling his wheelchair toward an isolated corner.

Price turned toward Tokaido and Delahunt. "I need more information from Venezuela," she said, shifting gears. "The response and speed of deployment to Able's snatch operation was too good, too smooth. Something is wrong. I want you online and up Caracas's ass with a flashlight to find out why we've been compromised."

"Will do," Tokaido said, turning to his screen and keyboard.

Delahunt didn't bother to verbalize her response, just tucked her chin in a nod of affirmation. She quickly slid her VR glove and helmet back on and began to tackle the encryption of the Venezuelan intelligence agencies.

Her troops deployed, Price walked past Hunt Wethers, who was busy setting up a transatlantic two-way informational link to the Middle East and pulled out her personal cell phone. She hit #2 on her speed dial and inside of three rings Hal Brognola had answered her call.

"This is Hal. Go." His voice was gruff as always.

"Just giving you an update," Price said. "It's not a happy one."

"Give it to me," he replied.

"Phoenix and Jack are down. Apparently, McCarter took a round to the head. He's alive but out. I don't how much time he has. Able has run into trouble in Caracas. They're still on schedule, but somehow Chavez's premier squad of bully boys managed to respond within minutes to their takedown. It's an impossible coincidence. Like Delta Force showing up to a drive-by shooting in Compton."

"We've been compromised, obviously. Have you got support rolling to Phoenix?"

"Bear's on with the Brits now. We expect cooperation but the infiltration of the local police by Iranian sympathizers brought a response on target completely out of proportion to what we initially briefed the area commanders on. They may feel like they were set up by us to be tricked into a massive display of unilateral force they were unprepared to deliver."

"Goddamn politics," Brognola muttered, voice dark.

In her mind's eye Price could see the big Fed sticking an unlit cigar in his mouth to chew on. There was a heartbeat of silence as the coordinator of the Justice Department's Sensitive Operations Group digested what his mission controller had just told him.

"I'm going to inform POTUS," he said. "If the Brits give you any flak, let me know immediately and I'll see if I can put some executive weight behind the request. For now all we can do is watch and hope Able can get clear. Otherwise we'll have to punt in South America."

"Understood," Price said. "But Phoenix is pinned down now. If the Brits balk, it may not matter what the President does, it may just be too late."

"Can we get them artillery or close air support?"

"Negative," Price said. "Every Shiite in that neighborhood is shooting at them, but if we go in with indirect fire there's going to be collateral damage. The rules of engagement were very clear on that."

"Understood. Keep me informed."

Both of the Stony Man officers hung up at the same time. Barbara Price spun on her heel and marched back through the door of the Farm Annex building's computer room to find Kurtzman.

The lives of Phoenix Force lay in the hands of gunshy and politically entangled professional bureaucrats. She could feel her stomach tie into knots as she waited for the answer.

It wasn't long in coming. As soon as she entered the room Kurtzman waved at her and put his connection on speakerphone.

"Commander," Kurtzman growled. "You recognize the code paroles I gave you—the level they represent?"

When the voice on the other end of the line answered it was very English and very collected.

"Yes, I do," the British general replied. "I know exactly what they mean, but that doesn't change the truth on ground." His voice was strained enough under the surface that Price knew he was being sincere. "This isn't like the bad old days," the man explained. "The troop surge worked. This isn't 'my' sector or a 'British' sector anymore. This is an Iraqi-controlled city and province. We are no longer occupiers or authority—we are guests and advisors. I have no authority to use military force without direct Iraqi approval, do you understand? Supplementing a covert op is a hell of a lot different than me rolling a tank platoon into a neighborhood to rescue people operating in a technically illegal matter. I was informed you were told all this by our liaison at Six before we started." The general referenced the infamous MI-6, the British equivalent of the CIA.

"Damn it," Kurtzman snapped. "That's not fair! When we started this we were going on the assumption that the Iraqi forces were nationalists and not Iranian puppets."

"Welcome to the truth on the ground in Basra," the general replied. "Look, I understand. But my ambassador is already fending off screaming attacks about murdered Iraqi policemen and collateral damage in a city that's been mostly peaceful. I have my orders from on high—do not intervene."

"You realize there's a British national in this trapped unit?" Price interrupted.

There was a pause on the other end of the line, then

the general continued in the same mellow tone. "If there's one of us with that team then, given the nature of your code paroles, he's either Regiment or Cross and knew what he was getting into." The reference to Cross, Price knew, was from Vauxhall Cross, the headquarters of Britain's MI-6, just as the mention of Regiment was an oblique acknowledgment of the Twenty-second SAS Regiment, which had in fact been David McCarter's unit.

"I'm sorry," the general said. "My hands are tied."

Basra, Iraq

JACK GRIMALDI HUNG out of the helicopter door.

Blood flowed from bullet wounds in his shoulder and thigh. His face was a mask of gore where exploding shards of glass had peppered his mouth and jaw in sharp slivers. Bullets streamed into the cockpit from enemy positions as a column of smoke roiled up from a smoldering engine.

As soon as the stray round had knocked McCarter down, the Stony Man pilot had powered down his bird to allow James and Hawkins to rescue their fallen commander. Two seconds later, a white Nissan pickup powered around a turn in the street, a Russian antiaircraft heavy machine gun mounted in the back.

The barrage had come from only fifty yards away, practically point-blank range for a weapon of the size, and had ripped apart the helicopter until Encizo and James had put two rounds each through the gunner's head, vaporizing it simultaneously.

Grimaldi suddenly lifted his head, his face a dripping mask of blood under his helmet. His hands came up and he found the release on his seat harness. He manipulated the device and dropped free, falling on all fours to the dusty, hard-packed earth. The hard amber light of dawn illuminated his motions and more fire was directed his way.

Hawkins had taken a Soviet AKM with a folding stock from an enemy casualty and was using it now. He scooped the wounded Stony Man pilot up with one hand under an armpit and sprayed covering fire with the Kalashnikov held in his other.

"How bad is it?" he yelled.

"Not bad, but I'm hurt," Grimaldi said, the oxymoronic statement making perfect sense to the veteran Army commando.

Hawkins took Grimaldi's weight onto his shoulder and felt his clothes instantly soaked with the other man's blood. The ex-Delta Force shooter killed a gunman who had popped up behind an abandoned hulk of a car to fire on them, then began dragging the pilot toward a four-story tenement building made of sun-dried brick.

Behind them the helicopter made a dramatic *whoosh* as the fuel tanks spilled out and splashed the burning motor mechanisms, igniting the vehicle like a bonfire. Gary Manning, running with the unconscious David McCarter scooped up in his arms like a child, felt the skin on his neck and face tighten with stinging intensity at the sudden rush of heat. Behind him Calvin James ran with the helicopter medic kit backpack in one hand while screaming into his sat-link hookup earpiece.

Encizo tried to cover their retreat, spraying his weapon wildly as the team ran for the dubious shelter of the building. Machine-gun and assault-rifle rounds burned through the air around the fleeing Phoenix Force, snapping next to their ears and kicking up gouts of dirt from the ground. The gunfire was relentless.

Operating calmly despite the danger, Encizo twisted and pitched a fragmentation grenade underhand behind him. As it bounced away he lifted his machine pistol and burned a burst at an enemy fire team using a narrow alleyway as an approach to the engagement. His rounds slowed their advance long enough for the grenade to explode and funnel a wave of shrapnel down the narrow enclosure.

A heavy-caliber slug struck the ceramic plate in the back pouch of his Kevlar vest. The plate shattered under the impact inside its bullet-resistant weave, stopping the round from penetrating. The blunt force of the bullet hit the Cuban commando and flung him forward, whipping his head back and sending him spinning.

Encizo picked himself up as Hawkins and Grimaldi made the door to the building. His weapon had spun away and as he pushed himself up off his hands and knees he tried desperately to find it. He spotted it just as a line of rounds cut across the dirt, slammed into the receiver and buttstock, busting them apart into useless fragments.

Carrying McCarter, Gary Manning plunged through the door kicked open by Hawkins and ducked inside the building. A searing-hot lance cut across Encizo's deltoid, plucking up his fatigue shirt and splashing him with his own blood as he spun around from the impact of the round.

Digging in his heels, Encizo sprang forward, sprinting for the building as several streams of gunfire poured out of the street behind him. He ran hard, lungs screaming and heart pounding as he cut for the open doorway. Beside the wooden frame a burst of fire pockmarked the wall with crater wounds. Putting his head down, Encizo sprang forward and dived through the opening.

He landed on one shoulder and rolled over, coming up inside the room to see Jack Grimaldi sprawled on the floor, bleeding heavily, his pistol in hand. T. J. Hawkins stood above him, wrestling with an AKM-armed insurgent.

Hawkins twisted the rifle up and slammed an uppercut elbow strike into the Shiite's face, knocking his head back. The Texan drove his knee into the man's midsection and doubled him over while pulling the Kalashnikov free. The terrorist fell backward, empty hands flailing as Hawkins spun his captured rifle around.

Calvin James fired past the poised Hawkins and cored the man's throat and jaw with a tight 3-round burst. The corpse spun farther back as it fell, spinning like a top and spraying blood out in a fat arc that splashed Hawkins.

Encizo came up and snatched up the AKM Hawkins had initially been using. He shuffled forward and took up a position by the open door even as more fire began to impact around the entrance. Almost immediately he was forced to duck his head back around the corner.

"The burning chopper is keeping them back for now," he shouted toward his unit. "But we can't stay here. Not for long."

"We may not have a choice," James yelled back. The team medic moved up to inspect the still unconscious McCarter. "The Brits have backed out. We're not looking at the cavalry coming anytime soon."

Manning took up a defensive position at an open window and looked back. "What's that mean for David?" The strain was clear even over the noise of incoming gunfire.

"Nothing good. I need help!" James snapped. "He's stopped breathing!"

Instantly, Hawkins knelt beside the inert form of McCarter as Calvin James used a size-3 Macintosh blade on a Paramedic Laryngoscope to intubate the unconscious man. Sliding the flexible plastic tube down McCarter's throat, he then secured an OD-green Bag-Valve-Mask to the slack muscles of McCarter's face.

"I can't get a peripheral pulse. Compressions," James instructed. Without hesitation Hawkins used his boot knife to cut the Phoenix leader from his body armor then found the appropriate spot on his sternum and began performing CPR chest compressions.

James crushed the rubber balloon of the BVM under his hand, forcing fresh oxygen into McCarter's still lungs while Hawkins performed CPR.

"People!" James snapped. From behind him the team used captured weapons to return enemy fire. Outside the building a grenade went off, rattling the basement so hard that dust came down from the ceiling. "I need another set of hands."

At that moment Encizo unleashed with his AKM at the doorway. "I'm hot! I'm hot!"

Almost frantic, James turned to where Manning was firing his weapon out of the window, but then Grimaldi, still dripping blood from his own untreated wounds, was by his side, taking the BVM from James.

"Slow," James told the pilot. "One, two, squeeze. Quick and hard. Stay calm."

Grimaldi nodded his understanding, operating the BVM with steady hands. "Is he gone?"

"He's got no circulation. I hope the heart stopped because his lungs couldn't get the oxygen it needed and not the other way around. I need to use my drugs."

Even as he explained the situation his hands were in

motion. "I'm pushing an amp of epi in now. Keep pumping hard, T.J.! I need to be able to find his veins without a central line."

Hawkins responded with renewed vigor. "I can feel his heart beating under my hands! But it feels funny." He stopped, searching for some way to describe what he was experiencing. "Like a rabbit running zigzag jumps," he said finally.

James just nodded as he pulled the epi syringe clear. "Hopefully this will kick-start him."

Behind him Manning dropped the spent magazine in his AKM and injected his last backup.

"It's like a damn anthill outside!" the huge Canadian snarled. "We have to get some height. We have to get above these bastards."

"If we move David he's dead," James said calmly.

"We've no time," Manning countered. He fired a burst from his window position. "We'll all be dead if we don't move."

Encizo had leaped to his feet and was firing the machine pistol from a Weaver stance, unusual for the situation. Past the burly shoulder of the Cuban, James saw a rushing figure, torso laden with canvas pouches he knew had to be filled with some form of plastic explosives.

Encizo fired a third burst into the man, and James felt his heart lurch with hope as the crazed suicide bomber began to fall. Then the man disappeared and the shock wave of the IED vest detonation rocked the battle. Smoke rolled forward and Encizo's body was catapulted backward and bounced off the floor. James hunched his shoulder and threw himself over the inert body of David McCarter as rubble and dust rained down and scattered across the men in the basement.

Manning was thrown against the wall and turned as he pushed himself clear. He swept up his stolen AKM and raced toward the door. At the edge of the now shattered doorjamb he threw the weapon up and began firing out the door and into the smoke.

His weapon suddenly cut short and he snarled in frustration, slapping upward on the magazine to try to seat the round in the breech. Encizo, still crawling on all fours, his left eye swollen closed and blood dripping from his right ear, came up beside him, his pistol in one hand and a grenade in another.

As Encizo lobbed the bomb, Manning snapped the bolt on his assault rifle back and cleared the misfeed. Snapping the stock into his shoulder, the Canadian special operations soldier began firing even as enemy rounds continued to strike around the opening.

Inside the room Calvin James lifted himself up off of the motionless McCarter. Immediately he and Hawkins and Grimaldi resumed the CPR.

Suddenly, McCarter spasmed. His chest hitched with involuntary motion as the lungs quivered and then drew breath. His heart suddenly began to beat on its own.

"You're back, you son of a bitch," James whispered.

Instantly he let his feeling of euphoria dampen. McCarter was still unstable and in extreme danger.

"McCarter's up, but he won't last!" James shouted.

Gary Manning turned to answer but a machine gun blast knocked him backward into the room.

CHAPTER EIGHTEEN

Caracas, Venezuela

Able Team picked themselves up and leaped to their feet.

Their weapons came up as the last echo of the shaped charge rattled through the room. Rubble and mortar and bits of rebar lay scattered everywhere in mounds and piles and a man-size breach had appeared in the basement wall.

"Go!" Blancanales shouted.

He brought his MP-5 around and triggered a series of 3-round bursts as harassing fire while the rest of his team hauled the prisoner up and shoved him forward. Schwarz leaped through the hole into the Caracas subway tunnel and Lyons shoved Kasim through the breach after him. Lyons saw a black-clad commando lurch to his feet next to a building support pillar and shot him through the head. The man's Kevlar helmet jerked to the side and the body spun away as Lyons turned and dived through the opening.

Scooting backward on his taped ankle, Blancanales

fired multiple bursts with the H&K submachine gun until he was close enough to spin around and dive through the breach himself. He landed on the other side and came up immediately, his muzzle tracking back toward the hole Schwarz had constructed to cover the egress point.

Behind him Lyons and Schwarz quickly surveyed the area. They were in a molded concrete tube flattened on the bottom to accommodate train tracks. They looked in both directions down the tunnel, unsure of their exact location in regard to the memorized schematics.

"There!" Schwarz shouted and pointed.

Lyons looked and saw the dim outline of the silent subway train standing dark about thirty yards away. He hooked his arm underneath Kasim's, applying leverage and putting the Iranian spy up on his toes. "Let's go."

Schwarz took the lead, letting his submachine gun drop to the end of its cross-body sling and rest against his body armor. He reached back and pulled up his PDA. He thumbed through the options until he had what he wanted, then he tucked in under his belt for quick access and hurried forward.

Lyons followed close behind using his intimidating physicality to cow the prisoner and keep him moving forward, his free hand wrapped around the pistol grip of his H&K MP-5. Behind them Blancanales pulled rear security, shuffling backward despite his injured leg and keeping his weapon trained on the breach hole leading back into the commercial tower basement.

Just as Schwarz reached the first in a line of subway passenger cars Blancanales saw a black canister arc through the hole in the wall and immediately recognized a flash-bang grenade.

"Grenade!" Blancanales shouted, partly to warn his team and partly to equalize the pressure he knew was coming. Mouth still stretched open, he spun and dropped an eyelid in a quick blink before the flash and explosion.

Beyond him in the subway tube Carl Lyons shoved Kasim to the ground and fell on him even as Schwarz cursed loudly and ducked up against the shielding bulk of the subway car.

The tunnel filled with light like a bolt of lightning followed by a sharp bang that battered the three Americans. The effect was negated by both the distance from the blast epicenter and the fact that each member of Able had trained with religious frequency against just such devices, allowing them to collect their wits in rapid fashion.

Knowing the flash-bang was intended to facilitate the Venezuelans' movement through the breach into pursuit, Blancanales swung over onto his belly and held the trigger down on his submachine gun, washing the blast hole down in 9 mm Parabellum rounds. His weapon kicked and bucked in a rhythmic, staccato pattern, and shell casings arced out of his ejection port and tumbled down to the tracks beneath him.

He saw a dark silhouette in the breach point stagger as the bullets struck him and then fall back. Behind him another man was dropped, but a third SWAT trooper dived forward, shouldering his way into the tube beyond the blast hole. The commando swung up an M-4 carbine and triggered a blast. Blancanales was forced into a reorientation of his fire from the breach toward the trooper. Already centered, his rounds struck the man from twenty-five yards and pummeled into him with merciless accuracy. The time it took for Blancanales to kill the Venezuelan allowed two more of the SWAT commandos to gain a position in the breach.

Their 5.56 mm rounds burned down the tube, forcing Blancanales more tightly down onto his stomach. He lifted his own weapon at an awkward angle and returned fire, spraying the area. Behind him Lyons risked rising to his knees despite the flying rounds and burned off bursts over Blancanales's body, laying out a wall of lead and throwing back at the attackers.

The big ex-cop pushed Kasim forward until the bound Iranian bounced off the rear platform of the subway car. Still firing, Lyons shouldered in behind the man and shoved him upward. Rounds pinged and ricocheted off the superstructure, spiderwebbing the reinforced glass of the windows and showering them with sparks.

Inside the subway car Schwarz sprang into his predetermined course of action, knowing that the survival of Able Team now rested in his ability to operate like the talented electronics genius he was.

He spoke into his ear jack as he charged down the central aisle of the car, his voice strained from his exertion, but remaining calm enough to replay the situational realities.

"Stony, this is Able," he said.

"Go for Stony," Price's calm voice responded.

"We are in the tunnel and I'm preparing to initiate takeover of the transit unit."

"Understood," Price acknowledged. "I'm giving you Hunt."

"Gadgets, I'm here," Wethers said.

His voice was warm and well modulated, and Hermann Schwarz knew he spoke with all the power of the Stony Man computers behind him. The effect to the embattled Schwarz was every bit as calming as an infantry soldier learning air support was en route.

At each car Schwarz was forced to use his fighting knife to pry open the doors, sliding the blade tip between the black rubber sealant, then leveraging them back until the automatic hydraulic switch engaged.

Sweat dripped from Schwarz's face and collected in pools at his belly, armpits and crotch, staining the fabric dark. He was in phenomenal physical shape, but the strain of sustained adrenaline bursts had left him winded and gasping for air. The oxygen in the shut-down subway car was stale and tasted artificial, contributing to his feelings of claustrophobia. The weapon hanging from its sling off his front had been so frequently and continuously fired that it radiated heat like a camp stove and the barrel glowed hot in his NVD mono-goggle lens.

He moved through four empty and dark subway cars after establishing his link with Wethers and arrived at the engine compartment. The doors here were of the same hydraulic dividers as the passengers cars with the addition of an electronic keycard security access system.

Behind him down the train he heard the sound of gunfire, then heard Lyons roaring curses. Concentrating intently, Schwarz tried to block all external stimulus from his mind, focusing sharply on the task at hand and the sat-link communication connection he had to Stony Man tech wizard Huntington Wethers.

For springing the simple civilian commercial security system Schwarz would not be called upon to utilize the power of Stony Man's supercomputers. For this task his PDA was more than equal to the challenge. Working quickly, he used a generic keycard imprint connected to the PDA by its earphone jack, allowing both the receiving and transmitting of information.

Using his thumb, the Able Team electronics specialist called up the appropriate program on his device, then initiated it. His screen winked into a green graph pattern and a bold line appeared at the top of the display. It blinked three times and began to slowly descend the screen. Each graph was filled with a number like a Sudoku puzzle. Each of the numbers began reducing or multiplying in rapid eyeblinks as the solid bar graph traveled downward over them before winking out one after another.

When the bar reached the bottom of the screen it blinked an additional three times and the electronically controlled door unsealed and slid open, allowing Schwarz to step inside the control room to the subway.

Behind him he could heard Blancanales and Lyons shouting over the bursts of gunfire. This was going to be tight, he realized.

"I'm inside," he said to Wethers.

"Copy, Gadgets," Wethers replied in his academically dry voice. "I am now shutting down the electrical grid for the subway system diagnostic program. They will not be able to track the process of your train. Set up the sat-comm link and I'll initiate the hack-and-slash protocol."

"Understood," Schwarz replied. "Give me fifteen seconds to hook the system."

"Copy," Wethers said. "We're standing by."

The interior of the subway was modern and ultratech. A panel system of gauges, displays and controls was arrayed in front of deep leather pilot seats and slanted view screens. Schwarz dropped into the engineer's seat and began powering the unit up, following a sequence he had practiced prior to deployment.

He shut the doors behind him and locked them down to prevent any stray or purposeful rounds from sabotaging his efforts. Humming softly to himself he connected his PDA to the engineer's CPU and then uploaded the signal to his sat-link relay system.

"Stony, we're good to go," he informed Wethers.

"Copy," Wethers replied. "Initiating knock program."

On the screen in front of Wethers a bar graph began to drop in segmented increments from the top of the screen to the bottom. Beside the display a statistical readout ran down from a flashing 100 percent to a steady-state 0.005 percent which blinked in rapid succession before filling the screen with a bright green 0 percent.

"The train is yours." Wethers's voice was smooth and cultured.

In Caracas, Schwarz heard the unmistakable sound of the hydraulic brake system releasing and then the hum of the powerful electric engine flood online in one smooth moment.

"I'm putting our airlift asset 'rotors up' to your extraction zone," Wethers said. "Good luck."

"Able out," Schwarz replied. He reached up and clicked his enhanced Bluetooth accessory over. "All aboard who's coming aboard. We're rolling hot."

THOUSANDS OF MILES away in the Stony Man computer room Carmen Delahunt and Huntington Wethers began initiating the complex attack on the Caracas infrastructure that would keep power flooding toward Able Team's hijacked train, black out any capability the Venezuelan authorities would have to track its progress and prevent equally fast subway systems emergency maintenance vehicles from giving chase.

Standing behind them, Barbara Price felt an immense weight lift off her shoulders. At least for now one of her teams appeared headed for safety. Now she had to go to Brognola on behalf of Phoenix because it was going to take intervention at the highest level to save the unit trapped in Basra.

CARL LYONS DUCKED his head as a hail of 5.56 mm rounds shattered Plexiglas next to him. Shards of reinforced glass sprinkled down around him and coated Kasim with the plastic slivers.

Crouched just in front of Lyons and the prisoner Blancanales fired his MP-5 in rapid aim-and-burst patterns that painted the subway tube with flaklike groupings of 9 mm Parabellum rounds. Venezuelan commandos, being driven forward by a massive officer in the rear of the unit, stubbornly pushed forward. Two burst groupings struck a shotgun-wielding police commando, shattering his ballistic glasses and leaving his eye sockets bloody fissures. The man's skull exploded outward and red spray struck the back of the man's Kevlar helmet and squirted downward to stain his black vest and fatigues.

Blancanales grunted with pain as he forced his injured ankle to support his weight long enough for him to leap back through the subway door. Lyons dropped to a knee and swept his own submachine gun up to his shoulder to trigger 3-round bursts as cover fire above the scrambling Blancanales. His rounds struck walls and ricocheted like buzz saws through the circular tunnel. There was a sound like a baseball bat on naked flesh, and a commando screamed as gouts of muscle were torn from his thigh. He collapsed forward in agony.

Hernandez was behind his men screaming updates on the Americans' movements. His angry gaze snaked out across the distance and found Lyons's cold eyes for a single instant. The subway train suddenly kicked into life and began rolling down the track.

Furious, Hernandez screamed his outrage and started forward, driving his men in front of him like a cowboy starting a stampede. The police commandos came up, all caution gone, and charged forward, firing their weapons wildly, hurtling a fusillade of lead down the tube to rattle and spark as bullets struck the supercarriage of the train.

Lyons threw himself flat and rolled to the side out the way of the barrage even as Blancanales tumbled over in the opposite direction. Unable to contain his enthusiasm, Schwarz, seated comfortably up front, hit the enter button on his secondary keyboard and laughed out loud as a train whistle sounded, taunting the frustrated Venezuelan commandos.

Hernandez stopped running as the train pulled away. His personal cell phone came out of an equipment pouch on his web gear and he quickly dialed a number from memory. In his role as leader of Chavez's premier direct-action unit he had found myriad ways to pad his paycheck.

It was time to pull a positive out of this disaster. "Tell Najafi his man has been taken by the Americans."

Basra, Iraq

MANNING RACED UP the interior steps and kicked open a door. Behind him, Hawkins and Encizo formed the other two-thirds of his fire team. Before they made the roof, the ground floor had to be cleared well enough to transport the unconscious McCarter.

Behind them Grimaldi and James held the ruined stairwell, guarding against the assault militia fighters and watching over McCarter. If a pathway was going to be punched through the interior defenses toward freedom, it would have to happen quickly to be of any use to the ex-SAS trooper.

Inside the room an irregular prepping a Claymore mine turned and reached for his weapon. There was a loud crack in the narrow hall and cordite filled the air like a flower bouquet. The militiaman's eyes crossed as they tried to see the sudden hole in his flat, low forehead, then he tumbled to the ground.

"Encizo, set the room on fire, and let's sweep toward the front," Manning said.

Rafael Encizo produced a lighter and ignited the UNICEF aid cardboard boxes stacked against the wall. Once he had a fire the three soldiers began to move farther down the hall, Hawkins covering their rear security while Manning led from the front.

He kicked open a door. Encizo covered his motion in one direction while Hawkins secured the hall in the opposite sector. Manning saw an empty office. He let the door close. From the end of the hallway he heard men shouting in Arabic. A door opened and Manning sank to one knee on the floor, bringing his stolen AKM up to his shoulder.

Three irregulars armed with AKM assault rifles charged into the hall. Instantly, Manning and Encizo opened up on them. Their tight, figure-eight-patterned bursts scythed into the knot of gunmen and ripped them apart. They tumbled over each other and fell in a pile on the ground. Blood flowed out from them in a red flood across the linoleum flooring underneath the fluorescent light.

"Let's go!" Manning said.

The fire team moved quickly down the length of the hall, weapons up until they got to the door the men had charged out of. The outflung arm of a dead militiaman held the door open several inches.

Manning stepped over the mangled corpse and snap-kicked the door open before moving inside. Enzico moved into the room behind him, weapon up and tracking as Hawkins took up a defensive overwatch to prevent a surprise attack.

Manning shuffled into the room, covering his vectors with tight motions of his weapon. He paused in the middle of the room and slowly lowered his weapon, taking in the scene. Behind him Enzico cleared behind the door and the ceiling before lowering his weapon and whispering a curse in Spanish.

The man hung from chains bolted into the wall. Inside the handcuffs attached to the chains the man's fingers stuck out at odd, painful angles, and he had only raw, bloody patches where his fingernails should have been. His mouth had collapsed inward like that of an old man, his cheeks hollow and his lips stained with blood. Most of his teeth had been yanked from his mouth.

A blindfold had been used to cover his eyes and a ball-gag shoved in his mouth. His head hung down limply between his outstretched arms. On a tray set on rollers, a butane torch, a pair of pliers and some blood-stained garden shears rested. Forgotten on the floor where the man rested on his knees was a three-foot length of black garden hose.

On a rickety card table set against the wall Manning saw an unzipped bowling ball bag. Even from his angle Manning could see it was filled with stacks of U.S. dollars. Next to it on the table was a blood-splattered blue Iraqi police uniform tunic and a Beretta 92-F automatic pistol. Scattered on the table like bloodstained dice, the long root nerves still attached, were the man's pulled teeth.

On the wall the man's body was covered with black patches where he'd been burned. His skin had bubbled and split at several points, including his genitals. From the ragged avulsion on his chest Manning could tell the man's nipples had been ripped off by pliers.

"They were videotaping it," Encizo whispered. "Look."

Manning looked up. He saw the little Toshiba mini-camcorder set up on a silver-legged tripod. "Take it. They might have been torturing him for information. Whatever they're interested in, Stony Man is interested in."

Encizo collected and secured the camcorder while Manning moved closer to the man. He leaned in close, ignoring the stench as he looked for signs of life. Manning reached out put two fingers against the man's neck at the carotid artery, searching for a pulse.

He could find none.

"Let's go," he told Encizo.

The two warriors headed for the room door as gunfire broke out again in the hallway.

Manning looked out the door of the room and saw Hawkins prone on the ground. The ex-Ranger fired his Kalashnikov in cool bursts, using the dead bodies of the torturers as a hasty fighting position. The Phoenix Force commando was positioned so that his fire was directed down the hallway in the direction they had first penetrated the building.

Manning threw himself against the right side of the door and angled his weapon outward to add his fire to that of T. J. Hawkins's. Encizo crouched on the left-hand side and swung the barrel of his stolen AKM around the corner. He began triggering long blasts of full automatic fire as the Stony Man task force fought hard to shift the momentum of the battle away from the attackers.

"I can't see them!" Manning shouted above the roar of the weapons. "How many are there?"

"Four!" Hawkins shouted back. "They must have come in off the stairwell opposite ours. There must be a coordinating officer outside the building directing them."

"Rafe," Manning said. "Check T.J.'s six."

Encizo stopped firing and repositioned his weapon so that it was articulated in the opposite direction. The Phoenix Force veteran threw himself belly down on the floor and peeked his head around the doorjamb to try to cover Hawkins's back.

Manning leaned out of the door and sprayed the hall. He saw two of the enemy irregulars firing down the hall from positions behind the open doors leading out toward the stairwell where the makeshift medical redoubt had been organized by James. The fighters aggressively answered the Americans burst for burst.

Hawkins suddenly lifted his Kalashnikov up at an angle, turning the weapon sideways. Manning heard the *bloop* as the commando triggered the Russian 30 mm grenade launcher slung under the barrel. The rifle recoiled smoothly into his shoulder and there was a flash of smoke as the round arced down the hallway.

Instinctively, Manning turned away as the HE round

rammed into the wall at the end of the hallway and detonated with a thunderous explosion and flash of light. The crack was sharp and followed by screams. The hallway acted like a chimney, filling with dark smoke from the detonation.

Manning seized the initiative hard on the heels of the grenade explosion. He leaped over the rifle barrels of both Encizo and Hawkins. He slid across the hall, bounced a shoulder off the wall and centered his weapon down the hall. He shuffled forward, firing his weapon in tight bursts toward the positions he had witnessed before the explosion.

Behind him T. J. Hawkins rose to his feet and began to move down the hall, as well, firing in tandem. Behind them Encizo rolled into position and covered their rear security with his drum-magazine-mounted AKM.

Manning caught a silhouette in the smoke and raked it with a Z-pattern burst of 7.62 mm rounds from his AKM battle rifle. Beside him Hawkins matched him step for step, his weapon firing. Manning's target spilled out onto floor, his chest and throat looking as if an animal had clawed it out.

"Magazine!" Manning warned.

Manning hit the release with his finger and dropped his almost empty magazine. His other hand came up with a fresh banana-clip magazine and slapped it into place. Manning's thumb tapped the release, and the bolt slid forward with a snap as a round was chambered.

Manning brought his weapon up, scanning quickly for a target. The smoke from the grenade blast hung in the air, reducing vision. Hawkins put a man down, then finished him off with a 3-round burst to the back of the head. Manning risked a look over his shoulder to quickly check on Encizo's status.

Just as Manning turned, he saw Encizo come up out of a crouch. The man lunged toward the open door where he and Manning had found the tortured man.

"Grenade!" Encizo screamed.

Manning saw Encizo stretched out as he dived, five feet up in the air, his weapon trailing behind him and one hand out ahead of him as if he were doing the crawl stroke.

Directly under the leaping man's boot Manning saw the black metal egg bounce once then get caught on a sprawled-out leg of a dead militia fighter. There was a flash of light and suddenly Manning was slapped down.

His world spun and he hit the floor hard enough to see stars. His vision went black for a heartbeat, then returned. Once again he had been struck deaf. He lay still for a moment, stunned by the concussive force of the blast. He blinked and the ceiling came into focus.

He saw a dark shape move beside him and turned his head in that direction. The hallway lit up as the muzzle-flash from Hawkins's weapon flared like a Roman candle. The ex-Ranger fired in one direction. Manning saw his face twisting as he screamed his outrage but he heard no sound.

Manning blinked. When he opened his eyes again he saw Hawkins roll onto his back and fire the Kalashnikov down the hallway between his sprawled-open legs. With a rush sensibility rammed into Manning and snapped him back into the present.

He sat up and his hearing returned instantaneously. He looked down and saw he still held his Russian weapon. He looked down the hall and saw starbursts of yellow light through the fog of smoke as militia fighters charged the position. Manning sat up and leaned against the wall before lifting his Kalashnikov and returning fire. He squinted and saw Encizo lying motionless, his legs trailing out from the doorway of the room.

The torn and headless torso of one of the torturers lay on top of the Cuban commando's body. Another one of the bodies that had been caught up in the blast had had its clothes lit on fire.

Manning sprayed the hallway. He saw his green tracer fire arc into the debris and dust and smoke and saw other green tracers arc back at him. Suddenly he saw a muzzle-flash to the right of the hallway and closer than before. He twisted at the hip and fired in response.

A man folded at the waist out of the fog and pitched forward. As he tumbled to the ground Manning put another burst of 7.62 mm slugs into his body. Beside him Hawkins rose up off the ground, keeping the barrel of his weapon trained down the hallway.

Manning held his fire moment and forced himself to stand. No enemy fire came from the hallway. Manning took a look behind him and counted the three dead men he and Hawkins had shot. The Phoenix Force commando had stated there were four when the ambush had begun.

Manning took a step down the hallway, weapon ready. He saw the crater where Hawkins's 30 mm round had impacted and the black scorch patterns spreading out from the center. He saw a severed arm lying in the hall in a puddle of blood and he turned back down the hallway.

Hawkins jogged forward, weapon up. Manning followed him, his weapon on his shoulder. The medic reached the still Rafael Encizo and reached to pull the torso off his friend's body. Manning drew even with him as Hawkins knelt beside the wounded Phoenix Force commando.

"Pescado," Hawkins said. "Pescado, can you hear me, brother?"

Manning passed the room without looking, his eyes searching for targets. As he passed a downed militia fighter he heard a moan and saw the man move. Manning whirled like a whip snapping and triggered a burst into the man, who shuddered and then lay still.

Manning snapped his weapon back around. At the end of the hallway, through the smoke and haze of dust he saw a door. He moved quickly to it and pulled it open. He sank to a knee and risked a look around the corner. The mosaic-tile hallway was a creamy-brown and stretched nearly thirty or forty yards toward the front of the building.

A bearded face peeked around a corner at the end of the hallway, and Manning instinctively fired a burst. The head ducked back to safety around the corner. Manning pulled himself back around his own corner.

"How is he?" he shouted at Hawkins.

"Out," Hawkins answered.

His voice was flat, lacking inflection. Manning felt a chill pass through him. Not another brother, he thought. He pulled his tactical radio from off his web gear H-harness fitted over his now filthy and blood-soaked black fatigues. He keyed the mike.

"How's your sit-rep?" he asked without preamble.

"Still in close contact, but no more suicide charges for now," James answered from the stairwell.

"Encizo took a hard one. He's unconscious, but I

think that's it. I'm sending him back to you with Hawkins before I finish this hallway."

"Time is a factor," James said. From out of the mike Manning could clearly hear the sound of gunfire.

"Understood," the big Canadian said.

Manning tucked his radio away and fired a blind burst down the hall. He turned back and saw Hawkins frantically working on the inert Encizo. What Manning saw made his throat close tight so quickly he almost gagged.

"We have to go," he said. "Get Rafe back to Cal."

Before Hawkins could answer, Manning heard a loud thump strike the door next to them. He didn't think, but simply reacted. Manning rolled up onto one hand, his leg curled beneath him, and leaped forward. He landed on top of the startled Hawkins and forced the Phoenix Force operator down over the unconscious and bleeding Rafael Encizo.

Behind Manning the hand grenade went off like a peal of thunder. It blew the door off its hinges and sent it flying into the hallway, followed by a billow of smoke. Manning lifted himself off Hawkins and Encizo as debris and dust rained down on the men. Manning swooned and shoved hard against the doorjamb to force himself upright.

He felt as if he'd just downed a bottle of tequila and taken a ride on a Tilt-A-Whirl. He gritted his teeth, snarling against the pain and disorientation. He scooped up his weapon and thrust the barrel around the edge of the door and pulled the trigger.

The weapon kicked and bucked in his hand and empty shell casings arced out and spilled across the bloody floor. He fired a 10- or 12-round burst, burning off half a magazine. Immediately machine-gun fire answered his burst and a maelstrom of heavy-caliber bullets sizzled through the blown-open door and hammered the wall behind Manning.

"Take him and go!" Manning shouted. "Get to the stairwell, get to Cal, I'll hold them off!"

Hawkins didn't argue. Letting his Kalashnikov dangle from its strap, he bent down and pulled Encizo up into a sitting position. The Cuban's head rolled loose on his neck and underneath a shroud of his own blood the man's skin was deathly white and starting to tinge with blue.

Hawkins squatted, tucking his butt underneath his shoulders and securing his grip on Encizo's shredded and smoking clothes. He grunted and lifted straight up, driving with the powerful muscles of his buttocks and thighs. Encizo rose as Hawkins did and at the top of the arch Hawkins ducked under the limp soldier, shouldering his weight easily.

Manning sprayed the hallway through the door without looking. Again his burst was answered with a long volley of heavy-caliber answering fire. Hawkins turned, Encizo's blood flowing out over him, and looked toward Manning.

"Go!" Manning shouted. "Go. I'm coming."

Hawkins nodded once and turned, running down the hall toward the back door by which the Stony Man task force had first accessed the building. He slid in the blood splashed across the linoleum, but did not go down, and Manning turned his attention back toward the door.

Whatever else happened he had to give the Phoenix Force commandos time to get to the stairwell. He would hold the militia fighters located in the front of the building off as long as he could, then make his own break.

A burst of machine-gun fire tore down the long hall. When the burst trailed off, Manning heard the familiar thumping bounce of a hand grenade coming his way. He looked down at the threshold of the doorway and saw the black metal sphere roll into the hall beside him.

He swung his left arm like a handball player and slapped the grenade back down the hall. He didn't look to see how far it traveled, but instead tucked his head between his arms and rolled away from the open door. He felt the shock waves traveling out of the hall slop over and push into his back.

He pushed himself up off his belly and swung back toward the door. He thrust the muzzle of his weapon around the corner and fired until he burned off the last bit of his magazine.

He turned and began to sprint along the hall away from the position held by his teammates. He dropped the spent magazine as he ran and fumbled for another in his web gear. His combat boot came down on a blue-gray loop of intestine and he went down hard, landing awkwardly on one knee. Pain lanced out from the hinge joint and he gasped in surprise at the intensity of it after all he'd already suffered.

He forced himself up and kept running, his Kalashnikov carbine forgotten behind him. He reached the open door leading into the hallway and drew his sidearm, a Beretta pistol, from his thigh holster.

Manning moved carefully through the room. He held his Beretta at the ready as he approached the door. His feeling of disquiet had not subsided. He couldn't place his unease, and that made it all the more bothersome.

He stalked forward, pausing at the door leading out into the hall.

He stopped, sensed nothing, moved forward.

All hell broke loose.

Manning was not a superstitious man, but when he stepped through the door and entered the hall, the soldier felt as if he had moved into a field of static electricity. The hair on his arms and the back of his neck lifted straight up as adrenaline surged into his body. The night fighter reacted instantly, without conscious thought. He dropped to one knee and leaned back in the doorway, sweeping up the barrel of his pistol and triggering a blast.

The unmistakable pneumatic cough of a sound-suppressed weapon firing on fully automatic assaulted Manning's ears across the short distance. Shell casings clattered onto the linoleum floor, mixing with the sound of a weapon bolt leveraging back and forth rapidly. Manning felt the angry whine of bullets fill the space where his head and chest had been only a heartbeat before.

Manning targeted diagonally across and down the office hall, firing his Beretta with practiced, instinctive ease. He moved back through the doorway behind him in a tight roll and reached for his carbine. From his belly Manning thrust the muzzle around the doorjamb and arched the weapon back and forth as he laid down quick suppressive blasts.

The 7.62 mm rounds were deafening in the confined space, and his ears rang painfully from the noise. Manning reached up and jerked his mono-goggle night-vision device down so that they dangled from the rubber strap around his neck. He heard the bullets from his assailant's answering burst impact the outer wall with audible smacks that rang louder than the muzzle-braked weapon's own firing cycle.

Manning guessed the shooter was using a submachine gun and not an assault rifle, though he was hard-pressed to identify caliber with the suppressor in use. Manning scrambled backward and rested his rifle barrel across the still warm corpse of a dead militia fighter. If there was more than one irregular out in that specific position, and they were determined to get him, they would either fire and maneuver to breach the room door, or possibly use more grenades to clear him out.

There was silence for a long moment. Manning's head raced through strategies and options. If the terrorist's intent had merely been escape, then why had he bothered to stay behind or try to take Manning out? If the unknown assailant was armed for a quiet kill, then that would indicate that he was probably not carrying ordnance much heavier than the silenced SMG being used now; perhaps it was the officer of the unit he and Hawkins had just wiped out.

The main thing, Manning's experience told him, was to seize the momentum. He quickly stripped an extra rifle from a dead bodyguard and hooked the sling over his shoulder. Conscious of how vulnerable he was, Manning high crawled back toward the door. He maneuvered the barrel of his AKM out the entrance and triggered an exploratory blast, conducting a recon by fire. Precious seconds ticked away.

Immediately, Manning's aggressive burst was answered with a tightly controlled one. Bullets tore into the wooden doorjamb and broke up the floor in front of his weapon. Manning ducked back; he had seen what he needed and found a way to exploit his heavier armament.

The gunmen had taken position across and two doors down the hall from the room where Manning was now trapped. From that location the gunman controlled the fields of fire up and down the hall, preventing Manning from leaving the room without exposing himself to withering short-range fire.

Again Manning triggered a long, ragged blast. He tore apart the door of the room directly opposite him, then ran his larger-caliber rounds down the hall to pour a flurry of lead through the sniper's door. Tracer fire lit up the hallway with surrealistic strips of light like laser blasts in some low-budget science fiction movie. Manning could smell his own sweat and the hot oil of his AKM. The heavy dust hanging in the air, kicked up by the automatic weapons fire, choked him. His ears rang and, over everything else, even the fever pitch of excitement, was the intoxicating smell of burning cordite.

Manning ducked back around as the gunman triggered an answering burst from his SMG. Manning heard the smaller-caliber rounds strike the wall outside his door, saw how they failed to penetrate the building materials. It confirmed his suspicions that the killer's weapon was a light caliber.

Manning snarled, gathering himself, and thrust his weapon out the office door a final time. He triggered the AKM and the assault rifle bucked in his hands. Manning sprinted out through the doorway hard behind his covering fire. His rounds fell like sledgehammers around the door to the room of his ambusher. Hot gases warmed his wrists as the bolt of his weapon snapped open and shut, open and shut, as he carried his burst out to an improbable length even as he raced forward.

Two steps from the room door Manning's magazine ran dry and the bolt locked open. Without hesitation Manning flung the empty weapon down and dived forward. The big man's hard shoulder struck the door. Already riddled with bullets, the flimsy construction was no match for Manning's heavy frame and he burst through it into the room.

Manning went down with his forward momentum, landing on the shoulder he had used as a battering ram and somersaulting over it smoothly. He came up on one knee and swung his second AKM carbine off his shoulder, leveling it at the wall separating his position from the gunman's. Manning triggered his weapon from the waist, raking the weapon back and forth in a tight, low Z-pattern. The battlefield rounds chewed through plywood, Sheetrock and insulation with ease, bursting out the other side with terminal velocity.

Still firing, Manning smoothly uncoiled out of his combat crouch, keeping his weapon angled downward to better catch an enemy likely pinned against the floor. His intentions were merciless. Momentum and an attacker's aggression were with Manning now. Coming to his feet, he shifted the AKM pistol grip from his right to his left hand. His magazine came up dry as he shifted his weight back toward the shattered door to the room.

The handle of Manning's Beretta filled the palm of his free hand as he fired the last rounds through the looted AKM. He was moving, lethally graceful, back out the door to the room. His feet pirouetted through a complicated series of choreographed steps as he moved in a tight Weaver stance. Out in the hall, smoke from weapons fire and dust billowed in the already gloomy hall.

Manning stepped out long and lunged forward, sinking to one knee as he came to the edge of his ambusher's door. He made no attempt to slow his momentum, but instead let it carry him down to the floor. He breached the edge of the enemy door, letting the barrel of the pistol lead the way. He caught the image of a dark-clad form sprawled out on the floor of the room.

The 9 mm pistol coughed in a double tap, catching the downed figure in the shoulder and head. Blood splashed up and the figure's skull mushroomed out, snapping rudely to the side on a slack neck. A chunk of cottage-cheese-like material splattered out and struck a section of bullet-riddled wall.

Manning popped up, returned to his feet. He moved into the room, weapon poised, ready to react to even the slightest motion or perceived movement. After the frenzied action and brutal cacophony of the gun battle, the sudden return of silence felt deafening, almost oppressive. Approaching the dead man, Manning narrowed his eyes, trying to quickly take in details. Muzzle-flash had ruined his night vision.

Frustrated, Manning snuggled his NVD back into position and turned the IR penlight on. The room returned to view in the familiar monochromatic greenish tint. Manning looked over at the dead gunman's weapon. From its unique silhouette Manning instantly recognized the subgun as a PP-19 Bizon. Built on a shortened AKM-74 receiver, it had the signature cylindrical high-capacity magazine attached under the fore grip and the AKM folding buttstock. The weapon was usually associated with Russian federal police or army troops, but international arms merchants had been marketing more and more as the Russian economy went through its series of crises.

"I'm clear on this end," Manning said into his radio, his voice hoarse from strain.

"Just in time," James answered back. "Encizo has a bump on the head, but he's up and about. With that hall clear, I say let's get the fuck out of here."

"I'm rolling to your twenty now," Manning answered.

As he ran through the building the sound of gunfire echoed louder and louder until it drowned everything else out.

CHAPTER NINETEEN

Caracas, Venezuela

Carl Lyons held the sat phone to his ear. "That's it," he said. "I just turned Kasim over to the boys in black. He's on a one-way ticket to a black site for interrogation. Once we clear up this matter we can start rolling north."

"I think you should reconsider hitting Kasim's arms dealers," Price said. "Let a CAG or ISA team do it. You've just been through the ringer."

"We want to finish this up ourselves. We're good. Besides, we have Mott right here with a Little Bird. We can hit 'n' git in five minutes. In and out, no loose ends. We wait for JSOC to scramble a team, the Iranians might get word of Kasim's snatch and go to ground. We go now or we might never get 'em." Lyons paused. "Besides, Charlie's got that present basket for us from Kissinger. I can't stand to let good ordnance go to waste."

"No, I suppose you can't," Price replied, voice droll.

"This is why people love me, Barb."

"What people? Where?"

"Well, just humanity in general."

"Ten minutes, Carl," Price instructed, voice serious.

"Ten minutes, boss lady," Lyons acknowledged and signed off.

Putting the sat phone away, he ducked into the team vehicle behind the steering wheel.

"They're on the fifth floor," Schwarz said. "Room 519. There's at least three of them in there, but I think more like twice that."

"Building materials?" Blancanales asked.

"Reinforced concrete for load-bearing structural, but only Sheetrock covered by wood between rooms. The doors have a lock, single dead bolt, and chain."

"Windows?"

"Commercial variety. Set in the wall with no balcony. They open inward with a metal-clasp locking mechanism. Set into four even quadrants of windowpane around molding and wood frame. High quality, but not security."

"Wall penetration will be a problem even with our 9 mm weapons," Lyons said.

"C-2 breaching charges on the door and shotguns with buckshot or breach-shot for the takedown?" Blancanales suggested.

"What's security like in the hotel?"

"They have a single Caracas uniformed police out front armed with a pistol and submachine gun. They liaison with hotel private security, who have a heavy presence in the lobby and restaurant area. They have hourly passes through the room halls. They have 9 mm side-arms," Schwarz answered. "I think we could get in and do the takedown. It's getting out without slugging it out with security forces I'm doubtful of."

"Position to snipe on the window?" Blancanales asked.

"Negative. The Caracas Pan-American Mall is across the street. It's eighty-five thousand square feet. No defilade and no angle other than up trajectory. Lousy for shooting."

"Yes, but does it have frozen yogurt? You know how I feel about my frozen yogurt." Blancanales laughed.

"That kind of exposure rules out rappelling down the outside, even if we could get to the roof." Lyons rubbed at his chin, thoughtful. It was going to come down to Charlie Mott.

"Bait and switch followed by a bum rush?" Schwarz suggested.

"How do we get out?" Blancanales countered.

"I think I SPIE a way." Lyons smiled. "Schwarz, I'll need you to find us a good covert LZ on the edge of Caracas, toward the east, and pinpoint the GPS reading."

"That'll work. Depends on how fast Mott can get us his bird. This'll have to be fast with the city alive with cops and military. And did I mention fast? Very goddamn fast," Blancanales said.

"Has Charlie ever let us down yet?" Lyons answered.

SCHWARZ WALKED OUT of the hotel and dodged traffic as he crossed the busy street to where Blancanales was parked at the curb. Schwarz opened the passenger side door and slid into the seat.

"It's a go," he said.

"Good," Lyons replied from the backseat. "Let's do it."

Driving quickly, the Stony Man task force circumnavigated the luxury hotel and pulled into the parking lot of the Pan-American Mall, quickly losing themselves among the acres of parking for up to 3,500 vehicles. A State Department courier with no association with the mission would pick up the vehicle five minutes after Able Team left the area.

Over the horizon, in the hot Venezuelan night, Charlie Mott was already inbound in an AH-6J Little Bird attack helicopter from a Navy ship offshore. The clock had started running on a tightly scheduled and overtly aggressive Able Team operation. Dressed in their civilian clothes, the men moved fast toward their objective.

The hotel loomed up above them as they crossed the street. Lyons was presented with an opportunity to do what he did best: go blood simple. He intended to seize the chance to vent his frustrations in righteous wrath against violent international criminals. It was a relief, a short-lived blessing.

Walking fast, Able Team moved onto the Caracas sidewalk. They sweated freely, dressed in black body armor under their casual clothes with various weapons and tools attached for instant use once the dynamic entry began. The ornate wall ringing the hospitality structure was broken by a gate opening upon the loading dock where deliveries were made.

Caracas was a security-conscious city in a criminally volatile region. Yet its problems were minor compared to other neighboring narco-states, and the well-developed sense of paranoia evident in some other Central and South American countries was largely missing despite sporadic narco-terrorist attacks. As such its security was as capable of being exploited as those in other, more violent nations.

They reached the back gate, hands sliding into black driving gloves of kid leather. As one the three men reached up and swept their long coats to one side. The tan or black coats tumbled to the ground. Under the blue jeans and tan cargo pants black-leather-and-canvas combat boots trampled the coats as they sprang into action.

Black balaclavas were pulled into place, obscuring the Stony Man commandos' faces from internal CCTV cameras. Schwarz pulled a pair of short-handled bolt cutters from under his vest as Blancanales grabbed the chain and padlock looped around the chain-link fence gate and held it up.

Schwarz cut through the chain in one easy motion. Blancanales pushed the fence gate open as Schwarz dropped the bolt cutters next to the raincoats abandoned on the ground. The Stony Man task force rushed through the opening, Schwarz taking the lead.

As they ran the three commandos swung out their implements and firearms so that by the time they reached the fire door Schwarz had scouted earlier they moved in only their body armor and rappel harnesses, weapons out and at the ready.

Each man carried the 9 mm Viper JAWS pistol at either shoulder or hip, and all three wielded Saiga 12K Russian .12-gauge assault shotguns with folding stocks and shortened barrels. The 8-round box magazines went into a weapon designed on the AK-74M paratrooper carbine. Loaded with sixteen pellets of .30-diameter buckshot, the rounds were considered the most effective man-stoppers. They were also considered generally more efficient at causing blunt trauma through protective vests or even in general when compared to the fléchettes round loads.

The first two shells in Schwarz's Saiga 12K were breaching rounds designed to penetrate the civilian locks on interior doors. The outer fire door was made of metal, reducing the effectiveness of the rounds and potentially signaling the team's presence before they had fully exploited their advantage of surprise.

As they reached the fire door Blancanales allowed his combat shotgun to hang from its strap across his torso. He pulled a two-foot-long titanium crowbar fitted with rubber grips at the end from a carbiner holster on his rappel harness. While Lyons and Schwarz covered him, shotguns at port arms, he went to work.

Without preamble Blancanales wedged the comma-shaped end of the cut-down Hooligan tool under the overlapping lip of the steel fire door. Throwing one big boot up on the other door, he grabbed the crowbar in both of his gloved hands and yanked back sharply.

There was a screech of metal and then a loud pop as the door snapped open. A fire alarm began to wail. Blancanales dropped the crowbar and grabbed the door with one hand as he scooped up the pistol grip of his Saiga with the other. Lyons went through the door, shotgun high, followed hard by Schwarz.

Once the other two were inside the hotel Blancanales stepped through, letting the fire door swing closed. Able Team took the stairs in a rapid leapfrog pattern. The stairs themselves were metal and set into the wall with a three-rail guard running along the outside edge. The staircase ran up in a squared spiral with a flat landing at each level where the doors opened off on the guest hallways. The cacophony of the midnight fire alarm was deafening.

Lyons bounded up to the second floor, then covered the area as Schwarz and Blancanales raced past him, the pounding of their boots echoing up and down the vertical shaft. At the third floor Schwarz provided rearguard protection as Blancanales and Lyons charged past him.

The skills of the commando or the paramilitary operative existed in a form like an inverted pyramid with each level of skill resting on the small, more fundamental level below it. Communications, medical, explosives, computer and other specialties such as scuba, free-fall parachuting or piloting were all coalesced around certain core abilities.

At the heart of these abilities were physical fitness and personal-weapon marksmanship. Conditioning to the level of a professional athlete was the entry-level trait necessary for inclusion in the fraternity of special operations troops, as was the ability to put bullets downrange with a superior level of accuracy.

The Stony Man commandos were no different, and their fitness routines were exacting. Loaded down by implements and equipment, in addition to carrying weapons, the three elite operators raced up the steep stairs with all the cardiovascular endurance of triathletes.

Blancanales covered the landing on the fourth floor, and Lyons followed Schwarz. At the fifth floor Lyons stepped onto the landing, and off to the left as Schwarz rushed forward. The Able Team operator snatched open the public-access door leading onto the guest floor hallway.

Lyons rushed through, weapon up and in place at his shoulder, his teammates hard on his heels. A few hotel guests, eyes sleepy and hair mussed, had opened their doors and stuck their heads outside in response to the fire alarm. At the sight of the night-suited and bala-

clava-masked intruders they screamed or shouted in
terror and slammed their doors shut tight.

Lyons knew that security, already alerted by the fire
alarm, would now have guest reports to guide their response protocols. He began to race faster down the hall.
Speed, aggression, violence of action, superior firepower remained the holy mantra of conducting raids.

The hotel decor was dark wood and thick carpeting
with soft lighting and gilt-worked mirrors. The place
paled in comparison to Escondito's suites, but was still
four-star.

The occupants of Room 519 hadn't opened their door
in response to the alarm. Lyons streaked past their door,
ducking under the spy hole set at eye level in the muted
wood tones of the door. He spun around and put his back
to the wall on the handle side of the door, weapon up.
Schwarz ran up and halted in the middle of the hall at
a sharp angle to the door as Blancanales slid into position against the wall on the side of the door opposite
from Lyons.

Schwarz's shotgun immediately roared. The breaching shot slammed into the door just behind the handle.
A saucer-size crater punched through the solid building
material. Schwarz shifted the semiautomatic combat
shotgun's muzzle and fired his weapon again, blowing
out the dead bolt.

The Stony Man hitters had been inside the hotel for
less than three minutes.

THE DOOR SHIVERED under the twin impacts of the
special shotgun rounds. The booming of the assault gun
banged sharply in the narrow hallway over the wailing
fire alarm. The door shook open, trailing splinters of

wood and pieces of stamped metal. Schwarz stepped forward and kicked the door wide before peeling back.

Blancanales leaned in and pumped two loads of buckshot around the corner high for covering fire as Lyons squatted and let his flash-bang device roll over the threshold. The canister-shaped grenade bounced into the room as Lyons swung back and leg pressed himself up out of his crouch.

A flash of light like a star going nova followed the deafening concussion of the grenade's bang with a brilliant flash. Lyons swung through the door, Saiga shotgun held at his hip and ready. Rosario Blancanales followed hard behind him as Schwarz brought up the rear.

Lyons saw an opening to his left and covered it with his shotgun. It was a door to the hotel room's bathroom, and he caught a glimpse of a shoeless man in trousers and a white cotton tank top T-shirt staggering against the sink. A Skorpion machine pistol lay on the tile by the European-style toilet.

Lyons's shotgun blast punched the Venezuelan narco-mercenary in the chest and cracked his sternum. The man was knocked across the bathroom counter, and blood splattered the mirror and sizzled on the lightbulbs.

The suite was a luxury suite with two big bedrooms opening up on a common living area and bar. Blancanales, second in line, raced past the engaged Lyons and peeled off to the left, followed hard by Schwarz, who sidestepped to the right.

A wet bar and service sink took up the front part of suite while toward the far wall three couches and a massive ottoman had been set up like an E around a large-screen television. When Escondito had footed the bill for the Venezuelan cell's logistical support he hadn't skimped. Three men in various stages of undress were in the room, attempting to scramble back up to their feet and recover various submachine guns.

Rosario Blancanales took the man on the left. He wore a huge gold hoop in his ear and his long hair was swept back in a ponytail. He wore silk boxers and a stunned expression on his face as he looked up into the gaping muzzle of Blancanales's combat shotgun. Blancanales pulled the trigger and the man no longer possessed a face to place any kind of expression on at all.

Still firing from the hip, Blancanales swiveled as a second man rose, fumbling with his H&K MP-5. A trickle of blood flowed from the broken drum of the gunman's right ear and splashed the bare skin of his shoulder. Blancanales's point-blank shot knocked him back to the carpet and tossed his jaw into the television screen behind him.

The third South American in the room lifted his Skorpion and turned it toward the balaclava-covered killer who had just gunned down his fellow gang members. Schwarz's load of buckshot hit the man with sledgehammer force in the neck and left shoulder, and the man folded at the knees and flopped like a fish to the floor.

The muzzle of a second MP-5 thrust around the door of the left bedroom. Schwarz fired a blast from the hip, tearing through the wood frame and wainscoting around the door. Lyons stepped between Blancanales and Schwarz, firing a blast of harassing fire as he charged the bedroom. Blancanales moved to cover him as Lyons entered the room. The Saiga bucked hard in Lyons's hands as he stood in the doorway and finished off the killer.

Schwarz moved quickly to the door of the second bedroom. He kicked the door open and entered the room. He fired a blast through the closet and then checked under the bed, finding nothing.

"Clear!" he shouted, using Spanish to mislead any potential witnesses and reduce any sense of an American footprint on the operation.

"Clear!" Lyons answered from the other side of the suite.

The Stony Man hit team folded back into the room. A haze of gun smoke hung in the air and trailed from the barrels of their shotguns. Cordite stink was a bitter perfume, and the metallic sent of blood was pungent.

"Let's shake it down," Lyons said. "Gadgets—" he indicated Schwarz "—cover the door."

Schwarz was already in motion as Blancanales and Lyons began looking for paperwork, cell phones and laptops to loot. They had discovered nothing other than three unattended cell phones when Schwarz alerted them from the room door.

"Company. Security," he said. "Time to roll."

"Which side?" Lyons demanded.

Schwarz dropped his box magazine from the Saiga. "Elevators," he replied. "Two, with pistols and radios." He slammed a fresh 8-magazine into the shotgun, this one with a short strip of green tape on one side.

"We go out to the right. Let's roll," Lyons ordered as both he and Blancanales replaced the magazines in their assault shotguns, likewise marked with the same green tape.

Schwarz thrust his Saiga 12K around the corner of the door and unleashed three blasts of specialty ammunition. Hard-packed, nonlethal beanbags spread out down the hall and knocked the startled security officers to the carpet like wild haymakers.

Schwarz rolled back around the door and Blancanales stepped around him, tossing a concussion grenade. The bang as it went off rang even the Stony Man commandos' ears inside the room. Schwarz turned the corner and entered the hallway. Lyons and Blancanales spilled out of the room, turning to their right as they raced for the staircase.

Lyons sprinted hard down the hallway, Blancanales hard on his heels. Behind him he heard Schwarz fire his shotgun twice more and he was able to pick out the brutal smack of the riot-load beanbags as they struck flesh even over the hotel's blaring fire alarm.

Lyons kicked open the door and held it against the wall as Blancanales went through. Schwarz caught up and all three team members raced up the staircase. Three stories up Lyons heard an angry voice shout out from beneath them. He leaned over the railing and triggered a double blast of his shotgun, hoping the thunderous sound would spook anyone following them.

Schwarz yanked the pin on a flash-bang grenade and let it drop down the spiral well. It fell three floors and detonated, the echo-chamber effect of the stairwell redoubling its effect on the security forces below Able Team.

They reached the top floor forty-five seconds later, breathing hard, but not disabled. Lyons pulled a road flare from a cargo pocket as Schwarz dropped his shotgun's magazine for a second time. It clattered as it hit the concrete landing in front of the roof access door.

Blancanales covered the stairwell as Schwarz triggered his shotgun, firing a breaching shot into the door. The team, moving with well-oiled precision, rushed through the door and out onto the roof of the hotel.

The lights of early morning Caracas blazed around them and they could hear the cars and horns of commuters from below. The plaza towers shone like beacons in the distance. Police sirens rushed closer, sharper and more staccato than the blaring fire alarm wailing below them. Lyons popped his flare and tossed it through the air ahead of him.

It fell on the roof, burning brightly. Rosario Blancanales pulled a spring-loaded door wedge from a pocket and dropped it down in front of the blown door. He kicked it into place and triggered the spring. Instantly a V-shaped wedge of hard rubber locked into place, jamming the door shut.

From overhead they heard the *whump-whump-whump-whump* of a helicopter sweeping in toward them. They looked up as the Little Bird flared hard and settled over them. A long, thick rope uncoiled and hit the ground. Loops of canvas had been sewn into the rope and the three commandos moved forward and hooked on at two points with their D-ring carbiners.

The technique was called SPIE, or Special Patrol Infiltration/Extraction, and was common among recon troops and special operations forces. Lyons gave the signal once Schwarz and Blancanales showed him thumbs-up and the Little Bird shot straight up out of its hover. The three men went into the arms-spread position to avoid spinning.

The helicopter pilot swung the nose of the Little Bird around and pointed it toward the northeast. The tail rotor elevated above the main blades it sped off toward the LZ whose GPS coordinates had earlier been programmed by Schwarz. A vehicle and clothes awaited them there.

The raid had lasted seven minutes from the time they had cut the padlock on the fence to the time the Little Bird had pulled their SPIE rope off the hotel roof.

CHAPTER TWENTY

Basra, Iraq

With the pathway to the staircase cleared, Phoenix Force raced for the roof the building.

T. J. Hawkins kicked open the door to the building's staircase and swept up his rifle. The stairs ran up four stories to a door perched atop a set of scaffolding stairs that led to a roof. Quickly scanning for movement, Hawkins sprang forward and began sprinting up the stairs. Behind him Calvin James grunted along, carrying McCarter.

The ex-SEAL was afraid to carry the big Briton in a fireman's carry over one shoulder because of McCarter's injuries, and the close contact with the militia fighters made a two-man improvised stretcher carry a virtual impossibility; Phoenix Force needed every gun swinging if they were going to make it to the roof.

James cradled the Phoenix Force commander like a baby in his arms. The weight was debilitating, causing his biceps and low back to scream in protest. Each step felt as if his thigh muscles were going to rip clear of the bone at the knee. His lungs worked like bellows and sweat soaked him, sliding down his face in rivulets of stinging salt. His will, his discipline, were all that kept him moving. In his arms McCarter lay unconscious, a single jostle away from death.

Behind him Rafael Encizo and Gary Manning were firing continuously to keep the rushing militiamen from gaining a foothold on the stairs. Twice Encizo dropped HE grenades down to destroy the staircase and make it impassible, but each time the screaming zealots below them managed to scramble past. Jack Grimaldi, reduced to his sidearm, fired his magazine empty, dropped it out of the well and slapped another one home in the pistol butt.

Ayub stumbled up the stairs, his hands still bound behind his back. The Iranian ran, willing to escape the hellstorm of fire pouring through the building around him. The intelligence operative realized that their attackers were not trained commandos with precision strike capability. Rather they were street militia, uncoordinated, poorly trained—loose cannons who would cut him to ribbons with their grenades and wild automatic fire. Perversely, he knew his only chance at survival lay now in running with his captors.

Pistol and subgun fire hammered up the angled stairway, ripping through Sheetrock and twice striking the already pummeled Encizo in his flak vest. The Cuban and big Canadian's aim were telling, and below them blood flowed in rivers down the smoldering stairs as more Shiite irregulars paid the ultimate price.

Hawkins sensed motion from a door in the third-floor stairwell. He spun, swinging his rifle up, but the militia gunner was already through the doorway, a

Czech Skorpion VZ-83 in his hands and chattering out a point-blank hailstorm of 9 mm Markarov rounds.

Four rounds struck the spinning Hawkins, clawing through his outer flak vest and slamming into the Kevlar weave of his NATO body armor. The Texan grunted under the impact and rocked back on his heels. His finger was on the trigger of his looted rifle as he fell backward and struck the wall.

He triggered a blast from the hip and the round caught the submachine gunner under the chin, hacking out the flesh of his neck and coring out his spinal card. The man plunged backward through the open door and, still gasping from the bruising impact, Hawkins sent an 8-round burst through the opening after him.

Manning, climbing up the staircase backward, fired a long burst over Encizo's head. His finger found his throat mike. "Stony, how's our ride coming? A little update might raise our morale!"

Barbara Price responded immediately. "Official channels have closed off. You need to gain the roof and hold out. We have contracted a private military contractor with airlift assets. Their rotors are spinning at the Basra International Airport right now. As soon as they verify the funds transfer to their bank, they'll roll. At that time you'll need to pop smoke. I'll provide a comm link between you and the pilot."

Manning risked a glance up the stairs and saw James struggling with the slack weight of McCarter. The fox-faced British commando's head lolled on the end of a loose neck and his skin was ashen-gray from blood loss and shock. Jack Grimaldi, gasping for breath, held his pistol in a two-fisted grip and pulled the trigger three times.

"They have to have level-one trauma assets. James needs the gear," Manning shouted into his throat mike. "Can they swing that?"

"They do close protection and route security for British diplomatic assets so they have a full combat medic contingent and a medium-heavy-lift helicopter." Price paused then continued, voice dry, "Frankly, it's a better deal than we could have gotten from the government there."

"Copy!" Manning shouted over the firing of weapons. "We are en route to roof."

Three steps below him Encizo hurled two more HE grenades into the stairwell. The black metal spheres bounced off the wall and rebounded down the stairs with sharp, metallic clunks. The explosion rocked the building's foundations, and black smoke poured up the stairs, enveloping the team as Hawkins managed to finally reach the roof-access door.

Hard morning sunlight slammed into the ex-Ranger's eyes, blinding him momentarily as he stumbled forward. Behind him James staggered through the door and eased the limp McCarter down onto the roof, his mouth hanging open as he gasped for breath. Black smoke roiled out through the doorway as first Manning and then Encizo gained the roof.

Manning reached out with a hand the size of a dinner plate and shoved Ayub down to the roof with a single hard push. The intelligence operative and terror paymaster struck the roof hard enough to split his lip and draw blood. Terrified and helpless, the man stayed down, his eyes closed and his mouth repeating a mantra of childhood prayers.

Behind Ayub, Encizo dropped to his belly and burned

off the rest of his magazine into the smoke of the stair-well. Manning shuffled forward and pulled an OD canister from his web gear, popping the spring on a green smoke grenade before rolling it away from the group toward the corner of the building roof.

Grimaldi went to a knee just outside the door, keeping the muzzle of his pistol orientated toward the prisoner even as his eyes scanned the adjoining rooftops, hunting for threats.

Hawkins immediately took a knee and swept his sniper rifle, scoping the rooftop topography surrounding the trapped team, hunting for targets and scanning for threats. For one long, impossible moment there was silence. The morning sunlight rising out behind the silhouettes of the city turned the scene a pleasant, mellow gray.

Then from below them a voice screamed in fury and a barrage of weapons fire poured up toward them from the street. Around them the cinder-block facade parapet circling the roof began to disintegrate. Concrete chips flew out like shrapnel in jagged shards as rifle and machine gun rounds tore into it. Automatic weapons fire poured lead over the edge and marksmen began firing on the group from elevated positions in nearby buildings. The unmistakable sound of rocket-propelled grenades striking the building sides came from below the team's position.

Hawkins turned in tight circles, stroking his trigger with calm detachment and repeating the pattern in a seemingly endless loop: transition, acquire, engage, transition. Militia snipers armed with SVD Dragunov Soviet sniper rifles fell, two-man machine gun teams deploying RPK automatic weapons and RPG crews all fell in a harrowing forty-five-second stretch as the Texan put heavy-caliber round after heavy-caliber round through a succession of faces and skulls appearing on rooftops and in windows across from the building.

Even as Calvin James monitored the comatose McCarter, Encizo and Manning took up positions behind industrial conduit vents on the roof. Using stolen Kalashnikovs, they burned the barrels soft with continuous fire to suppress the moving teams. Grimaldi huddled belly down, one eye never leaving the terrified prisoner.

A random round arced out of nowhere and struck James between the shoulder blades, shattering the ceramic plate held there in a pouch on his Kevlar vest. He tumbled forward, but pushed himself up, gasping for breath at the shock the muscles of his back spasming in protest at the blunt-force trauma.

He threw himself prone over McCarter's body as more rounds began to chew up the gravel-and-tar roof. "Jesus Christ!" he snarled, looking up.

He saw Hawkins jerk back as a sniper round burned past his shoulder, ripping fabric and gouging a crease through his deltoid that splashed blood like syrup onto the roof. Hawkins recovered, cursing, then reorientated his weapon and squeezed off a round.

"I got a RPG-29 team!" Hawkins suddenly shouted. "RPG-29!"

Manning felt himself grow cold at the words. Both he and Encizo threw themselves flat, almost instinctively. The RPG-29 was larger extension of the more common RPG-7 Soviet-era weapon. Produced in 1989, it packed a considerably larger warhead and was more accurate than its low-tech little brother.

The heavy RPG warhead streaked low over the roof, leaving a contrail of brown smoke like a linear fog just inches above the team's sprawled bodies. Encizo began swearing in rapid-fire Spanish as he rolled over and began spraying the building housing the RPG team. Using the distinctive smoke line left by the rocket, the members of Phoenix Force brought all of their fire-power to bear on the fifth floor of a Basra tenement in frantic hope of suppressing the next round from the high-explosive grenade.

"Phoenix, this is Stony Man," Price broke in. "Your team is rotors up over Basra International. ETA under two mikes. Repeat, ETA under two mikes. Pop smoke! Pop smoke."

"Copy!" Manning replied. "Smoke is good."

Suddenly an RPG-29 round erupted from a rooftop. Hawkins swiveled in his shooter's crouch and killed the gunner, but the round was already shrieking toward them, eight metallic fins popping out like switchblades to stabilize flight. It slid over the top of the parapet facade and pushed across the roof just missing a line of dirty white PVC pipes to explode against the cinder blocks of the parapet on the fire side.

The antipersonnel TBG-29V thermobaric round spread flame out, pushed hard by the concussive force of the 10 mm warhead. The parapet burst outward, spraying chunks of masonry into the street below. On the roof the members of Phoenix Force were pushed hard into the gravel-and-tar-paper roof, their bodies bruised under the explosion. James used his body to shelter the helpless McCarter as Hawkins was jerked off his knees and slammed into the low wall around the roof.

Encizo lifted his head, his vision blurry and his ears ringing from the blast. He felt half a dozen stinging wounds from shrapnel on his scalp, arm and exposed leg. He saw Jack Grimaldi sprawled out like a rag doll. The Stony Man pilot lifted his head and his face was awash with fresh blood. Encizo's own blood coated him in a sticky mess. He blinked hard against the effects of the blast and forced his vision to focus. He saw Ayub.

The Iranian had been between him and the RPG-29 warhead and had taken the brunt of the blast. The left side of his body looked like ground hamburger. The broken corpse lay in a pool of blood and the entire purpose of their mission was missing half his skull.

"Ayub is dead, goddamn it!" Encizo snarled, pushing himself up.

"Christ!" Manning echoed from only a few feet away. A long gash had been opened in the Canadian's forehead and he was bleeding freely.

"There's the chopper!" James shouted from across the roof.

Encizo and Manning turned to look and saw a fat, powerful Chinook CH-47D rolling toward them over the rooftops of the Basra slum. M-61 Vulcan cannons opened up from each side of the war bird and burped out 6,600 rounds a minute of 20 mm ammunition. Around Phoenix Force the city block began to disintegrate.

Dinner-bowl-size craters exploded from the buildings around them, the ballistic gouges coming one right on top of the other almost faster than the eye could follow, collapsing structural supports inside the buildings and causing floors to sag and crash downward. On the streets knots of fighters and vehicles were ripped apart by relentless strafing from the Vulcan autocannons as the big helicopter swooped in.

Gary Manning dropped his stolen AKM and grabbed the mutilated corpse of Ayub. With a grunt the big

Canadian picked up the dead Iranian and rushed him toward the edge of the building. He snarled and heaved the body over the edge of the building to let it tumble down to the street below.

The message was clear as it was simple.

The Chinook hovered into place next to the building and Manning saw a bearded door gunner in OD flight suit and nondescript helmet smile at him from behind mirrored aviator glasses, a burning cigarette dangling from his mouth.

Manning turned and ran toward James as the medic struggled to lift the unconscious McCarter up. The far-side Vulcan continued to fire, but even with that cover enemy fire still burned across the roof. The rotor wash battered into them like hurricane winds and the roar of the engines was deafening.

Manning reached down and lifted in unison with James, bringing McCarter up as Encizo rushed past them, half dragging a disorientated and bloody T. J. Hawkins. The Canadian and the ex-SEAL turned and jogged toward the Chinook. Through the open cargo bay James could see the Vulcan firing in a virtual sheet of flame.

They made the edge of the building and saw Encizo on the helicopter reaching out for the inert McCarter between two civilian dressed men, one white, the other Asian. The private contractors helped yank McCarter into the safety of the helicopter and immediately James scrambled in afterward as the medic team began setting up IVs and cutting his bloody clothes clear. A second later the blood-smeared Grimaldi had made his way into the helicopter.

The door gunner nearest them spit his burning cigarette out and cut loose with the Vulcan as Manning got into the helicopter. On the building four militia gunmen had gained the roof-access door and were racing forward, Kalashnikovs up and firing. Rounds arced through the open door and pinged off the armored super-structure of the Chinook. A stray round struck some interior hosing and pressurized fluid began to spray outward.

The pilot gunned the engine and lifted the Chinook upward as the door gunner used the 20 mm rounds to blow the militia fighters into bloody chunks. Manning looked over and saw James working feverishly alongside two medics in a state-of-the-art medic station.

He felt the powerful helicopter surging upward and he looked out through the open door, his adrenaline bleed-off leaving him numb and exhausted. He saw buildings torn to rubble or riddled like sieves. Bodies and parts of bodies were splattered across the street in the hard light of morning. Vehicles and buildings smoked like chimneys as flames ripped through them.

It was a hollow feeling that filled him as he watched the Shiite slum fall away. Phoenix had failed, he realized. His mouth tasted like blood and ashes. He turned to find the British mercenary grinning at him from behind the Vulcan autocannon.

"You're bloody lucky your check cleared in time, mate." The man laughed.

CHAPTER TWENTY-ONE

Tehran, Iran

Brigadier General Abdul-Ali Najafi studied his fingernails. He sat perched in a metal folding chair on a concrete floor in the middle of an airplane hangar. Hooded members of his elite Ansar-al-Mahdi Protection Corps stood sentry around him, submachine guns dangling from weapon straps.

On the floor in front of him sat a stainless-steel drain stained scarlet by the dripping blood trickling down the body of the hanging man and splashing onto the floor. The man was naked, his body covered in livid bruises and abrasions. He hung by the wrists from a length of chain attached to the blade of an industrial forklift, his arms stretched so far above and behind his head that his shoulders had popped out of their sockets. The muscles of his abdomen worked to help his lungs feed his body oxygen. His left eye had completely swollen shut and his right eye had been reduced to a slit. His cheeks looked hollow and sunken because over the course of a week every tooth in his mouth had been knocked out of his head.

Najafi opened a file folder in front of him and began leafing casually through the contents. His eyes flickered across neat rows of information and over several photographs of varying quality.

"You are Gunnery Sergeant Brian Hollister," Najafi said. "United States Marine Corps, six years. You are assigned to the Marine Expeditionary Unit, Special Operations Capable, of which a reinforced platoon tasked with scout-sniper operations has been deployed to Al-Amarah, Iraq."

Najafi looked up from his file. He cocked his head to one side and studied the tortured man hanging in front of him. He lifted his right hand and used the thumb and first finger to smooth his fastidiously trimmed mustache.

"You were, roughly speaking," Najafi continued, "discovered in Dezful sixty-five kilometers away from home and well inside the border of Iran. Your presence here constitutes an act of war on the part of the United States government against the Islamic peoples of Iran."

Bloody drool spilled out of the Marine's mouth as he tried to make his mutilated lips and broken jaw into a smile. "I told you before," he said in perfect Farsi, "I got lost in a sandstorm while tracking Iranian arms smuggler violating the border of Iraq."

"So you said," Najafi allowed. He turned and nodded once to the hooded, shirtless man standing behind the prisoner.

The Ansar-al-Mahdi Protection Corps noncommissioned officer stepped forward and lifted up a ham-size right hand. The fingers of the Iranian's fist were covered with a pair of stainless-steel brass knuckles. The interrogator dropped into a boxer's crouch and fired a hard hook into the helpless Marine's kidney with a sound like a baseball bat striking a side of hanging beef in a slaughterhouse.

Hollister moaned in shock and swung wildly on the end of his chain. He made a sound like an animal low in his chest.

"General Najafi!" a voice called from the hangar door. "General Najafi, I have a message!"

The Iranian spymaster turned away from the American. His personal assistant hurried into the hangar carrying a briefcase Najafi knew contained a secured laptop capable of a satellite uplink. As the thin man in tan robes crossed the fifty yards of open concrete toward the scene of the interrogation, Najafi removed a silver clasp case and withdrew a Turkish cigarette. He used a gold lighter to light it and exhaled a cloud of blue-gray smoke.

"What is it?" he snapped in Farsi as the man drew close.

The assistant eyed the American, then the hooded figures standing in a loose circle around the grisly scene. "It's…delicate," he said finally.

"Fine, give me the rundown," Najafi answered, speaking now in French. It was a second language he shared with the assistant and one the two men had used many times before to discuss sensitive subjects in the presence of underlings, lower-ranking organization members and, at times, members of their family.

"Our representative at Credit Suisse contacted us."

Instantly, Najafi was on alert. The second largest Swiss bank was the primary holder of money used as operational funds for the Revolutionary Guard and the more clandestine Ansar-al-Mahdi Protection Corps. Najafi managed these funds, and several of an even more covert and personal nature, beyond the oversight of the Revolutionary Council. Instantly he was keyed into what his aide-de-camp was saying.

"There is a problem?" Najafi demanded.

"Certain inquires have been made through back channels at the SIS about specific numbered accounts," the aide said, referring to the Swiss Intelligence Service. "Our representative at Credit Suisse suggests we may want to alter some of our procedures. New international antiterrorism laws have hampered banking privacy."

Najafi frowned. "Which accounts, primary or secondary?" Primary accounts were those large accounts containing funds used by the Revolutionary Guard. Secondary accounts held the black funds used by the Ansar-al-Mahdi to conduct operations beyond Iran's border.

The aide paused, clearly reluctant to admit something he knew his volatile boss was going to be unhappy to hear. His eyes shifted away from Najafi's intense gaze, and the pink tip of his tongue darted out to lick at his dry lips.

"The accounts numbers were those comprising the tertiary interests," the aide whispered.

Najafi sat back in his chair as if he had been slapped across his face. The color drained from his face and his stomach cramped into knots as cold squirts of adrenaline flooded his system. The banking representatives had been so convincing in their promises of anonymity.

Their assurances had been iron-clad, his guarantee of secrecy absolute….

Najafi lifted his cigarette to his lips and drew deeply. The end flared brightly as he inhaled the strong tobacco smoke. His eyes blinked quickly as his thoughts raced.

"The tertiary?"

The aide merely nodded.

Najafi suddenly leaped from his seat and flicked his burning cigarette to the ground. It landed in a pool of Gunnery Sergeant Hollister's blood and extinguished with an audible hiss.

"I am tired of this!" Najafi snapped in Farsi. He jerked his manicured finger at the hooded guards. "Get this infidel out of my sight!"

Instantly the Mahdi commandos sprang to obey, lowering the forklift until the American was allowed to crumple onto the blood-stained concrete floor where they began to unhook the prisoner from his chains.

Najafi stalked back and forth, pacing relentlessly. As custodian of billions of dollars in operational and covert funds utilized for purchasing power beyond Iran's border, he had very quickly discovered that opportunities abounded for him to personally enrich himself. He had approached such opportunities with vigor and used the resulting funds to acquire even greater influence and power. But such actions were treason to the Revolutionary Council and if found out, his personal wealth was his own personal death fatwa, most likely from the Ayatollah himself.

Damn those bankers! he thought furiously to himself. They had promised and now everything was in jeopardy. He stopped. It had to be the Americans. Perhaps the

Israelis, but even then only as agents to the Americans. He choked on his fear and rage as the Mahdi guards lifted Hollister.

With a strangled cry of anger the Iranian rushed forward and yanked a 9 mm pistol from the belt of one of his commandos. Cursing wildly, Najafi racked the slide and shoved the barrel against Hollister's head.

The exhausted Marine looked at the Iranian with his single eye. He pulled back his swollen and split lips in a ghastly, bloody semblance of a smile. "Fuck you," he whispered.

The pistol shot echoed off the hanger walls.

The guards dropped Hollister's corpse and backed away as the furious Najafi emptied his pistol into the broken body of the American. The Iranian intelligence manager screamed with each shot, cursing furiously and venting his anger. The gun went empty in his hand he pumped the trigger several more times, producing nothing more than a dry *click-click-click*.

Najafi threw the pistol aside in disgust and turned on the Mahdi troops. "Get out!" he screamed. "Get out now!"

Instantly the squad turned on their heels and hurried toward the door of the hangar, leaving the bloody body behind them. As the last hooded commando exited the vast, open building Najfi turned toward his aide, still breathing heavily. He lifted a shaking finger and pointed toward the laptop the slender man was carrying.

"We must hide those funds," Najafi said. "Do it. Do it now."

Fifteen minutes later he got word that his top man in Caracas was missing and his personal representative in

Basra dead. Najafi picked up the phone and dialed El Salvador. The Americans had struck and it was time to return the favor.

CHAPTER TWENTY-TWO

Washington, D.C.—the Capitol

Hal Brognola was not having a good day.

He sat in front of the Senate Panel Subcommittee on Anti-Terrorism, cursing furiously to himself. The Farm's teams had just returned and there were afteraction briefings to perform, reports to read and important decisions to make. Instead of doing that, he was sitting behind closed doors begging for his money. It made him disgusted.

He had just answered a question about presidential authority obtained for a recent mission in Russian Georgia. He had had to tell the curious senators that the operation was sealed by executive order and that their clearances were not high enough for him to disclose details to them.

Such a revelation had gone over like a loud fart in a quiet church, and when he had subsequently submitted his special access program paperwork as evidence in the hearing, the situation had just grown more tense.

"Mr. Brognola." Donald Hascomb, the senator from Virginia, spoke up. "I just have a few more questions."

"Of course, Senator," Brognola acknowledged.

The big Fed kept his face perfectly neutral. Hascomb was no friend to direct-action special operations. Hascomb performed a watchdog role to help dampen what he saw as administration excesses in counterterrorism and covert actions. If they knew the half of it, Brognola thought wryly to himself.

"My briefing indicates you work for Justice. Is this correct, Mr. Brognola?"

Brognola leaned forward and spoke into the microphone. He sat at a hardwood desk covered with his papers. The senators on the subcommittee sat at elevated positions arrayed in a half-moon in front of him. The Inquisitional accoutrements reminded him vaguely of something out of Author Miller's *The Crucible*.

"That is correct, Senator."

"What is your position?"

"As I said in my introduction, I am the head of the Sensitive Operations Group."

Hascomb made a show of reading a paper in front of him over the edges of his bifocals. He frowned, obviously displeased with what he was seeing. He lifted his eyes and regarded Brognola.

"I do not see Sensitive Operations Group listed along with any of the standard divisions, agencies or offices falling under the departmental organizational umbrella. Does the designator 'Group' mean you are a subdivision?"

Here it comes, Brognola thought. Any time politicians or lawyers started asking questions to which they already knew the answers, a setup was coming. He picked up his pen and used it to highlight three letters from among the words of the first sentence of the memorandum used to summon him to the meeting: *A-S-S.*

"Yes and no," Brognola said.

"Yes and no?" Hascomb repeated.

"SOG was intended and organized as an extra-channel formation. We existed apart from other Justice Department divisions, agencies and offices. We, in fact, as designed, bypassed the attorney general and became a cabinet seat."

Hascomb sat up as if hearing something new for the first time. Brognola gritted his teeth. "Excuse me? You are a group of the Justice Department and you bypassed the cabinet head of the Justice Department, the attorney general?" Hascomb sounded incredulous.

The only thing this circus needs now is a bearded lady and a donkey. Brognola scowled. "As head of SOG I am an adjunct but de facto member of the President's cabinet. Subordinate to the attorney general except for all matters relating to SOG deployment, personnel, funding and scope of mission. In those matters I remain subordinate only to the head of the executive branch." Brognola paused. "That's the President," he added helpfully.

"Yes," Hascomb replied, voice leaded with dryness. "I realize the President is the head of the executive branch, thank you, Mr. Brognola."

"You're welcome, Senator."

"You make yourself sound like an autonomous warlord slipping through the cracks of our bureaucracy."

Brognola remained silent. The statement had not been a question, and he would not let himself be sucked into giving away easy points. It was clear Hascomb was head-hunting now. The man took a deep breath, let it out and immediately began attacking again. For the next forty-five minutes Hal Brognola underwent the interrogation, leaving his inquisitors stymied, frustrated and angry.

During the course of his interview he received a text message that changed everything.

Washington, D.C.

BROGNOLA STOOD ON THE STEPS of the Washington Monument and looked out over the thin crowd of tourists milling around the length of the Reflecting Pool. The sky above him was the color of lead with a low cloud ceiling and the promise of rain on the chilling breeze that whipped up the edges of his tan Burberry coat. He shifted his briefcase to his off hand and dialed a number on his iPhone. He could have been a lawyer or a lobbyist or a minor bureaucrat in some anonymous government alphabet soup agency.

He plugged in the number on his speed dial and slid his iPhone back into the case on his belt, using the Bluetooth attachment to continue his conversation. While he waited for the connection to go through, he let his gaze travel over the groupings, looking for his contact.

"How are things going, Hal?" Barbara Price asked.

"Other than Senator Hascomb crawling up my ass with a magnifying glass?" Brognola returned. "Not bad. Of course, getting a text message from the Chinese consulate during my subcommittee meeting put me a little off my game."

Instantly, Price was keyed in. "The Chinese? What do they want?"

"All it said is that a representative wanted to discuss the fallout from Caracas."

Price cursed foully. "Able…Chinese involvement might possibly explain how Chavez's bully boys could end up on scene so damn fast."

"It's a possibility," Brognola admitted, still scanning the crowd. "But if they were in bed with Hugo Chavez, why contact us? For that matter, how did they trace the op to us and not the Agency's Special Activities Division or a Pentagon outfit?"

"I don't know, Hal. Maybe you could ask them when you meet."

"Very funny. Has Wethers got me up on the Key-hole yet?"

"We're locked on to your GPS signal, but we're working through the cloud cover. I still think you should have let a team of blacksuits roll backup."

"I'm not in danger. They want something."

"Everybody does."

Suddenly on the edge of the stairs Brognola caught a flash of movement out of the corner of his eye. "Going silent," he murmured.

A tall Chinese man in an immaculate Dunning & Usher executive business suit beneath a camel-hair coat approached. The man's hands were covered against the damp by black, kid leather gloves, and his Italian shoes had been polished to a high shine. His face bore an inscrutable expression.

The man walked up to the much taller Brognola and nodded once, not offering to shake hands. Hal concealed his surprise and realized why no greeting was necessary; he knew this man. He was standing in front of the deputy attaché to the Chinese ambassador—or, as it was understood in intelligence circles, the man at the top of the food chain who was responsible for all Chinese espionage efforts inside the United States.

"This is a surprise, Nung," Brognola said.

"I am here to do you a favor," the man said.

"Really?" Brognola was not going to insult the man's intelligence by claiming to be a minor functionary in the Justice Department. This was an extraordinary meeting and the sheer audacity of it made Brognola want to shiver.

"Your team did exceptionally well in Caracas."

"It seemed Chavez's top unit was onto them from the beginning. Many people would say it was an extraordinary intelligence coup for them."

Nung snorted and looked away. "Chavez is a monkey. Propped up by Moscow and not ready for prime time on the world stage. It was our agent who intercepted your communications and triangulated the signal."

"I see," Brognola said. It was surprising that Nung had so readily implicated Chinese involvement.

"Our advisers in Venezuela do their job because it is imperative that Beijing counters Russia globally, lest an imbalance of power worldwide threaten our border stability."

Brognola merely nodded. There didn't seem to be anything for him to add and he wasn't going to talk simply to hear the sound of his voice. Whatever Nung had to say, he would get to soon enough.

"The world is a very complicated place, Mr. Brognola. It is my job to help guide my country through treacherous political waters. I understand well that you and I share similar vocations, which often puts us on different sides of the same issue."

"But not in this case?"

"My superiors do not believe that a second attack of the magnitude of 9/11 would be advantageous to our relationship. A shift toward more conservative political thought by your nation could only serve to strain our national interactions."

Brognola felt a cold chill surge through his body. "You have knowledge of a planned attack on the America homeland?"

Nung nodded and reached out his hand. Brognola responded in kind and took an envelope from the Chinese intelligence operative.

"The Iranians are furious about Caracas and Basra. More volatile elements in the regime there want action. Everything you need to know is on the flash drive inside that envelope."

Nung turned his back on the big Fed and began walking away. He paused and looked back over his shoulder. "China has acted in their own best interests just now, not America's. You would do well not to forget that."

Brognola remained silent and watched the Chinese operative disappear into the crowd. He looked down at the envelope in his hand, contemplated it for several seconds, then turned and began to move toward his car at top speed.

Stony Man Farm, Virginia

BARBARA PRICE ENTERED the War Room in the basement of the main farmhouse. She found a rumpled-looking Hal Brognola sitting at the conference table reading something off his iPhone. A cup of coffee sat beside his elbow, untouched, and he needed a shave.

"You look like hell," she said, sitting next to him.

He gave her a wan smile and put away his phone. "Truth in advertising. How's Bear doing with that flash drive?"

"There was a Trojan virus inside it. Akira caught and killed it."

Brognola snorted. "Figures. But the info?"

"I've already alerted the teams," Price answered. "It

seems our Iranian friend Najafi has alerted an El Salvadorean cell. There's an attack coming. We're running on short notice and two steps behind. The Agency boys down in Camp Xray have given us some info that, when we tie it to the Chinese information, puts them in our crosshairs."

"That's our SOP," Brognola said. "Send Able after the cell. I've just been texting the Man. He wants a message sent. I want you to mobilize Phoenix and get me a plan to bring Najafi down."

Price smiled. "We're on it."

San Salvador, El Salvador

THE BARGE RODE THE WAVES on the Pacific. Its lights were blacked out, its silhouette low as it held a bearing just off the coast. The five blades of the MH-6J Little Bird began to turn. The engine started to whine as the blades began picking up speed in long, looping rotations that rapidly spun faster and faster.

Jack Grimaldi watched his rpm climb to a fever pitch, then reached over and hit the engine baffle, effectively muting the helicopter's engine noise. He took the slack up out of the yoke and felt the landing skids lift off the heavy metal plating of the barge deck.

"Airborne," he announced into the PA system.

Carl Lyons, sitting beside him in the copilot seat, looked out the blackened glass of the Little Bird's door and watched the dark shape of the barge fall away. Behind him the other two members of Able Team adjusted themselves in their three-point harnesses, primary weapons kept muzzle down between their feet.

As the lights of San Salvador swept closer, Lyons felt

the aches and pains and exhaustion of his past combat melt away. He was a hungry predator on the hunt. He was in a race and to the fleet would go the contest.

In this city, the second largest in Central America, an Iranian mission controller had launched a terrorist cell north in the United States. Able Team was here to take the man out and discover the location of the death squad now operating on American soil.

Grimaldi banked the helicopter hard, running south down the coastline toward the rural outskirts of the sprawling topography. Below them the water was dark and the jungle line a black smudge against the shoreline.

CHAPTER TWENTY-THREE

The Stony Man pilot looked up to scan the readout from his GPS display, then cut in hard toward the mainland. The Little Bird hopped over the canopy of trees and entered a small valley dotted with isolated farmhouses and acres of pasture and fields.

"We're rolling close," Grimaldi warned the team over the intercom.

"Copy," Blancanales and Schwarz echoed from the back. Lyons lifted his fist and gave a thumbs-up gesture.

Grimaldi reached out with his left hand and flipped up a red switch cover, revealing a flip-toggle guns systems ignition. He clicked the silver metal switch in the on position, and instantly the nose-mounted electronic chain gun hummed to life.

Twin FLIR spotlights clicked on, painting a two-story ranch-style villa into brilliant illumination through the team's night-vision devices. The building was solidly built and adjoined by a barn, animal pens and two large corrals filled with several horses now frightened into frantic movement by the Little Bird's approach.

The Iranians had used Escondito's connection with the infamous Salvadorean gang MS-13 to move their agents north. The farm belonged to members of the international criminal group who had managed to survive the violent ordeals of their teenage years and invest their drug and extortion profits into real estate.

In exchange for cash and weapons the MS-13 middle management crew had provided the Iranian terror cell with a safehouse. The safehouse was a crime scene with potential evidence and Able Team intended to secure the property.

The helicopter swooped in low, avoiding power lines as Grimaldi banked the Little Bird and put the skids down on the crushed gravel of the driveway. Immediately, Able Team exited the cargo bay, the bullpup Pancor Jackhammer automatic shotguns up and ready as they charged the house.

Grimaldi instantly powered the chopper up, climbing as the ground team raced forward toward the house. From his superior position the Stony Man pilot let the Little Bird drift over the sprawling one-story ranchero until his nose gun was covering the side and rear entrances.

A line of dark SUVs was parked in front of the house, the automobiles in stark contrast to some of the surrounding rural poverty. Cocaine flowed up through San Salvador toward Houston and San Diego from South America, and cash flowed back the other way. The Salvadorean bosses of MS-13 had figured out a way to secure their cut and it showed.

Lyons raced forward, breaking into a sweat in the heat and humidity of the Central American tropical zone. As far as Brognola and the Stony Man crew could ascertain, the Iranian terror cell was already boots down on homeland soil and when presented with a race for time Carl Lyons always chose blunt-force trauma as his preferred fallback play.

Even with the mufflers engaged the Little Bird's engine noise was obvious. Rotor wash beat down on the team in a persistent gale. Their plan for the surprise advantage in this case relied not on stealth, but on speed and violence of action.

Able Team jogged forward in a loose triangular phalanx, cutting through the rows of parked SUVs, their autoguns up and ready to unleash a torrent of .12-gauge metal storm at the first sign of resistance. Once the scene had been pacified, then mercy was an option, but until then Able remained as keyed up as a school of sharks on the verge of a feeding frenzy.

Lyons shifted his gaze back and forth as he jogged up the lawn toward the front door. The house was quiet and dark, a discrepancy to the coke-fueled activity he would have assumed customary to a MS-13 gang haunt. The hairs on the back of his neck stood on end with an almost preternatural suspicion.

He watched the front door set up off the lawn by a low, wide veranda. Curtains obscured dark windows; nowhere was there a sign of motion. Over the house the Little Bird hovered like a Jurassic insect bathing the structure in IR spotlights visible only through their night-vision devices.

Lyons felt Schwarz and Blancanales drift out farther toward his flank in unspoken agreement. He drew a breath and felt his body ache in response from the battering it had taken. His torso, as well as those of his teammates, was covered with deep, punishing bruises.

Two steps more and he was around the canopy of a Ford F-350 on monstrous tires. He slowed and narrowed his eyes against the gloom. He came to a stop, looking down. Schwarz and Blancanales caught his motion and held up themselves.

The body lay sprawled on the ground, the limbs splayed out. The dark-skinned, muscular figure was dressed in a white ribbed-cotton tank top perforated with bloody divots. An M-16 A-2 lay a yard off in the dark grass. The man's jaw was slack and his pink tongue lolled out, his eyes bulging until the whites seemed big as saucers.

"Shit," Lyons whispered.

He lifted his head and looked toward the house. On the low veranda he saw a second corpse, partially obscured by an overturned piece of patio furniture. The top of the corpse's head had been cored out and a Remington 870 pump shotgun lay just out of reach of noodle-slack fingers.

"They've been hit already!" Blancanales swore.

Glass broke as the picture windows on the front of the house exploded outward. Starfish patterns of muzzle-flashes winked from the darkness and the metallic crescendo of full-auto weapons fire erupted.

Hermann Schwarz went down instantly, dropping face-first onto the lawn without a word, his weapon unfired. Blancanales had the bullpup Jackhammer up and returning fire even as Lyons unleashed his own combat shotgun. The twin .12-gauge autoguns burped a lead net toward the structure. Bullets whined off the luxury SUVs to either side of Blancanales as he walked his own fire across the front door and dumped four rounds through the first window. The curtains jumped and danced as his blasts cut through the hanging fabric. He saw a dark form stagger backward, the unmistakable outline of an H&K MP-5 SD-3 in one wild thrown hand.

Blancanales held up his fire long enough to adjust his

aim and Lyons triggered his weapon into the lull, shredding the front of the house with his shotgun blasts. A large-caliber rifle on full auto suddenly burped out of the darkness of the house with a sharp staccato of overlapping bangs. The heavy metal slugs ripped through the air in spinning tornados, forcing Lyons onto the ground and sending Blancanales spinning off behind a vehicle.

With sledgehammer blows the 7.62 mm rounds smashed into a car behind Lyons and walked up the body of the vehicle. Divots the size of golf balls crumpled the frame and shattered the glass of the windows before a tracer round scorched into the gas tank and ignited the SUV.

It exploded in a ball of yellow flame and black smoke, sending heat and car parts rolling out with lethal force. Lyons, already on the ground, felt the flesh of his exposed skin redden and then tighten instantly as the heat burned him. His face was driven into the gravel of the driveway and he heard Blancanales curse in fury at the sudden assault.

Hermann Schwarz remained unmoving.

Suddenly the Little Bird was overhead, the beat of its rotor wash blowing the flames back as Jack Grimaldi swung the helicopter around. The nose gun opened up with relentless, merciless fury, and empty shell casings rained down like hail. The machine-gun rounds tore into the building, ripping it apart.

The walls and roof were ripped open as if a chainsaw had been taken to the structure. Glass shattered into slivers and shards, and stucco was cracked and battered into craters and chunks the size of plates. Lyons forced himself up and forward to take advantage of the cover offered by Grimaldi's guns to make his approach.

His body screamed at him in protest even through the adrenaline surge that powered him. The Pancor Jackhammer .12-gauge felt heavy in his hand, and the metallic curve of the trigger was slick with his sweat as he made the porch.

Muzzle up Lyons entered through the bullet-riddled remnants of the front door.

Stony Man Farm, Virginia

HAL BROGNOLA SURVEYED Phoenix Force with a sour eye.

The team looked exhausted, beat to the bone and heavily abused. In the vernacular of his early days with the FBI, they looked rode hard and put away wet. And, he reflected, if wet meant bloody then by God the cliché was an aphorism.

Setting down his coffee mug Brognola eased back into his seat. His eyes flickered to the wall screen above Kurtzman's head. A map of the Middle East, centered on Iran, was up on the HD screen. A digital readout in the lower left-hand corner showed the current time in Tehran.

Just as impressive in his diligence and sense of duty had been the heavily battered Jack Grimaldi. The pilot had upon return simply swallowed a fistful of painkillers with a couple of go pills the military prescribed pilots on long missions and had taken off to support Able Team in Central America.

At the huge conference table in the farmhouse's War Room, Calvin James studied his PDA intently, reading David McCarter's updates and medical charts, committing the information to memory. Manning was going over Kurtzman's report on Najafi, page by page, as

Encizo discussed the situation quietly with a tired-looking Barbara Price.

T. J. Hawkins sat a little apart from the others, his brow furrowed as he read the U.S. Army Special Forces Detachment—Delta, also known as the Combat Applications Group, manual on in-flight takedown protocols.

Everyone in the room was drinking Kurtzman's coffee without the usual round of mandatory quips and sarcasm—a sure sign of overwork. But, Brognola noted to himself, overwork was the primary operational zone for Stony Man. He took out his iPhone and sent a text message of instructions to his secretary back in the Justice Department. He had an 8:15 a.m. meeting with a liaison from Homeland Security he would have to bump to just after lunch.

The door to the War Room opened and every head turned to watch Carmen Delahunt as she rushed into the room. The redhead looked slightly breathless and her hair was mussed from where she'd obviously been wearing her VR helmet.

Unfazed at finding herself the center of attention, she turned and addressed Kurtzman where he sat in his chair next to the broad form of Gary Manning. "We pulled it off," she said simply.

Kurtzman's grizzled face split into an evil grin. "You guys managed to hack a Swiss bank?"

"It was the battle of supercomputers." The ex-FBI agent smiled. "That firewall in Berne was better than what the Russians are using. But the contents of Najafi's personal accounts have been transferred and warning systems sent to update him on the transfer. Akira is inside the Ansar-al-Mahdi system." She paused, then added, "The Swiss could teach that crew something about encryption and ICE measures."

"Did Najafi take the bait?" Brognola leaned forward and demanded.

Delahunt flashed him a vicious, triumphant smile. "Yes, he did, Hal. You bet your ass he did. Once he thought his personal money was in danger he went into overdrive. He's making his excuses now—in order to close out and transfer an account of that size he'll need to be on site, in Berne."

Barbara Price leaned forward, eyes glittering and bright with her excitement. "That means a plane, and that means the Caspian Sea which means international water and airspace, which means once the son of a bitch is airborne he's ours."

Brognola leaned forward, face grim. "That's just exactly right. The Man could not have been any clearer on this. If the Revolutionary Guard wants a shadow war, then we're going to give them one at every turn. And we're not going to burn ourselves out killing foot soldiers, either."

"Conflict by coup d'etat," Manning said with grim satisfaction. Next to him Calvin James and Rafael Encizo both nodded their heads in agreement. At the end of the table T. J. Hawkins looked primed, the left side of his face a massive blue-black bruise.

"Exactly," Brognola agreed. "Precisely."

Barbara Price turned and took in Phoenix with an encompassing, motivated gaze. "You boys ready to take a plane ride?"

THIRTY MINUTES LATER Stony Man auxiliary pilot Charlie Mott ferried the prepped and primed Phoenix Force to the secured-access landing strip of Wright-

Patterson Air Force Base within spitting distance of the infamous Hangar 18. There the team boarded a special-operations-capable version of the B-2 Spirit Stealth Bomber.

The bomb bay had been modified into a personnel transport area, and ten minutes after loading their weapons and gear onto the clandestine aircraft they were en route toward their Atlantic crossing.

San Salvador, El Salvador

MOVING IN A PRECISE DRILL the Stony Man duo advanced under fire toward the lavish house. They approached a long series of Italian doors issuing smoke through the blown-out glass. They moved in a bounding overwatch, modified to exploit speed, but basically consisting of one commando holding security while the next leap-frogged forward to the next point of offered cover.

Twice their path was cut by armed men rushing to help engage the swooping Little Bird. The first time Blancanales took the shirtless man down with a short burst, followed up immediately by Lyons's finishing shot to the head. The second time a shoeless, bearded fighter with the build of a professional bodybuilder sprinted around a tight cluster of native Brazilian walnut trees with a drum-fed AKM in his massive fists.

Both Able Team warriors turned and fired simultaneously from the hip without breaking stride. The two-angled fire cut the giant of a man into ribbons and knocked him back among the decorative stand of trees.

As Lyons and Blancanales ran they could hear people screaming from around the compound and once they heard a ragged machine-gun burst answered immediately by Charlie Mott's M-134 minigun. Lyons cleared the deck over a line of concrete pillars supporting a low, wide stone rail encircling the patio. The explosive force of hand grenades had cracked and pitted its surface, but failed to break the stone railing.

Lyons landed on mosaic tile, waves of heat from the burning building washing over him and casting weird shadows close in around him. He saw a flat stone bench and took up a position behind it, going down to one knee. He began scanning the long line of patio doors with his main weapon while Blancanales bounded forward.

Blancanales passed Lyons's hasty fighting position in a rush and put his back to a narrow strip of wall set between two ruined patio doors. He kept his weapon at port arms and turned his head toward the opening beside him. From inside the dark structure flames danced in a wild riot.

Blancanales nodded sharply and Lyons rose in one swift motion, bringing the buttstock of his M-4 up to his shoulder as he breached the opening. He shuffled past Blancanales, sweeping his weapon in tight, predetermined patterns as he entered the building. Based on what he was seeing, Lyons made the snap decision that this wasn't a rival criminal network raid but was, in fact, an elite Iranian cleaner crew.

Blancanales folded in behind him, deploying his weapon to cover the areas opposite Lyons's pattern. It felt as if they had rushed headlong into a burning oven. Heavy tapestries, Latin rugs and silk curtains all burned bright and hot. Smoke clung to the ceiling and filled the room to a height of five feet, forcing the men to crouch.

In a far corner the two men saw a sprawling T-shaped stair of highly polished Mexican woodwork now smoldering in the heat. A wide-open floor plan accentuated groupings of expensive furniture clustered together by theme.

The bombs had rendered much of the floor plan superfluous. Slowly the two men turned so that their backs were to each other, their weapon muzzles tracking through the smoke and uncertain light. Smoke choked their lungs and stung their eyes. They saw the inert shape of several bodies cast about the room among the splinters of shattered furniture. One body lay sprawled on the smoldering staircase, hands outflung and blood pouring down the steps like stream water cascading over rocks.

Lyons moved slowly through the burning wreckage, amazed that it had been unobservable from the outside. Approaching twisted bodies, he searched the bruised and bloody faces for traces of recognition.

From the beginning of this campaign Lyons had felt more like a frontline soldier on this battlefield than on others in his endless campaigns leading Able Team. His combat was directed not against a specific, identifiable enemy led by a single powerful or charismatic figure, but rather an army with officers and troops but no single embodiment of the evil he faced. Like an assault force smashing through emplaced defenses to sweep behind enemy lines, Lyons had killed the enemy as they appeared in front of him with little information to personalize his struggle by. He grasped that this man Najafi had put everything into motion, but the layers between the Iranian and Lyons seemed huge.

Now he had driven his enemy in front of him, battered him into a final, defensive stand and Lyons risked all to deliver the knockout blow that would shatter the organizational capability of the Iranian's terrorist syndicate. His engagement would not be finished until he had assured that the dragon's head was cut off and cauterized. Any clue that could lead him to the location of the terror cell now operating within the Homeland had to be pursued at any cost.

Lyons searched the dead for the faces of his enemy's leadership cadre. Around him the heat grew more intense and the smoke billowed thicker. Blancanales moved with the same quick, methodical efficiency, checking the bodies as they vectored in toward the stairs.

Lyons sensed more than saw the motion from the top of the smoldering staircase. He barked a warning even as he pivoted at the hips and fired from the waist. His shotgun lit up in his hands and his blasts streamed across the room in violent swaths of lead.

CHAPTER TWENTY-FOUR

Lyons's .12-gauge rounds chewed into the staircase and snapped railings into splinters as he sprayed the second landing. One of his rounds struck the gunman high in the abdomen, just under the xiphoid process in the solar plexus. The massive slug speared up through the smooth muscles of diaphragm, ripped open the bottom of the lungs and cored out the left atrium of the gunman's pounding heart. Bright scarlet blood squirted like water from a faucet as the target staggered backward.

The figure, indistinct in the smoke, triggered a burst that hammered into the steps before pitching forward and striking the staircase. The faceless gunman tumbled forward, limbs loose and his head made a distinct thumping sound as it bounced off each individual step on the way down, leaving black smears of blood on the wood grain as it passed.

Lyons sprang forward, heading fast for the stairs. Blancanales spun in a tight 180-degree circle to cover their six as he edged out to follow Lyons. He saw silhouettes outside through the blown-out frames of the patio doors and he let loose with a wall of lead.

One shadow fell sprawling across the concrete divider and the rest of the silhouettes scattered in response to Blancanales's fusillade. Blancanales danced sideways, found the bottom of the stairs and started to back up it. Above him he heard Lyons curse and then his weapon blazed.

To Blancanales's left a figure reeled back from a window. Another came to take its place, the star-pattern burst illuminating a manically hate-twisted face of strong Middle Eastern features. The Phoenix Force commando put a double tap into his head from across the burning room and the man fell away.

"Those were the Iranians," Lyons shouted.

"Clean 'em out and loot the bodies—it's all we have," Blancanales answered immediately.

Lyons nodded and let loose with three bursts of harassing fire aimed at the line of French doors facing out to the rear patios and lawns as Blancanales spun on his heel and pounded up the steps past Lyons. Outside, behind the cover of the concrete pillared railing, an enemy combatant popped up from his crouch, the distinctive outline of an RPG-7 perched on his shoulder.

Down on one knee, Lyons fired an instinctive blast, but the shoulder-mounted tube spit flame in a plume from the rear of the weapon and the rocket shot out and into the already devastated house. Lyons turned and dived up the stairs as the rocket crossed the big room below him and struck the staircase.

The warhead detonated on impact and Lyons shuddered under the force and heat, but the angle of the RPG had been off and the construction of the staircase itself channeled most of the blast force downward and away from where Lyons lay sprawled. Enough force surged upward to send Lyons reeling even as he huddled against the blast. He tucked into a protective ball and absorbed the blunt waves.

He lifted his head and saw James standing above him, feet spread wide for support and firing in single blast of savage, accurate fire. Lyons lifted his Pancor and the assault shotgun came apart in his hands. He flung the broken pieces away from him in disgust and felt his wrist burn and his hand go slick with spilling blood as the stitches from his Caracas wound came apart under the abuse, and his injured ankle screamed in pain.

He ignored the hot, sticky feeling of the blood and cleared his .357 Magnum pistol from its underarm sling. He pushed himself up and turned over as Blancanales began to engage more targets. As he twisted he saw something move from the hallway just past the open landing behind his fellow Stony Man operator.

Lyons extended his arm with sharp reflexes and stroked the trigger on the big pistol. A single .357 Magnum round found the creeping enemy high in the chest, just below the throat.

The killer's breastbone cracked under the pressure. The back of the target's neck burst outward in a spray of crimson and pink as the massive round burrowed its way clear.

"Go! Go!" Blancanales shouted. He bent and snatched up a fallen M-4, then swung it back and forth in covering fire as Lyons scrambled past him to claim the high ground.

Lyons pushed himself off the stairs and onto the second floor. Stepping over the bloody corpse of his target, he turned and began to aim and fire the .357 Magnum in tight blasts.

Under his covering fire Blancanales wheeled on his heel and bounded up the stairs past Lyons. At the top of the landing he threw himself down and took aim through the staircase railing to engage targets below him in the open great room.

From superior position the two Able Team warriors rained death on their enemies.

"Hold the stairs!" Lyons growled, rising to his feet. "I'll check the site, then we'll un-ass the AO."

"Get 'er done," Blancanales acknowledged as he coolly worked the trigger on his stolen M-4.

Lyons moved quickly down the hallway. Smoke burned his throat and irritated his eyes, obscuring his vision as he hunted. He worked quickly, checking behind doors as he moved down the hall. Flames kept the corridor oven-hot and the hair and clothes on still, broken bodies smoldered as Lyons moved to verify the dead.

In several places he found that the collapse of the two floors above had penetrated down onto the second story, cracking open the bedroom ceilings and dumping broken furniture and flaming debris like rockslides. Lyons scrambled over mounds of rubble and skirted charred holes dropping away beneath his feet.

Behind him Lyons heard Blancanales's smooth trigger work keeping the enemy at bay. He refused to waste energy on being angry, but deep inside of him he was frustrated at his own intelligence failure that had missed such a huge number of combatants in the compound. He couldn't afford to let it cloud his attention now.

He came upon a body and picked up the head by the hair. The face looked as if it had been taken apart by a tire iron and was puffy, bruised and covered in blood, but Lyons was still able to identify the man as a leftover MS-13 street soldier.

He turned the corner in the L-shaped hallway and saw the corridor blocked. An avalanche of ceiling beams, flooring, ruined furniture and body parts had dropped through the third floor and completely obstructed the hall. Flames ran in fingers off the cave-in, spreading heat and destruction with rapid ferocity. The Iranians had been liberal in their use of thermite and HE grenades, and Lyons realized the primary assault on the compound could have only been finished mere moments before his own untimely arrival.

A bit of debris fell through the roof and Lyons looked up. His eyes widened and he stepped forward to get a better look. Dangling from the hole was a mahogany Savali Pristine briefcase made from dyed crocodile hide, a prized status symbol in EU boardrooms and just the sort of thing a man like Juan Escondito would have given out to his couriers. The Savali case hung from a pair of blue steel handcuffs attached to a blood-smeared arm.

"Well, look at that," he murmured.

Lyons raised his arm and touched the bottom of the crocodile hide case. He stood on his toes and grasped the Savali Pristine case with a firmer hold. Realizing he was going to have to yank the whole body down to get the case, Lyons pulled hard.

There was a brief moment of resistance, then the case came loose in his hand so suddenly he was overbalanced and went stumbling back. His heel caught on a length of wood and he almost fell. He back-pedaled like a pass receiver then cut to the side and came up against the wall.

He looked down at the case in his hand. The case was still attached to the blood-smeared wrist by the dark metal handcuffs. A man's arm hung from the dangling chain. It ended in a ragged tear at the elbow. Bloody muscle and tendon hung in scraps from the open wound.

Sweating, Lyons looked up through the hole and saw only more flames. He felt a grudging acceptance that it was unlikely anyone in the floors above could have survived the intensely burning fire. He dropped his gory artifact onto the hot ground and knelt to one knee, pinning the disembodied forearm to the ground with his leg.

He drew his boot knife and went to work to free the arm from the handcuff. When the hand dropped out of the handcuff to one side, Lyons clutched the Savali briefcase under one arm and rose. He used the back of his web harness to secure the potential find and continued on.

He backed up to the edge of the corner and pulled a grenade from his web gear suspenders. The AN-M14 TH3 incendiary hand grenade weighed as much as two cans of beer and had a lethal radius of over 20 meters that spread its burning damage out to 36 meters; in the hallway its destruction would be concentrated, spreading fire and contributing greatly to the overall structural instability of the building.

Lyons yanked the pin on the hand grenade and let the arming spoon fly. He lobbed the compact canister underhand and let it bounce down the short stretch of hall before ducking around the corner to safety. The delay fuse was four seconds, which gave him plenty of time to achieve safety.

Both he and Blancanales carried the incendiary grenades. They were heavier than some other, more modern hand grenade versions but their power was undisputed and they made a nice compromise to more powerful but larger satchel charges.

Lyons moved in a fast crouch toward the once ornate landing where Blancanales fired down from his defensive vantage point to cover Lyons's search-and-destroy mission. Lyons spoke into his throat mike.

"Able to Stony. I have a structural blockage. Our operation is finished. Site destruction verified to acceptable factor of certainty. Over."

Caspian Sea

THE B-52 STEALTH BOMBER streaked across the night sky.

The black wedge dropped out of the cloud ceiling and came into a trajectory of a the Boeing 777 flying two thousand feet below them. Inside the cockpit the black-helmeted, black-visored pilot crew began their preparations for final approach.

The copilot reached over with a black-gloved finger and hit the intercom button. Instantly his voice was transmitted to the cramped troop transport area, where Phoenix Force was huddled close together in the staging bay. All four men raised their heads as the internal communications system broke squelch.

"Heads up, Phoenix," the copilot said. "We have the target in sight and will be initiating an approach."

"Copy, Nighthawk," Manning replied.

The Stealth aircraft suddenly shifted sharply to starboard and plunged downward so precipitously that the drop was felt acutely in the pressurized staging area. Rafael Encizo, oxygen mask in place, reached out with one hand and grabbed a maneuvering handle set into the wall above their folding canvas bench seats to compensate for the sudden shift. The closed, cramped environment of the staging area reminded the Cuban more of immersion launch chambers in submarines than the troop area of an aircraft.

Next to him in the crowded launch bay, Gary Manning swung around in his seat and powered up the digital control panel for the hydraulic umbilical air-to-air access tube. The inertia of the rapidly shifting Stealth aircraft caused him to sway slightly in his seat, pulling against his restraint harness.

Next to him T. J. Hawkins, the designated breach trooper on the insertion, unlimbered his H&K MP-7 and gently rested the muzzle of the sound suppressor on the floor between his black canvas jungle boots. As the B-52 leveled out, Calvin James placed his own silenced submachine gun at the ready and then leaned forward and bumped knuckles with the Texan.

"You ready to do this?" the ex-SEAL asked.

Hawkins offered an evil grin, his eyes dilating as adrenaline flushed into his system like amphetamines. "Hey, diddle-diddle, right up the middle, baby."

The pilot's voice came over the intercom. "We have achieved synchronistic pattern, Phoenix."

"Copy," Manning replied, his voice like cold gravel. "Initiating breach procedures."

"Understood," the pilot replied. The faceless voice seemed to hesitate, then the Air Force flyer added, "I'll keep it tight, Phoenix. You can depend on me, but if they shift orbit I have standing orders to use the emergency detach."

"I understand, Nighthawk," Manning said. "We're on top of it."

"Good copy," the pilot replied, and the intercom clicked off.

"In the hole, Phoenix," Manning said to the team. "Let's go up and get some payback for David."

Hawkins slapped him hard on one massive shoulder and pulled himself into a standing position. He reached up and placed his left hand on the safety lever to the egress hatch set into the roof of the B-52 airframe. Encizo unbuckled his seat belt and reached up to grasp an overhead strut and eased into position directly behind Hawkins, checking to secure the 40-round box magazine of 4.6 mm hardened steel bullets. Calvin James dialed the focus on the Zeiss scope attached to his own MP-7 into alignment and took his own place.

Manning flipped on the external camera. Instantly the massive belly of the Boeing 777 appeared in the viewfinder. The Canadian reached out and used a switch on his control panel to aim a laser at the cargo hatch. The feedback readout placed the hatch in precise metrics and an indicator light on the panel blinked from red to green.

"Initiating umbilical," Manning said.

His gloved finger found the button and depressed it. Instantly there was a whir of powerful servo-motors from overhead. Inside on his screen Manning watched as the tube lifted out of its streamlined housing and rose straight up for two yards to attach to the bottom of the much larger 777. He struck the enter button on his keyboard and sent a small ionized charge through the inert magnets—causing them to click from passive to active.

The Stealth bomber was now linked to the much larger aircraft. A mishap or discovery at this stage could send the smaller plane tumbling off through the air. A line of sweat broke out on Manning's forehead. He typed a command quickly and the whoosh as the umbilical was pressurized was clearly audible.

He turned toward Hawkins, who stood with his hand ready on the level. "Go," he snapped.

Hawkins squeezed the release lever and the hatch popped open with a soft, dull thunk as the rubberized prophylactic seal was broken and the lid popped up. Without hesitation Hawkins moved upward, his MP-7 dangling as his hands found the rungs of the umbilical's internal ladder.

The Texan scrambled up the ladder, almost overcome by intense vertigo as he realized it was only a thin polyurethane synthetic housing between him and 35,000 feet of open sky. He frowned and pushed himself upward. Below him Encizo appeared in the mouth of the umbilical.

Hawkins reached the cargo hatch of the 777. The roar of the Boeing jet's big engines was overwhelming, turning everything into white noise. He grasped the clasp to the cargo handler latch and unsealed the door. Below him at the control panel Manning worked the keyboard, adapting to the swiftly changing air pressure. A red bar graph screen flashed open in the upper right-hand quadrant of his monitor and he held his breath as he waited for it to flash green. The red line dropped in a free fall down to a readout of 34 percent then blinked twice, switched to green and the line began to climb, hitting 98 percent in seconds before blinking out. The secondary display screen folded inward and disappeared a moment later.

Manning activated the plane's intercom. "Nighthawk, we have engagement and transfer."

"Copy, Phoenix."

"I'm leaving this station and sealing aircraft egress hatch."

"Good luck and godspeed," the pilot replied.

"Copy. Phoenix out," Manning replied, and shut down the intercom.

The Phoenix Force commandos were on their own.

CHAPTER TWENTY-FIVE

Manning shut down the egress hatch on the B-52, feeling the vibration of the Stealth aircraft's powerful engines through the metal. As soon as the seal was engaged the sensory units inside the doorway tripped the binary code and control of the umbilical switched automatically to the Stealth's copilot.

Manning looked up in time to see the soles of Hawkins's combat boots disappear into the dark belly of the Iranian 777. Quickly, Encizo crawled up after him and pulled himself into the cargo bay. James turned and looked down at Manning.

"You good?" James asked.

Manning nodded. "Hit it."

James turned and scrambled up into the enemy aircraft. Manning climbed up a few rungs, listening for any indication that the team had been compromised during their breach. Hearing none, he finished converting the system and crawled through the opening.

It was hot and dark in the hold of the 777. Manning saw the hunched forms of his team pulling security and quickly worked to secure the cargo hatch. As the link sealed, the air pressure in the umbilical changed, alerting the aircrew of the Stealth to the team's successful transfer. Instantly the copilot gave the command and deionized the magnetic couplings. The servo-motors whined as the seal broke and the tube collapsed backward into its housing. The pilot eased off his propulsion and twisted to the starboard. The Stealth aircraft dropped away and banked out into the blackness, gone.

Manning lifted his eyes and found his three teammates looking at him. He nodded once. "Let's roll," he whispered.

Stony Man Farm, Virginia

OUT ON THE LANDING STRIP, the rotors on the Osprey turned in slow loops. They swung around in a lumbering rhythm, pushing the branches of the orchard trees down, knocking leaves to the grass. The whine of the turboprops stirred in the background, drowning out the other sounds of the night.

Hal Brognola stood on the runway, back to the rotor wash that picked up the ends of his trench coat and pushed them around like kites on a string. Beside him the smooth silhouette of Barbara Price stood in counterbalance to his blocky form. Her honey-blond hair stirred and fanned out like a flag in the wind of the Osprey V-22 VTOL machine.

Carl Lyons and Rosario Blancanales got out of the Chevy Blazer that had ferried them up from the Farmhouse barracks. The two battered veterans were bulky in their battle armor and festooned with weapons. It had been a hellish eighteen hours that had brought them to this point, but their gait was still athletic, their faces still determined.

And miles to go before I sleep, Brognola thought yet again to himself. The refrain was with him always at Stony Man. The lines by Robert Frost played themselves in an endless loop through the big Fed's mind.

"How you feeling?" Brognola called out to what remained of Able Team.

"Just peachy, boss," Lyons snapped. "More word on Gadgets?"

Price nodded, her features almost aquiline in the stark light of the landing field. "He's fine—they saved the eye. We arranged to have him in the same room as McCarter at Bethesda. They are both expecting full recovery."

Lyons nodded then looked at Blancanales, who nodded back. The Puerto Rican was unusually silent, and Brognola could read his worry over the wounded Schwarz like a billboard.

"We have the FBI's hostage-rescue team positioned to serve as the anvil to your hammer," Price said. "D.C. SWAT will be doing security operations outside the building and the Man will be watching the takedown from a closed-circuit feed." Price paused, then offered the grim-faced commandos a wry smile. "So don't fuck up."

Despite themselves the two men returned the grin. Tracing the terror cell to the D.C. ghetto with the information they had obtained in San Salvador had proved almost surprisingly easily. Forged credit cards originating from the same Swiss bank account as the one Kurtzman and his team had hacked to put Brigadier General Abdul-Ali Najafi onto an emergency flight out of Tehran had been traced to the purchase of a loft apartment on the second floor of a partially renovated textile factory in an industrial section of the Potomac.

For the past forty-five minutes the Washington Metropolitan Police Special Weapons and Tactics teams had been infiltrating the area, keeping the platoon-size terror cell under surveillance and putting roadblocks in place. The Department of Justice plan, formulated out of Brognola's SOG offices, had been simple. The FBI's elite counterterrorism unit, the Hostage Rescue Team, would strike from the ground floor while Able made entry into the building by rappel to the roof. In a classic pincer movement the two U.S. elements would work together.

The elements linking the terror operatives to their command and control was already established. No investigation or interrogations would be necessary. Because the continued survival of the terrorist had the potential to be a liability Able Team had been given the nod over the FBI's HRT.

The Stony Man rules of engagement were considerably more flexible than those of the FBI.

Brognola and Price watched as Lyons and Blancanales boarded the VTOL aircraft, each of them lost in their own thoughts. Then the hatch closed on the Osprey and they were snapped from their private reveries. Behind them they knew the Farm was bustling with activity and that even as they returned to the Stony Man Annex that Phoenix Force was engaged in a life-and-death-struggle almost forty thousand feet in the air.

Behind them the massive Pratt-Whitey turboprops screamed and the Osprey jumped up into the air, headed for Washington, D.C.

OUT ON THE EDGE of Potomac, the Osprey began to power down and the turboprops began to change with the whine of the big engines. The angle of propulsion changed and Carl Lyons felt his center of balance shift in a sensation he associated strongly with helicopters. The back hatch of the V-22 was open and the lights of the nation's capital stretched out below him in a checkerboard pattern.

The Osprey slowed even further and the ex-LAPD detective swung the barrel of his sniper rifle around while beside him Blancanales, serving as a spotter, used a pair of Zeiss binoculars to walk him around his target.

The 7 mm bolt-action rifle was fitted with a powerful scope capable of ambient-light amplification. Blancanales read off the wind speed from the gauge display on his binos and Lyons dialed it into the scope, adjusting the crosshairs. The pair repeated the procedure, factoring in altitude, as well.

On the roof of the target building a figure suddenly filled Lyons's scope. "Gotcha," he whispered, and dialed in.

The man's face, sharp-featured under longish black hair with a full mustache that made Lyons think of a 1970s Burt Reynolds, filled the viewfinder. The Iranian had turned toward the sound of the lumbering Osprey and his questioning look was readily apparent on his face through the powerful scope.

Lyons squeezed the trigger and turned the expression into a bloody crater.

The Iranian sentry jerked under the impact and tumbled to the roof, as loose as a rag doll. The sniper rifle recoiled smoothly into Lyons's shoulder and he automatically pulled the bolt back, kicking the brass shell out and seating a second one out of habit though it was obvious a second shot wouldn't be necessary.

Beside Lyons, Blancanales gave a low whistle of appreciation at the shot. The Puerto Rican reached up and hit the push-to-talk button on his flight helmet's mike.

"All clear. Bring us in," he told the pilot.

"Copy," Grimaldi replied. "Prepare to initiate ropes."

Blancanales and Lyons heaved the fast ropes out of the rear of the Osprey. The thick hemp ropes were as big as fire poles as their free ends dropped to the rooftop fifty feet below. Beside them a blacksuit with a M-249 SAW machine gun covered the two members of Able Team as they plunged downward, holding on with welder's gloves to reduce friction burns.

Lyons jolted onto the roof, bending at the knees to absorb the impact. He stepped clear of the rope and swept his Pancor Jackhammer up, tracking the muzzle of the automatic shotgun. Blancanales hit the roof next to him and quit the rope, swinging his own Pancor up to cover Lyons on the flank and rear. The Osprey gunned hard and flew away.

The roof of the warehouse was flat and wide, like a hundred Lyons had been on before. Conduits, air vents, pipes and coaxial housings covered the flat plane, punctuated by the occasional skylight. It was an obstacle course that lent itself readily to tripping up and slowing down anyone moving across the space carelessly. An industrial crane about the size of a subcompact car was perched at one edge and a small shack housing the building access door was positioned dead center.

"Let's go." Blancanales nodded, thrusting his chin toward the door.

Lyons nodded and began moving quickly toward the building egress point. The Pancor was a comforting weight in his hands, its bullpup design giving the heavy weapon a balanced feel.

"Able in position," Lyons said into his throat mike.

"Copy," Price answered immediately. "HRT has been alerted and are moving into ground position to seal exits."

Almost immediately, as if on cue, gunfire rang out from terrorist sentries. Rounds tore from the building access door, sweeping Blancanales to his belly. Luckily his body armor absorbed the impacts, but Blancanales had also been hit on his shoulder.

Lyons spun, pumped two .12-gauge blasts into the single shooter, then dropped to his knee beside the moaning Blancanales. His partner's voice was strained and he was cradling a shoulder, his arm now useless.

"Evac! Evac!" Lyons shouted into his throat mike.

"Copy," the FBI helicopter pilot answered. "En route."

Blancanales lifted a hand and put it on Lyon's arm as the man scanned the rooftop for further threats.

"Go," he told Lyons. "They're coming, I'll be fine. Go."

Lyons looked up, saw the inbound EVAC chopper and nodded once curtly. "I'll finish this," he promised.

Then he went.

Caspian Sea

HAWKINS WORKED QUICKLY while the rest of Phoenix waited, poised with weapons up and ready. The Texan inserted det cord into a special shaped lining designed to concentrate the explosive blast into a knife edge of force. Once the yard or so of cord had been inserted into the sleeve, he pulled the tacking of the adhesive surface and placed it in a coil pattern directly on the aircraft door.

"Ready," he warned.

Immediately, the other three men moved outward, clearing a lane for the backblast from the breaching charge. Hawkins yanked out the timing cord on the ignition primer and let it fall back. The charge quickly burned down as the ex–Delta Force operator scooted into the cargo hold and clear of the explosion.

As a unit Phoenix Force turned their heads away from the blast and opened their mouths to compensate for the violent change in pressure while stuffing their fingers into their ears.

The bang was sharp and violent and the cargo hold filled with white smoke as the door was thrust forward off its hinges and cracked perfectly down the middle. The pieces of the hatch shot forward into the lower passenger section of the massive Boeing 777.

Hawkins swung around and brought his weapon to bear, lifting the H&K MP-7 and charging up the molded metal scaffolding stair. He gained the doorway and pushed through, folding left and sweeping the muzzle of his submachine around. Directly behind him, Calvin James sprinted through the opening and folded right.

Rafael Encizo peeled off behind Hawkins as Gary Manning copied James's motions. The team found themselves in a narrow access hall leading to the storage area behind the banquet dining compartment. It was crammed and narrow with wall-mounted hatches. White smoke from the breaching charge hung heavy in the air, and the cracked eggshell of a door lay in two smoldering pieces on the cross-checked rubber matting of the floor.

A uniformed figure rose up from the ground still stunned by the unexpected explosion. Hawkins, keyed up in his dynamic entry, put a 3-round burst into him and knocked him back down to the floor.

Shuffling forward, Hawkins led his teammates out of the service area and into the banquet area. He rounded the service hallway corner and snapped his submachine gun into position. Behind him the muzzles of his teammates' weapons tracked for targets, and James pulled even with him.

Entering the lounge area, they immediately stepped into a firestorm.

Men charged forward or twisted in seats, caught in complete surprise by the airborne assault. Bodyguards gathered for a meal clawed at handguns as Phoenix poured out of the funnel of the access hallway. Support personnel caught in the crossfire scrambled and dived to get out of the killing field, but the air was thick with lead as Phoenix forced their way right into the belly of Najafi's personal plane. Handpicked Special Revolutionary Guards attempted to react to the impossible ambush, but the surprise was almost total and the Iranian commandos paid with their lives.

Washington, D.C.

ON THE TOP FLOOR of the converted textile mill, Fowzi Nejad stood at the bottom of the stairs, looking up toward the roof access, a Kalashnikov in his sweating hands. He called again, confused by the commotion and then the lack of commotion as the first team of bodyguards had rushed up the stairs that ran like scaffolding to the main floor of the house.

On the ground floor the FBI HRT squad had taken out the Iranian cell members easily in the moments before the helicopter had showed up, using stun grenades with merciless efficiency. Suddenly a black apparition appeared quickly in the roof doorway and he barked out a single word before opening fire.

He saw a black-clad, balaclava-covered man and screamed, "Yankees!"

His assault rifle blazed in his hands as behind him the rest of the Iranian cell, already poised and on edge, exploded into action. They had been betrayed somehow only blocks from their target, and nothing was left but martyrdom.

The American pulled back from the edge of the doorway as he saw Nejad level his weapon and open fire. The muzzle-flash obscured the black-clad man's vision as the Iranian poured lead into the shadows above him.

The terrorist didn't see the deadly black sphere as it floated down toward him.

It arced in a gentle lob over his head and struck the oil-stained concrete of the floor. The impact-detonation grenade immediately exploded. Shrapnel fanned out, riding the edge of the concussive blast, and tore into Nejad's flesh seconds before the explosion sent him spinning like a rag doll over the safety railing, his weapon spinning off.

Behind him razor-sharp shards of metal buzzed into unprotected flesh and a ball of billowing fire mushroomed out behind it. Men were screaming in the oversize production room as they were thrown or swept aside. Clothes burst into flame and blood ran in rivers across the filthy floor.

Lyons stepped out of the doorway and rushed down the stairs, his automatic shotgun up and ready. He caught a flash of motion and pivoted smoothly at the waist. He put two rounds into one stumbling kidnapper, then a second into a another one fighting to stand.

He saw a screaming man staggering, clutching at a torn and bleeding stump where his arm had been—no threat. He turned away, raced down four more steps and saw a black-clad figure crawling along the ground in agonizing pain, his guts strung out behind him like garters. The man was reaching for the blood-smeared grip of a machine pistol—threat. Lyons used a .12-gauge burst to hollow the man's skull clean.

He thundered down another half flight of stairs and saw movement beyond the edge of the blast radius. He vaulted the smoking railing on the stair as heavy-caliber slugs chewed into the wood where he'd been standing. He landed in the middle of his grenade kills. He tried to spin and drop, but his toe came down in a puddled smear of intestines and he slipped.

He went down hard and felt blood soak the side of his uniform. The gunner who had fired on him rushed out from behind fifty-five-gallon industrial barrels, weapon blazing. Lyons shot him with a blast low in the stomach, and the man doubled over, firing a burst into the ground and causing ricochets to whistle and whine madly around the room. Riding out the recoil of the last burst, Lyons pushed himself up. His body was soaked with blood along the right side and his ribs felt bruised from the tumble but his adrenaline was running through like currents of electricity.

He sensed movement and turned his head, the muzzle of the smoking pistol shifting in tandem and steel steady in his grip. His finger lay welded on the smooth metal curve of the trigger taking up the slack. He saw a shape crouched under a metal desk and his arm straightened, his finger tightening on the trigger.

The little girl's eyes were such a brilliant blue they looked incandescent and big as saucers and rimmed with tears. Her lips were quivering with fear and her thin cheeks smeared with dirt. Her lower lip was split and swollen so that a trickle of blood had run down her chin and dried like chocolate syrup.

Narrowing his eyes, Lyons lowered the pistol. He pushed himself to his feet and looked around him. Off to his left on the edge of a pile of corpses strung like toys by the grenade blast a gang member pushed himself up and staggered away. Lyons shifted, seeing only the motion at first. His eyes went to the hands. In hostage rescue situations the shoot teams always looked to the hands in their split-second decisions. Empty hands—no shoot. Full hands—shoot. It was a simple binary code that allowed the best to operate in close-quarters battle.

The shuffling figure grasped one of the ugly, utilitarian machine pistols. The handgun in Lyons's fist seemed to cycle of its own accord. The bullets burrowed into the man, cracking the wing-shaped shoulder blade like hammers on a plate.

The man spasmed then, arching his back like a landed fish, and the machine pistol clattered and bounced off the concrete. The man stumbled forward toward a line of barrels. He screamed once in pain and staggered, close to going down. His arm came out and Lyons figured it was a last, desperate attempt to stop his fall before he died. The hand came down and too late Lyons saw the apparatus attached to the industrial barrels by coaxial cable.

There was a sharp, dry metallic click, and suddenly glowing red LED numerals blinked on in the swatch of gloom as he put a second 3-round burst into the man and dropped him dead. The numbers glowed dark red and stood out stark against the gloom: 00:60.

CHAPTER TWENTY-SIX

Lyons leaped forward. The demolitions a group like this seemed capable of couldn't be that difficult. He was no Gary Manning or Hermann Schwarz, but he could defuse most simple trigger explosives easily.

He had almost reached the charges. The number read 00:55. His eyes fairly danced across the apparatus taking in the details of the construction, hunting for connection points, trailing wires.

Then the little girl shot him in the back.

He grunted hard at the impact and spun even as the echo of the burst was still bouncing through the warehouse. He felt a sting like a razor slice along his left arm and the middle of his back felt as if he'd been blindsided by a sledgehammer.

He didn't have time to question why it had happened. Would have doubted something like Stockholm Syndrome anyway. He was a man with a gun and the only men with guns the little girl had seen, he understood intuitively, had been the ones intent on using her up and throwing her away.

He spun and dropped and fired quickly. His bullets found the floor in front of her and there was a risk of ricochets, but he was unholy good with his weapons. Concrete chips sprang up and slapped the little girl with slivers and she screamed, but held on to the dead terrorist's machine pistol.

Lyons shifted the muzzle and punched a burst through the desk beside her head, already starting to move forward. The rounds flattened out as they punched through the cheap metal and the girl screamed.

From the top of the stairs a terrified woman screamed.

Lyons felt adrenaline flood his system as he realized there was more than one hostage. He didn't know who the people were or why the Iranians had been forced to kidnap them, but they had just multiplied the difficulty quotient on this mission by a factor of a hundred.

Then Lyons felt relief like a punch in the gut when the little girl finally panicked enough to drop the machine pistol. No time to reflect on why the situation was crazy, only time to act. He leaped forward and kicked the weapon until it skidded across the floor, and snatched her up by one stick-thin arm.

"I'm American!" he growled. "I'm here to take you home."

The little blond-haired girl looked at him and more tears came, but he could feel her tense in his grip as her fear and confusion overtook her.

The girl clung to him for a moment and he felt hope. She let out a sudden, piercing scream and her little fists began to windmill as she fought him with desperate energy. He looked to the digital timer, which was counting down relentlessly: 00:45.

He wanted to yank the girl free and disconnect the bomb, but she was glued to him like a wildcat, scratching and clawing and trying to bite. He forced himself to hold on despite the hurt in his back where the Second Chance ballistic vest had stopped the slug. He yelled for the woman who had screamed to run and then turned away, scanning the big room for the way out he'd seen on his initial assault.

His finger found his throat mike. "This is Able," he barked. "I have explosives. Clear the building! Repeat. I have cooking explosives, clear the building!"

"Copy, Ironman," Price answered. "I'm clearing HRT. You get out now!"

"Copy. Scramble medics. I'm bringing at least two hostages out!"

He turned, saw the door and saw the padlock hanging off the chain from the inside door. He'd shot the man charged with manning the entry post on his own way down the stairs. The sentry's body was sprawled out loosely on the floor, outflung hand inches from an assault rifle.

"Lady!" Lyons barked for a second time. "Oh, Christ! Lady! I'm a cop!" It seemed a small enough lie considering the situation.

"I'm coming!" the woman answered, and he could hear her running down the stairs now.

"I'm Karen, we were taken—"

"Not now!" Lyons snapped. "Are there any more hostages?"

"Just us," the woman sobbed. "I own the building. I don't know who the girl is—"

But the clock was burning fast and Lyons was already tucking the wildly flailing little girl under his arm and moving toward the door.

He brought his handgun up as he did so, approaching the lock at an angle. He was stunned by the ferocity with which the terror clique had been prepared to defend its base of operations. These men were committed jihadists and even if he died in the next half a minute, Lyons knew the attack that would have been perpetrated by such mad animals had been stopped. His life for thousands—it was a trade he would make.

Then the little girl, still crazed with fear, kicked hard and he redoubled his efforts to escape.

He saw more clusters of fifty-five-gallon drums connected by television cables designed to carry electronic impulses and digital signals. The terrorist cell had cobbled together a devastating mixture of low and high-tech. What it lacked in complexity Lyons felt sure it would make up for in raw explosive power.

00:37.

Squeezing the girl tightly, Lyons lifted the pistol and fired into the big padlock holding the thick links of chain together. The metal padlock jumped up at the impact, but split apart. Lyons stepped forward and struck out with the tread of his boot, catching the mechanism and ripping it down.

Behind him the woman, Karen, ran up and the chain dropped to the floor. The little girl was almost epileptic in her spasms now and she kept shrieking a word over and over again, the same liquid syllables in screaming repetition, but Lyons didn't know the word, couldn't understand what in the hell the girl was shrieking. He stuffed his pistol into its shoulder holster to better control the twisting girl and reached out to pull the warehouse door open.

00:26.

From behind him Karen ran forward and threw herself against the handle, heaving her weight against the sliding structure. It came open easily and she stumbled forward. Lyons came out after, running hard. The little girl bucked in his arms.

He was on the ground floor of the building and the front door to the building was hanging open as the last armored HRT trooper exited the building. Lyons heard a car door open and saw the flash of a dome light out of his left across the open space of the old textile mill even as he was turning. He saw an Iranian man in a leather coat with a long, greasy ponytail hopping out of a sleek black Lexus, a machine pistol coming up in his hands.

Lyons dropped the twisting little girl as he brought up his handgun. Karen was screaming, hands around her face and standing directly in his way. He struck her with a heel-of-the-palm blow in her shoulder blade as the gunmen lifted his machine pistol and she spun away.

He leveled his silenced weapon, just catching a sense of the little girl darting away from him. His finger found the trigger a split second before the other man's, and a 3-round burst struck him center mass. The man staggered under the triple impact and came up against the edge of the car. Lyons pulled down and stroked his trigger again. The man's face was ripped off his skull and he hit the broken pavement of the parking lot.

Lyons turned, reaching out for the little girl as she darted back into the building. His fingertips just missed her, coming close enough to feel the feather brush of her hair as he grasped nothing and she slipped past him.

"Sister!" Karen suddenly shouted. "She's saying her sister's still in there."

But Lyons was already running.

He hit the doors of the warehouse three steps behind the frantic girl. His eyes were drawn to the LED display and what he saw flooded his system with jolts of adrenaline.

00:13.

He sprang forward, growling with the exertion and caught the girl as he dived toward the hiding spot he had first pulled her out of. She turned like a ferret and sank her teeth into his palm.

00:08.

He swore and let go instinctively as blood pooled up out of the cuts. He reached out with his other hand and caught the little girl by her shirt. Doll in hand, she came away easily now and he drew her to him.

A doll, he realized, and the incredulity of the irony slapped him as hard as an iron bar. They were going to die for a goddamn baby doll.

00:05.

He saw the readout and knew he couldn't make it. His feet hit the ground as he drove with his legs against the concrete like a running back breaking for open field after a handoff. He cut around an overturned barrel and cursed the half second it cost him.

The girl was babbling now at him, but he was too keyed up to catch her words. He went out through the building divider and hurtled past the parked Lexus, seeing the dead bodies of terrorists killed by the HRT unit lying on the floor.

He saw the door standing open and he put on the last burst of speed left in his body. His heart was thumping hard in his chest, just banging against his ribs with the exertion and his breath was coming fast and hard.

00:02.

He hit the door at a dead sprint just as he felt the air around him suddenly drawn backward in a vacuum rush that stung his eyeballs. He covered the girl up tight against him as he felt the flash of sudden heat come rolling up behind him like a locomotive.

Then he was hurtling through the air, twisting as he flew to catch the angle out of the doorway and the orange freight train of a fireball rushed past him and the concussive force sent the doors flying off like tumbling dice. Lyons twisted as he fell to protect the girl and landed hard along one arm and shoulder. He grunted with the impact and recoiled slightly off the pavement before sprawling wide to cover as much of the little girl's flesh with his own body as he could.

Jets of flame shot out windows and air vents and punched holes through the roof. Black smoke appeared instantly and debris began to rain down.

CHAPTER TWENTY-SEVEN

Caspian Sea

Rafael Encizo leaned into his weapon and fired off a tight burst. The rounds sailed just past Hawkins at a tight angle and sliced into the Iranian military guard struggling to rise from a dining table. The bullets punched into the soldier, mangling the flesh and cartilage of his throat and crushing his upper vertebrae. The soldier tipped backward as blood gushed, then he slowly spun and fell to the floor.

At that point the fundamental nature of the encounter changed.

They had been an elite unit storming an aircraft with the advantage of complete surprise and the capability to decimate through extreme aggression. In an instant they were a grunt line platoon, nose to nose with an entrenched and tenacious enemy.

Hawkins entered the middle section of the plane and realized in a horrifying moment that their intelligence had been wrong. A squad of bodyguards was actually a platoon and the reactions of the Iranian Ansar-al-Mahdi gunmen were well disciplined and instantaneous.

Hawkins did not falter.

Training, condition, courage was too strong, too ingrained. He darted forward, clearing the door like a stormtrooper coming over the trench. His weapon was up as he hugged the left side of the aisle of seats and he was firing.

His target acquisition was instantaneous despite the adrenaline that flooded his system like a superdrug. Precision had been drilled into him until it was a reflex, and in the face of withering fire he charged.

Behind him Calvin James entered the room, his own weapon blazing. Then came Manning, followed by Encizo. They raced hard into the aisle, each two-man team taking down targets to either the left or the right.

They moved with fluid precision into a devastating killing spree, putting elite Iranian bodyguard after elite Iranian bodyguard down forever. Ahead of them the parallel rows of seats suddenly ended and gave way to a plush sitting area with low couches and desktop tables.

The inner circle of Brigadier General Abdul-Ali Najafi's Ansar-al-Mahdi Protection Corps scrambled to throw themselves away from the man as the bodyguard unit was decimated. People died in classic triple-taps of two rounds to the body followed by a single shot to the head.

Najafi was screaming, cowering in terror. He made no move to reach for the fancy Signature Grade SIG-Sauer pistol under his suit jacket. Everywhere he looked he saw blood splashed: across the crushed-velvet upholstery, the porthole windows, the smooth grain of the custom white-oak tabletops. Mouths gaped in silent screams and eyes bulged blindly, showing the whites, covered in the film of death. Tongues lolled and limbs were twisted in grotesque parodies of life.

Najafi the terror merchant looked up from the carnage and saw black-clad demons hurtling toward him. Their faces were hidden and distorted by masks, their bodies bulging with armor and weapons and the kind of dense, frightening sinews men couldn't earn in weight rooms.

He heard someone screaming, then realized it was himself. His bladder let go in a sudden liquid rush and he could smell himself. Two of the biggest men raced toward him and he cringed. They pummeled him hard, beating him mercilessly. He felt buttstocks strike his kidneys and he screamed only to be struck in the mouth hard enough to knock out his front teeth.

Fingers like steel claws intertwined themselves in his hair and yanked his head cruelly back. A dark, wild-eyed demon leaned in close, his voice a hoarse whisper. Najafi moaned and his lips tried to form prayers.

"Brigadier General Abdul-Ali Najafi of the clandestine Ansar-al-Mahdi Protection Corps," the faceless commando said. "Your time has come."

Steel bracelets clicked into place around his wrists and ankles. Najafi screamed as his shoulder was wrenched to facilitate his being hog-tied with the high-tensile handcuffs. He lay trussed up like a pig for the slaughter.

He saw a man with impossibly wide shoulders step forward, a pistol in his hand. The man leaned down and gently rested the muzzle against Najafi's forehead right between his eyes.

There was a horrifically loud click as the hammer on

the pistol was cocked back. Najafi closed his eyes tight shut; here it was, the end. He heard the hammer fall and he jerked.

"Bang!" the devil shouted, and Najafi soiled himself for the second time.

I'm still alive, he thought. How? Why?

"We have not taken the cockpit," Najafi's mock executioner growled. "You have been given a message. This is your only warning. Tell the Revolutionary Council what happened here. Let them know that no one is safe, that we can get to anyone, anywhere. No one is beyond our reach."

Najafi looked up in time to see the toe of the boot that bludgeoned him into darkness. For the rest of his life the Iranian would carry the half-moon-shaped scar in his eyebrow so that each time he looked into a mirror he was reminded of his humiliation. Then he would feel rage but then, just as quickly he would remember the terror and his will for revenge evaporated.

He always remembered the terror.

FLOATING GENTLY DOWN toward the Caspian Sea in his glider-style parachute, Gary Manning lifted a finger and touched his sat-link comm unit.

"Stony, this is Phoenix," he said.

"Go for Stony," Barbara Price replied, voice as dry and calm as ever.

"Tasking accomplished. Phoenix out."

"Good copy. Stony out."

The Executioner®

Don Pendleton's

DEATH RUN

A dangerous sport masks a deadly threat....

For a group of fundamentalist extremists, stealing a shipment of weapons-grade plutonium from Pakistan was almost too easy. Now they have everything they need to construct a terrifying weapon on U.S. soil. They believe their plans are virtually undetectable—but Mack Bolan is on their trail!

*Available in May
wherever books are sold.*

TAKE 'EM FREE

2 action-packed novels plus a mystery bonus

NO RISK

NO OBLIGATION TO BUY

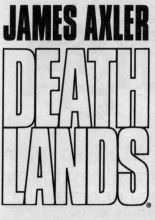